BOSTON METAPHYSICAL SOCIETY

BOSTON METAPHYSICAL SOCIETY

A STORM OF SECRETS

MADELEINE HOLLY-ROSING

Enjoy the story!
Best,
Madeleine

Brass-T Publishing

Los Angeles

Contents

Dedication

This book would not be possible without
the support of the fans of *Boston Metaphysical Society*.
Special thanks to my beta readers James Boyd and Dover Whitecliff,
and to my editor, Leslie Peterson.

And a very special thanks to my husband, David, who has
believed in this project since the beginning.

Introduction

This is an American story.

It is a story about the men and women in American society who had no voice, but still dream the American dream. It is about you and me, and where our society came from and perhaps where we are going. This is an American story told through the lens of the privileged, the persecuted, and those who walk between those worlds.

Boston Metaphysical Society began with a script called *Stargazer* that I wrote while I was working towards my MFA in screenwriting at UCLA. The story was about Mina Fleming, a Scottish-American woman, who arrived in Boston pregnant, penniless, and abandoned by her husband in the late 1800s. She was hired as a maid to work in the house of the director of the Harvard observatory. Later, she became one of his female computers and eventually discovered over 10,000 stars and developed a new stellar classification system. (And yes, they were called female computers.) That script won the Sloan Fellowship.

What I didn't realize then was that I had the foundation for what was going to become *Boston Metaphysical Society.* I had no idea what was in store for me. It began as a TV pilot, then became a six issue graphic novel mini-series. While we were in production for the comic, I also wrote a series of short stories and novellas to dig deeper into the world.

It became obvious that the next step was to write novels which further explored this world, while continuing the comic as standalone stories. Many of the characters in my novella, *Steampunk Rat,* and the short sequential art story, *Hunter-Killer,* (which is part of the graphic novel trade paperback,) will be featured in my next series of novels about the House Wars, which is my version of the American Civil War.

This novel, *A Storm of Secrets,* is the first *Boston Metaphysical Society* novel. It takes place five years before the start of the original graphic novel series.

Welcome to the Great States of America and a Boston that never was, but could have been.   Madeleine Holly-Rosing ~ 2018

Foreword

Steampunk, the "Future That Never Was", has many forms of expression, from books to artwork to fashion to philosophy. The steampunk community which creates all those fantastic items is just as diverse, incorporating a variety of media, perspectives, and experience. The authors, artists and other creators draw on the rich global history and cultures from the nineteenth century, adding in their personal, modern day interpretation to create something new but still a bit familiar.

Creativity is a hallmark factor of steampunk, motivated, in part, by the wide range of outlook and awareness in the community. There is a constant and ever-changing juxtaposition of ideas which drives the innovation of the aesthetic and narratives, and proposes a response to the unfamiliar, and possibly the uncomfortable, with "Well, why not?"

Steampunk stories, while entertaining, can be educational, including revealing the histories not taught in schools, and exploring how 'what might have been' can be used as 'what can be done now'. They can champion the value of individual actions when challenged by adversity, and exemplify the benefits of integrity and dignity. They teach us how to look inward at ourselves and outward at society in order to better understand the common ground which unites us and the issues which can be overcome before they divide us. They can show that "Us" and "Them" may just be reflections seen in a mirror.

The broad appeal of steampunk to its participants is partly due to that use of knowledge in new combinations, and the resulting possibilities. From ages eight to eighty, and from every corner of the world, steampunks share their history, culture, and most importantly, ideas. We grow as individuals when we collaborate together by extending our knowledge, expanding our frame of reference, and engaging our imagination.

As the creator and editor of the steampunk news and information website, Airship Ambassador, I'm constantly reading and searching for content to share. *Boston Metaphysical Society* appealed to me instantly when I came across it. In the steampunk checklist, it had historic people, anachronistic technology, prevailing scientific and paranormal theories of the time, and engaging ideals and philosophies which were not popularly adopted in the 1800s. It confronts some of the realities of those days, and uses it well to tell a gripping story.

Madeleine Holly-Rosing has crafted a captivating alternate history world which I have enjoyed again and again in each new publication. With science, action, history, and more wrapped around compelling characters and their peculiar circumstances, this is certainly a gift for your imagination.

Happy reading.

Kevin Steil
Airship Ambassador ~ 2018

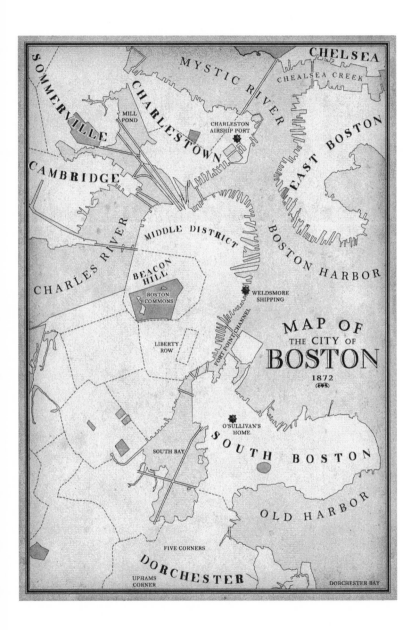

MYSTIC RIVER

CHELSEA

CHEALSEA CREEK

SOMMERVILLE

CHARLESTOWN

MILL POND

CHARLESTON AIRSHIP PORT

EAST BOSTON

CAMBRIDGE

CHARLES RIVER

MIDDLE DISTRICT

BOSTON HARBOR

BEACON HILL

BOSTON COMMONS

WELDSMORE SHIPPING

LIBERTY ROW

FORT POINT CHANNEL

MAP OF
THE CITY OF
BOSTON
1872

O'SULLIVAN'S HOME

SOUTH BAY

SOUTH BOSTON

OLD HARBOR

FIVE CORNERS

DORCHESTER

UPHAMS CORNER

DORCHESTER BAY

xiii

1

"I'd rather face a firing squad," Samuel Hunter announced with all the sarcasm he could muster as he gazed down the gangplank and cringed. It looked as though all of Boston had arrived to watch him and his wife, Elizabeth, disembark the *Hermera*. If he appeared the least bit awkward, the gossip mongers would skewer him both publicly and privately. He was, after all, now the husband of the heir to House Weldsmore and they were disembarking a Crystal Class passenger steamship built and owned by her father, Jonathan Weldsmore.

"Stop acting so silly," Elizabeth replied as she peered up at him from under her black silk hat with a brim just wide enough to shield her eyes from the sun.

On the dock, dozens of Bostonians waved and cheered as they waited for the other passengers, but moved aside when Samuel and Elizabeth walked through the crowd. A few women curtsied when Elizabeth stopped to greet them, ogling her magenta silk brocade ensemble with gold filigree woven throughout the corset and half jacket. Though he loved his wife with all his heart, Samuel was appalled when people treated her like royalty. And this wasn't the first time. It had been a weekly occurrence in almost every major city in Europe they'd visited during their honeymoon.

A Middle District man, Samuel had been astounded when the "real" royalty fawned over her and attempted to bribe him because they thought he had Jonathan's ear. When they learned he was useless to them, he was shunted aside.

"Elizabeth," he called to her. "The car will be waiting."

She said her goodbyes and moved out ahead of him.

Samuel followed but not before he tugged at his long dark-brown woolen coat with two copper strands woven into the lapel. He had to make sure no one saw the gun in his shoulder holster. No need to alarm anyone. Though Elizabeth was safe on her father's premier ship and the docks, his old Pinkerton habits were hard to break.

An older woman gave Elizabeth a variegated violet rose as they wound their way through the throng. Elizabeth patted the woman's hand and smiled. Her butterfly-shaped fascinator of silver and copper filaments accented with pearls glittered in the sunlight as she waved goodbye. Most waved back in adulation. Elizabeth Weldsmore Hunter was not only well loved for her generous philanthropy, but defined fashion among the Great Houses on the East Coast as well.

A midnight-blue steam-powered car with silver trim chugged toward him. Polished to a high sheen, it sparkled when the sun hit it at the right angle. As it slowed, a rush of steam poured out the exhaust pipe. Brendan, the chauffeur, stopped before any toes were crushed then hopped out to assist them. Two Weldsmore guardsmen in long silver coats trimmed in copper with the emblem of House Weldsmore—a sailing ship with three masts—embroidered on the upper left side of the chest flanked the car. Both of them peered into the throng of people as if expecting the worst.

"Brendan! I'm so happy to see you!" Elizabeth gushed.

A stocky man with graying hair, he gave her a short bow as he opened the back door of the car for them. "Always a pleasure, miss. I mean Mrs. Hunter," he replied with a hint of an Irish lilt. He nodded at Samuel. "Geoffrey is picking up your trunks."

As Elizabeth got into the car, Samuel noticed dark circles under Brendan's eyes and tension in his face. "I hope all is well with you."

"Nothing for you to worry about, sir," the chauffeur replied with a stiff smile.

"Brendan?" Samuel raised an eyebrow at him, not believing a word he said.

"Let's just say Mr. Weldsmore is a happier man when Mrs. Hunter is present."

"Well, he and you can come visit us after we find our new home." Samuel made a mental note to talk to him in private later as he stepped into the car.

"Yes, sir."

One guardsman sat in the front with Brendan while the other entered another car that followed behind them.

After negotiating the crowd, the trip back to House Weldsmore would take about thirty minutes. Brendan took a slight detour up Tremont so they could drive through the park and avoid the cobblestone streets. Elizabeth had rolled down the front windows to let the air in. She gazed out the back, noting the various changes that had occurred over the past year. How the trees were taller, the flowers more vibrant, even the streets cleaner. Samuel only had eyes for her.

"I want to expand my philanthropic work, like my mother did. Perhaps plant a new garden in the park for the school children. A new wing at the hospital. Or even something on the South Side," she commented, rubbing a smudge off the window.

Samuel chuckled. "South Side? I think your father will have an opinion on that."

"My father has an opinion on everything."

She sat back in the seat, took his hand, and squeezed it. "You know I haven't had any visions for a whole year. I think the honeymoon may have had something to do with it," she said with a lowered voice as she snuggled closer.

"Honeymoons are good." He grinned. "We should do one every year."

Her face lighted up in joy. "That's a wonderful idea." Her eyes then narrowed as she pondered the idea. Samuel loved watching her plan. "One month out of every year, we shall go on a honeymoon. Away from Father, the business, everything," she announced.

"I particularly like the part about being away from your father. Which reminds me, you've put off deciding where we're going to live long enough." Samuel remarked. "We could find a house near Beacon Hill in the Middle District."

Elizabeth turned to gaze out the window again. "I'm tired of talking about that. We can decide all that later."

"You keep saying that, but—"

She gasped.

"What is it?" He leaned forward to see what had upset her. She pointed out the window.

The police were cutting down the effigy of a man hanging from an elm tree with the words *Great Houses* painted on it. Nearby, a small group of protesters were being arrested.

"Oh, hell," Samuel muttered under his breath. "Someone will pay for this."

"I don't understand. We help them."

"Elizabeth, you've seen the dark side of this city in your visions. Not everyone believes in the benevolence of the Great Houses. Not even you."

The childlike enthusiasm vanished as the mature and sometimes troubled woman returned. "I know."

He had met Elizabeth when Jonathan Weldsmore hired him to be his daughter's body guard. They'd been returning from a social event when Elizabeth had fallen asleep in the car and had a vision of them being attacked. When she awoke, she'd realized the attack was imminent and warned him. The men were swift and brutal, but Samuel's Pinkerton training had paid off and he'd killed all of them with only their driver being injured. When Jonathan had learned that Samuel now knew Elizabeth's secret, he had threatened to shoot the former Pinkerton detective.

A bang against the window surprised them both. Samuel reached for his gun when he saw an elderly Irishman with rheumy eyes and rotting teeth beating on the window next to him, screaming, "You be the one! You be the one!"

The car jerked to a stop, and the Weldsmore guardsman leapt out, dragging the man away.

The anguish and madness in the man's eyes tugged at a memory Samuel had kept at bay during his honeymoon. A speck of inky darkness bloomed in his vision. It wormed its way into his subconscious, chipping away at his self-confidence. Samuel could swear it was alive and had an intelligence of its own. Sometimes he imagined it called his name, luring him deeper into despair. Samuel refused to let that happen and squeezed his eyes shut.

"No! You will not control me!" he muttered.

A hand touched his shoulder. "Samuel? What's wrong? Is it happening again?"

He opened his eyes to see his wife, Elizabeth, staring at him with worry etched on her face. He reached out and caressed her cheek with the tips of his fingers.

"I'm fine now."

She gave him a queer look, then smiled. "All right." She turned her head toward the chauffeur as the guardsman returned. "Brendan, take us home."

"Yes, Mrs. Hunter."

***

By the time the car pulled into a smooth paved driveway lined with a hedge of pink and yellow roses, Samuel had recovered from his episode.

Before he could open the door for his wife, one of the younger underbutlers had done it and gave him a quick head bow. Samuel sighed. "You don't have to open every door, Charles."

"But, sir. It's my job." Aghast, the young man blinked at him.

Samuel looked back at Elizabeth. "I will never get used to this."

"Yes, you will." She gestured for him to exit.

The Weldsmore mansion was more than a house; it was a tribute to the power and influence of the families that dominated American politics and business. Four stories tall and designed in the Federalist style, it was built of red brick with high narrow windows set with amber-colored glass. A remnant of the House Wars, an elaborate wrought-iron fence with decorative ship designs welded at various points surrounded the property as a deterrent against forcible entry. A side and back garden with a gazebo and several ponds softened the more austere portions of the house. At the entrance stood at least two guards who wore long silver coats trimmed in copper and boasting the emblem of House Weldsmore. That same emblem, about hundred times larger, hung above the double oak doors that led inside.

Those doors swung open as if the weight of the world pushed back. Out pranced Mrs. Owen, the head housekeeper. Behind her, walking at a much more dignified pace, came the house manager, Sampson. They both beamed at Elizabeth with love and pride.

"Miss Elizabeth." A petite woman close to sixty with ocean gray hair bound up under a cap with the Weldsmore emblem on it, Mrs. Owen gave her a quick hug. "I mean, Mrs. Hunter. We are so pleased to see you home safe." She gave Samuel a warm smile. "And you, too, Mr. Hunter." Her light Irish accent was not surprising considering she was the wife of Brendan, the chauffeur.

"Thank you, Mrs. Owen," he replied. "I hope Mr. Weldsmore behaved himself while we were gone."

The head housekeeper rolled her eyes. "That man can be a trial."

"Your father will be overjoyed to see you." The deep bass voice of Sampson interrupted them. "As am I." He grasped Elizabeth's hands, patted them, then turned to Samuel to shake his proffered hand. "Good to see you, sir."

A former underbutler for the Weldsmores when Jonathan was a boy and his grandmother Beatrice ruled the family and the business, Sampson would never admit to the power and influence he had over Elizabeth's father, but Samuel knew better. He had watched the sixty-three-year-old house manager protect Elizabeth like his own daughter. The entire staff would be lost without him. Jonathan might be the captain of this Great House, but Sampson was its anchor.

"When will the both of you call me Samuel?"

Mrs. Owen and Sampson glanced at each and said in unison, "Never."

Sampson motioned for them to enter. "Come. Your father is waiting for you in his study."

The newlywed couple followed the house manager inside.

Samuel watched as Elizabeth waltzed in as if her feet barely touched the floor. It amazed him that she never noticed the grandeur of the mahogany staircase or the chandelier that cascaded down from the top landing. Nor did she seem to appreciate the Italian paintings that graced the walls or the exotic birds-of-paradise that sat in crystal vases in the salon and library. A host of servants buzzed and hovered around her like a queen bee. Then he remembered: she *was* the queen bee.

"Elizabeth!" The voice of Jonathan Weldsmore boomed across the room.

Samuel watched his wife fly into her father's arms.

Taller than Samuel by two inches, Jonathan's lanky physique belied a physical and mental strength of which he was all too aware. He wore a long forest-green wool coat over matching trousers. Like those of his class, Jonathan's lapels and cuffs were accented with three copper-and-gold wires woven into the fabric. His ensemble was finished with an iridescent gold satin cravat tied around his neck. Jonathan's dark brown hair and mustache had turned almost completely gray over the year they had been gone, but none of the fierce protectiveness he had for his daughter had diminished, judging by the way he hugged her and glared at Samuel.

He knew that look. The man still wanted to shoot him.

"Samuel." Jonathan released his daughter. "It's about time you brought my daughter home."

"Father, stop that." She teased. "We are here now and that's all that matters." Elizabeth gave Samuel a wink behind her father's back. Samuel struggled to keep from laughing.

"Fine. Come along both of you. We have much to discuss." Jonathan turned and headed toward his study.

"But, sir," Mrs. Owen called out after him. "Shouldn't the lady rest first after such a long journey?"

Jonathan said nothing and marched away.

Mrs. Owen shrugged. "Off you go. I'll get you both unpacked."

Elizabeth reached out her hand toward Samuel. He took it, though he had the feeling that whether he liked it or not, the next few minutes would define the rest of their lives.

2

Elizabeth was worried as she walked into her father's study. She was entitled to be married, happy, and have a life of her own, but there was always a fear in the back of her mind: Would the visions return? And if they did, what future would she see? And whose?

She had been nine when her first vision occurred in her sleep. At first Elizabeth had thought it was a dream—until she realized that some the events she'd experienced came true. After that, the dreams had continued, always in the same way. As she slept, her mind would enter someone else's, and though she had no control over their body or thoughts, she could feel, hear, and even smell what they did. The vision could be years, days, or even hours ahead. Elizabeth had kept her ability a secret, fearing how her father would react if he discovered it. It wasn't until one of her visions showed her Samuel's murder that she decided to reveal her secret to her father. His reaction had not been pleasant.

"Elizabeth?" Samuel tugged on her hand.

She reached over and brushed a lock of his tobacco-colored hair off his forehead. "I'm fine. How are you?" She knew that some kind of melancholy plagued her husband from time to time, and it worried her.

"Nothing a good night's rest won't take care of," he replied. "So let's go talk to your father before he reneges on his promise not to shoot me."

"Very funny." Elizabeth took his arm as they walked into her father's inner sanctum together.

A relic of the House Wars, Jonathan's study had once been called The Sanctuary and was used to protect the family in case of an attack. The entrance to the room was barred by two massive steel doors with gears the size of a small carriage attached to the back. Each door was operated by Weldsmore guardsmen, who used a crank to rotate the gears to open and close them. They rarely closed those doors, but remained vigilant at all times. Though the war was long over, her father liked the historical significance of the room and kept many of the vestiges of that violent time.

Inside, one wall was lined with four amber-colored bay windows that could also be sealed and barred even though the massive gears that had controlled those mechanisms had been dismantled. A host of compound bows were displayed on another wall. Bookshelves took up a third wall from floor to ceiling with books on ship building in several languages. A loveseat was stationed off to the side while two matching walnut chairs with maroon velvet upholstery sat in front of Jonathan's mahogany desk. A large drafting table dominated the room while Jonathan's desk sat near the windows with a view of the bay. On it sat one of the first telephones in the city. A mouth piece perched on top of a long metal tube, which was itself attached to a wooden base. On the side was a handle that held the ear piece. All the Great Houses had one, and a few homes in the Middle District, but Jonathan's had been installed by Alexander Graham Bell himself.

Business papers lay stacked in files on his desk, yet the drafting table was astonishingly messy with engineering diagrams and partial drawings of ships not yet built.

What Elizabeth loved the most about the room were the mechanical animals displayed in a small glass cabinet behind her father's desk. There was an owl, two rats, a heron, and an automaton the size of a large doll. The owl he had built for her mother, Adaline, a few years after their marriage. The rats were a homage to a real one named Tinker that Jonathan had saved as a boy. Elizabeth had loved to listen to her mother tell the story of how her father had saved Tinker from an accident and then her cruel and stern grandmother. Even Sampson became complicit in the plot to save the rodent.

But her favorite part was hearing how a teenage Jonathan and his rat had snuck aboard one of the family's new ships and saved almost everyone when the steering system broke and the boilers blew up. It was a story of adventure, daring, and bravery. As a girl, it had sounded like a romantic fairy tale—cut short by the death of her mother from pneumonia. These days the mechanical rat served as a reminder of the time when her father had laughed and smiled more.

"Elizabeth." Jonathan's sharp voice brought her to attention.

"Yes, Father?"

"Sit."

Jonathan walked around his desk and stared out a window. Elizabeth sat at the edge of her chair with her spine straight and her feet tucked under her skirt while Samuel leaned back with practiced ease and no regard for his posture or appearance. Annoyed that he was comfortable and she was not, Elizabeth scooted back a tad to settle into the cushy part of the chair.

"I see no reason to mince words with the two of you. Europe is unstable, and I fear there may be another war coming. Maybe not next year or the next, but it will come. And we must be prepared." He turned around and gave them both a hard stare. "Neither one of you is suited to run this company alone. At least, not yet and not without help. Especially with this 'gift' of yours, Elizabeth."

"Father, I haven't had a vision in over a year," she protested.

"That doesn't mean it won't happen again. And if it does, and others find out about it, it will ruin your credibility."

"Sir—" Samuel began before Jonathan interrupted him with a wave of his hand.

"I know you will keep this secret, but secrets are often revealed whether we want them to be or not."

Elizabeth nodded. "I understand. What do you need of us?"

A slight smile tugged at his face. "An heir might be nice. I presume that won't be a problem."

Elizabeth glanced over at her husband, who threw up his hands in surrender.

"Your wish is my command."

"Samuel! Father!" Elizabeth sputtered. "This is most unseemly."

Samuel grinned, but Jonathan clasped his hands behind his back and studied his daughter thoughtfully.

"I admit that I do not have the education to run a shipping business, but Elizabeth most certainly does." Samuel added. "Perhaps you can find her a partner in case something happens to you while our children are still young."

Jonathan nodded. "My thinking exactly."

Elizabeth cleared her throat. "I agree, but I insist that I be included in the process, Father. I don't want to be stuck working with someone who is disagreeable."

"Of course."

"What worries me is that you think there will be a war." Elizabeth clutched her hands and sat up even straighter. "What has happened?"

"While we were in Europe, neither one of us noticed anything out of the ordinary. At least, where we traveled." Samuel commented. "However, we were a little preoccupied." He reached over and held Elizabeth's hand.

She was reluctant to let it go, but did anyway when she saw a fleeting look of sorrow cross her father's face. "Father, you know something, don't you?"

He pulled out the mahogany chair to reveal two small velvet pillows tied to it for back support. He paused, then sat down. "Yes, although it's mostly rumors and innuendos right now. Nothing specific. But we must plan for the worst and hope for the best. That's how this we survived the House Wars and . . . other things."

"Speaking of planning for a family, Elizabeth and I will need a house. I think we should rent first on the border of the Middle District and Beacon Hill. That way we won't be too far for her to come and visit. She could even walk," Samuel remarked.

Elizabeth stared at him, almost too stunned to say anything. She glanced over at her father, who sat hunched down with his hands folded in front of him. By the way his thumbs twitched, she could tell that he was going to let her deal with it.

"Samuel . . . darling."

Her husband flinched. "Ahh. You only call me 'darling' when I've said or done something stupid."

"No, it's that women like myself don't walk. We stroll. Like through the park or visiting foreign cities."

"Strolling is walking, last time I checked." Samuel failed to hide his annoyance at where this conversation was heading. "But this isn't about walking, is it? You want to live here."

Elizabeth nodded. "Yes. I'm sorry I didn't have the courage to tell you before, but I'm not ready to live anywhere else yet."

"But we're married. We deserve a house of our own."

"Of course you do, but that's not the point," Jonathan interjected.

"Then what is the point? If it's money you're worried about, I have enough saved up to find us something suitable. And I'll go back to work."

"As a bodyguard?" Jonathan shook his head. "Impossible. It would take you away from Elizabeth. You will work for me."

"Sir, with all due respect, that's not going to happen." Samuel's voice took on a hard edge.

"Samuel, please." Elizabeth reached over and squeezed his hand. "This is all my fault. I kept avoiding this conversation hoping I could find a better way to tell you. The truth is I'm too afraid to live anywhere else."

"What are you afraid of? We've already been through so much together."

"What if the visions come back?" The terror of those nights flashed through her mind. She slipped her hand out of Samuel's and clutched them in her lap again.

"Then we get you help. Someone to teach you how to deal with them."

Jonathan stood up abruptly, knocking his chair over. "Out of the question. You cannot trust those people."

"'Those people'?" Samuel stood and leaned over the desk, facing off with his father-in-law. "Who exactly are you talking about? Your daughter is one of 'those people' now."

Elizabeth realized she had made a difficult situation even worse. She reached over, grabbed Samuel's arm, and yanked him back into his chair.

"Both of you, sit down!" When her father remained standing, she glared at him. "You too!"

He growled at her, then righted his chair and sat down with a thump.

"Now, this is what we are going to do." She settled her shoulders back and held her head up. "Samuel and I will live in the house for at least one year. If the visions do not come back during that time, we will look for our own home."

Her husband and father opened their mouths to speak, but she cut them off with a sharp glare.

"If the visions do come back, and only if, Samuel and I will explore the possibility of someone teaching me how to control them." She turned her attention to her father. "And he will not work for you in any capacity unless he chooses to do so. Samuel will decide for himself what job he wishes to pursue."

Jonathan's eyes narrowed while Samuel put his hand over his mouth to hide a reluctant grin.

"However, if I decide to stay longer than a year, there will be no argument." Her husband's grin vanished. "But I promise you we will not live here longer than two. Do we have a deal? Father, shall I have your secretary notify the lawyers to write up a contract?"

Both men gaped at her. Jonathan recovered first. "I don't think that will be necessary." He reached for his glasses. "I will take you at your word."

"As will I . . . dear." Samuel followed up. Sarcastic undertones reverberated in her husband's voice.

"Are we done, Father?" Elizabeth asked. "I would like to help Mrs. Owen unpack my things and get some rest."

Jonathan gestured to Sampson, who stood outside the room holding a tray of coffee and sandwiches.

Elizabeth turned on the balls of her feet and marched out. "Sampson, if you could please send up tea instead of coffee, I would much appreciate it."

The house manager gave her a quick smile. "Already done, miss."

"Really? How did you know I preferred tea now?"

"You have a most attentive husband." Sampson responded with complete sincerity.

Elizabeth stopped and raised an eyebrow at Samuel. He gave her an "Aren't I perfect" look.

"Gah! You are the most infuriating yet wonderful man."

"And you, Elizabeth Weldsmore Hunter, are your father's daughter."

Samuel strode right past her, paused, and held out his arm. She sighed then took it. Together, they walked out of the study and toward the staircase with two servants trailing behind them.

3

Jonathan watched his daughter and Samuel exit his study before noticing that Sampson had placed a cup of coffee next to his right hand. Like all of their fine bone china, it had the house emblem painted on it in gold leaf.

The house manager's throat cleared, breaking his reverie.

"If you have something to say, Sampson, spit it out." Jonathan picked up a small silver spoon and dipped it into the sugar bowl to retrieve not one but three consecutive spoonsful of sugar, dumping each into his coffee.

Sampson leaned over to pour cream into the cup as Jonathan stirred with a teaspoon. It was such a well-practiced routine that not a drop of cream or a crystal of sugar landed on the desk.

"There is no reason that Elizabeth and Samuel cannot live in a house of their own. He is perfectly capable of protecting her, and . . ." Sampson put the cream down. "She needs to strike out on her own whether she wants to or not. You have far too much influence on her, if you don't mind me saying so, sir."

"I do mind, but say it anyway." Jonathan placed the spoon down in the saucer. "You're right. Elizabeth is stronger than I give her credit for. I hate it, but she did well by marrying that man. Anyone else would have been a disaster." He took a sip of coffee.

"Samuel Hunter is a man of honor, though he tends to suffer from what the Irish would call a 'soul tainted by darkness.'" Sampson placed a small matching plate of sandwiches in front of Jonathan.

"Is that what I sense about him?" Jonathan mused. "I suppose it has something to do with his time with the Pinkertons. I did hear there was some nasty business at the Homestead Steel Mill. He's never discussed it, though."

"Have you ever really discussed anything with Mr. Hunter other than your daughter?" the house manager asked.

Jonathan put the coffee cup to his lips then stopped and put it back down in the saucer. His eyebrows scrunched together. "He's not exactly the kind of man you can sit around the club and drink with."

"Neither are you, sir. You hate going to the club."

Jonathan thumped his fingers on the edge of his desk as he glanced around the room in thought. He spied the compound bows on the wall. "Hunting."

"Sir?"

"We can go hunting. I'm sure he's never hunted using a bow. That's a little too upper class for a Middle District man."

"Or too low class. Depending on your point of view."

"Sampson, why do you always have to be so—"

"Thorough?" Samson completed the thought for him. "That's why you have kept me on all these years."

"I thought it was because you saved my pet rat." Jonathan's face softened a bit at the memory. "Adaline cried for days after Tinker died."

"I seem to recall you did, too, sir."

He shoved the coffee and sandwich away. "I am not ready to let her go, Sampson. Not yet. But I agreed to her terms. Two years. No more. And I will hold to that."

"Yes, sir."

An underbutler rushed into the room carrying a wooden box about eight inches by eight inches. On the side where it opened sat an unbroken red wax seal. "Sir, this just arrived." The young man stopped in front of the desk. He handed Jonathan the box then stood up straight waiting for instructions.

Jonathan glanced at the box and smiled. Sampson gestured for the underbutler to leave. He went as fast as he could without running.

Jonathan picked up a letter opener and slid it under the seal, cracking it. He lifted the lid and looked inside, feeling a smile of pleasure warm his face at sight of the contents.

"Sir? What is it?"

"It's from the Abyssinian envoy. He should be arriving soon."

Jonathan reached in and pulled out a miniature replica of an ancient Axum ship. Traditionally made of papyrus and wood, this one was meticulously crafted out of woven threads of rose gold, silver, and bronze. It was shaped like a scorpion with a single sail amidships and an oar attached to the side that also served as a rudder.

"My God, that's beautiful." Jonathan examined it carefully.

Sampson leaned over to get a better look. "Do we have a gift for him, sir?"

"Oh, hell. Can you—"

The phone rang on Jonathan's desk. It startled both men. This was not a regular occurrence.

Jonathan frowned and picked up the earpiece.

"Yes?" The frown became a scowl.

"Sir, word is that we may have an unwelcome visitor shortly." His executive assistant, Mr. Evans said with urgency on the other end of the phone.

"Lock up all the new designs. I don't want anything out. Thank you, Mr. Evans." He slammed the earpiece back onto its cradle confident that his executive assistant would accomplish his duties with his regular efficiency.

"We probably have until tomorrow to get everything I'm working on locked away. I don't want any trace of it anywhere," he told Sampson.

"I'll make sure the ship and the engineering designs are locked up. Anything else?" the house manager asked. To his credit, he did not inquire as to why the sudden need for secrecy.

"Mr. Evans and I will take care of the Abyssinian contracts at the office. You and he are the only ones who know about those and I want to keep it that way."

"Yes, sir. Is Congressman Pierce coming to spy again?"

"No. It's much worse." Jonathan placed the ship back inside the box and locked it in a drawer. "My brother has decided to pay us a surprise visit."

***

Sampson hurried around Jonathan's study, picking up the new ship designs off the drafting table and locking them away in the wooden file cabinets that were kept in an unobtrusive closet near the desk. Mr. Weldsmore had left for his office on the wharf where he oversaw the building of both his passenger and cargo ships. Whoever had notified

Mr. Weldsmore that his brother was arriving had not been specific as to where and when he would arrive, thus all the commotion. Spies had their limits.

It didn't surprise Sampson that Hal Weldsmore would attempt to arrive unannounced. He liked to make his brother's life uncomfortable. Though he was older than Jonathan, Hal had lost the right to take over the business after he almost killed the entire family during the trial run of a new ship. Sampson remembered how Hal's reckless behavior had opened the door for a then fifteen-year-old Jonathan and his pet rat to save the day. On top of taking control of House Weldsmore, Jonathan was rewarded with Hal's future bride, Adaline. If memory served, Sampson recalled the young lady was very pleased by her sudden change of fortune. Adaline loved Jonathan and he her. It had been a very happy marriage.

Hal never forgave Jonathan or his grandmother for that.

Sampson stood in the middle of the room and inched around in a circle studying every desk, chair, and place a piece of paper could have fallen into. While Hal was in residence, this study must look like no one ever used it other than to entertain guests. He never came without a reason, and Sampson hoped he only needed money and would be gone in a day or two.

"Mr. Sampson?" Mrs. Owen waved at him from the doorway. "Shall I give it a good dusting? I hear we are to expect more company."

"Yes." Sampson nodded. "And prepare the guest rooms as well. But don't make them too comfortable. No need to encourage them to extend their visit."

"Already done." She turned to leave then stopped. Her head crooked around. "Wait. Did you say rooms? As in how many?"

"Mr. Hal never travels anywhere alone."

Mrs. Owen threw her arms up in disgust and stomped away. "That man!"

Sampson walked over to the door and inspected the two guardsmen who stood there. "No one is allowed into Mr. Weldsmore's study with the exception of Miss Elizabeth, Mr. Hunter, and Mrs. Owen. Is that clear?"

"Yes, Mr. Sampson," they replied in unison.

It was his duty to protect this family, even from each other if need be.

***

Jonathan made notes on some of his new ship designs as Brendan maneuvered the steam-powered car through traffic. The mix of horse carriages and steam-powered cars were a civic nightmare, one that city leaders had addressed by building a subway. The underground transport was not quite completed, thus the chaos. As one of those leaders, Jonathan knew he was as much to blame for all of this as his colleagues, but he'd much rather build ships than meddle in politics. Unfortunately, the world required that he remain involved or else it might come undone like it had in 1812 and during the House Wars.

The War of 1812 had changed the direction of the country. The Great States had used the pretense of British impressment of American sailors to launch an invasion of Canada. A war that was mostly fought at sea, it ended in a stalemate between the two warring nations. Afterward, a group of American industrialists had decided that democracy would not make the Great States of America dominant on the world stage. Their solution was a coup of sorts. Over the years after the war, these industrialists and their families had eroded civil liberties, changed laws, and allowed slavery to become entrenched in the South. Instead of the populace electing officials to Congress, they were selected from the leading industrial families. These families became known as the Great Houses.

The new Congress functioned more like a parliament, and they elected a president from within their ranks every six years. Jonathan had once considered running for a congressional position—until Adaline became ill. He'd always wondered whether, had he been old enough to hold office before the House Wars, he could have prevented it from happening.

Jonathan tapped his pen on his notebook. The more he thought about it, the more he doubted anyone could have stopped it. Slavery had become such an integral part of the southern Houses' way of life they refused to consider alternatives. Even when faced with hard and cold numbers that their method of doing business was inefficient and unprofitable, they refused to budge. Jonathan did not believe all men were created equal, but he had always thought slavery was irrational and self-defeating. A man worked harder when treated well and with respect, no matter what his class. Duty and loyalty were paramount, of course, and a fair salary didn't hurt either.

The war proved the northern Houses were right, but the cost was high. Much of the South was destroyed along with a number of their Great Houses. Abraham Lincoln had demonstrated his ability to lead a nation through war, but his republican vision of the future made him a marked man. His own House agreed to have him assassinated after he attempted to dismantle the Great Houses and return to a more democratic form of government. It had been a difficult period in his nation's history, and he sensed something equally bad was coming now.

The entire city of Boston was in the throes of change, as was the rest of the nation. It wasn't just the new technology and social change. Jonathan sensed there was something darker on the horizon. He had heard strange and unsettling rumors about demons fighting on the side of the South during the House Wars, but attributed it to propaganda. His whole world had upended when he learned Elizabeth had visions of the future—something he'd believed was Irish folklore.

Brendan slowed as they approached Chelsea Street. Jonathan glanced up and saw his chauffeur frown. "Brendan, why—"

An explosion heaved the car to one side, lifting half of it off the ground. Both doors on the driver's side bent inward, slamming Jonathan against the other side. The wheels crashed back down as flames swarmed the outside of the car like an infestation of ants.

"Get out!" Jonathan yelled at Brendan.

His chauffeur, bloodied and dazed, reached for the passenger's side door, but passed out.

Jonathan jerked on the door handle as the flames crept inside the car. Smoke poured in. He didn't have much time. He lay on his back and kicked the window with his feet. Once, twice, three times. It refused to break. That didn't surprise him. They were made with a special glass that, though not bulletproof, came close. The irony of dying due to his own security measures was not lost on him.

The window shuddered, but not because of him. It dawned on him what was happening, and he covered his eyes. The glass shattered as a tire iron burst through. Several hands reached through and yanked the door open. Two older Weldsmore guardsmen, Lewis and Kolb, pulled him out.

"Get Brendan!" Jonathan ordered as he was hustled away from the car and into another one. He glanced back to see the chauffeur being rescued just as the car and his paperwork went up in flames.

They sped down Chelsea Street, paralleling an eight-foot wrought-iron fence for a half mile before stopping at a gate with the sign *Weldsmore Shipping* over it. The gate was already open and flanked by a half a dozen guardsmen.

Whizzing by the gate, they drove a few blocks past several floating dry docks where men scrambled up and down the sides of two massive seagoing cargo ships making repairs. After another quarter mile, they skidded to a stop outside a five-story brick building the size of one of the Weldsmore's passenger ships. The glass in the top-story windows had been painted white so even if you had a ladder high enough, seeing in would be impossible.

Jonathan scrambled out of the car and was surrounded by more guardsmen. Two ran ahead to open the unassuming oak door into the building. He lurched through the entrance with Lewis holding on to his elbow.

This was the heart of his shipping empire. The crackling of welding filled the air as one of his foremen directed huge iron beams into place to frame a ship. Sparks lit up the mens' masks as they worked on the seams. Iron hulls were being prepared on the far side of the building. Hydraulic lifts underneath the main structure supported what would be the hull of the ship. Each corner bustled with activity as the work crew focused on their particular specialty. Even though the ship was in the early stages of being built, it was a sleeker, more elegant, design than the bulky ships that were the current norm.

Lewis released his hold to allow Jonathan to smooth back his hair and compose himself as he walked past the workers and headed for a set of iron stairs. They zigzagged up for five levels, each with a landing that overlooked a different section of the warehouse. Not wanting to become distracted, Jonathan sped up each level until he reached the open door to his office, which overlooked ship construction. Though this was the main office for Weldsmore Shipping, there were two other locations that handled payroll and procurement.

Here the rooms were split into three almost equal-sized spaces surrounded by glass windows on all sides except where the room sat flush against the outer wall of the building. Wooden file cabinets and four modest desks stood in the first room where the undersecretaries worked. Blinds were drawn on most of the windows so the four men could work undistracted. Jonathan's unusual appearance was enough for all of them to stop working and stare, then focus back on their work without comment.

"Mr. Weldsmore, sir! Are you all right?"

From the second room, a man about half Jonathan's height shuffled in carrying a stack of design drawings. He had a faint mustache and wore circular spectacles halfway down his nose. His apparel identified him as Middle District with a single brass wire woven through the cuffs and lapels of his dark-gray suit; however, his expression took on that of a worried old woman when he saw Jonathan's singed clothing and the blood running down his face.

"Should I call a doctor?" asked Mr. Evans.

"Yes, but not for me, Mr. Evans," Jonathan replied. "Brendan is injured. Make sure he's taken care of. And order another car from the house while I clean up."

"At once."

"And tell no one, including my daughter and son-in-law, of this incident."

Mr. Evans, his executive assistant, gave him a brief nod before he scurried out.

Jonathan stepped into a small and unadorned bathroom off of his office to change his clothes and clean up. When he looked in the mirror to see the extent of his injuries, he understood why his executive assistant was so alarmed. His face was covered in soot and the tips of his hair, eyebrows, and mustache were singed. A small gash on his forehead had left a copious amount of blood on his cheek, which had dripped onto his shirt. When he took his torn jacket off, he noticed the elbows were burnt.

This wasn't the first attempt to assassinate him, nor would it be the last. What bothered him was that his spies had given him no warning. They were usually quite good at ferreting out Great House plots, but now there was a weak link he needed to discover. However, there was the immediate problem of Hal and the Abyssinian envoy arriving at the same time.

He cleaned up and put on a fresh suit then exited the bathroom to see that Mr. Evans had returned with a tray of bandages, coffee, and sandwiches.

"How is Brendan?" Jonathan asked.

"Dr. Marley is taking care of him now. A few cuts, bruises, and minor smoke inhalation, but he'll be fine." Mr. Evans set the tray of food down on the meeting table.

"Good, good. Let's keep this quiet. I want a list of our current informants in every Great House. The minor ones too. Inform Mr. Kolb that I want to recheck the background of everyone who is working here. I'll have Sampson handle the house staff. In the meantime, we have until tomorrow before my brother arrives, but I'd rather be prepared now."

"Yes, sir. I understand. Anything you want destroyed?"

"No. Let's put the Abyssinian contracts in the main safe and the metallurgy reports in the other. I don't believe my brother's spies have discovered that yet."

"Yes, sir."

Spies were a constant source of annoyance to Jonathan. If it wasn't his brother trying to undermine him, then it was another Great House looking to discover his latest research and ship designs. Not that they would be capable of building it themselves, but they could either sell the plans to an overseas competitor or use it as insider information for their investments. Or try to kill him.

Jonathan entered his office to see every important piece of paper removed from sight. The only things left on his desk were a writing tablet, several pens, and the latest newspaper. He reminded himself to give Mr. Evans a raise.

"The meeting with the envoy is in two days, correct?"

"Yes, sir. The consulate promised to be discreet when he arrived and not put on their usual . . . display."

"Good." He admired the Abyssinians' resistance to the Austria-Germanic colonial efforts, but their monarchy tended to be a little ostentatious for his tastes.

Jonathan double-checked the locks on the file cabinets. "What can we distract Hal with when he arrives? I want him preoccupied."

"I have already procured him an invitation to Mrs. Gardner's salon and dinner tomorrow night."

"Get one for Elizabeth and Samuel too. That should make the evening more interesting."

Mr. Evans chuckled. "Yes, sir."

Satisfied that everything was in order, Jonathan turned to study the progress on his most recent ship design down in the dock. They were implementing his latest metallurgical techniques to lighten the hull yet keep it strong. It was still too soon to see what it would become, but the frame of it was in place. The bow had a sharper point than a normal ship that flared out amidships where it was three stories tall. It then dropped back at a sharp angle to form a flat surface to a squared-off stern. It had a shallow draft so it could maneuver in coastal waters. It was the perfect ship for the Abyssinian Navy to use against an invasion. Jonathan liked to think he had developed the modern world's response to the Spanish Armada.

What none of the men working on it knew was that he had also designed weapons unique to this ship to be installed at a later date and a different location. They were being built at a facility that only he and Mr. Evans knew the location of. The workers lived in barracks in northern Virginia and were transported in a secured and windowless steam-powered vehicle to the building site. They were allowed to write to their families, but any mention of what they were working on was edited out. Concerned they would become bored or homesick, Jonathan made sure they were compensated well for their trouble and temporary isolation.

One of the new weapons was an armor-piercing cannonball made of the new metal alloy Jonathan and his team of scientists had created. They also had to build the cannons to withstand the friction and heat the new cannonball produced. Jonathan was also tinkering with a torpedo with a guided propeller system. His first tests had been a disaster, but he was sure he would crack the formula soon. If he could manufacture such a weapon, it would change the face of naval warfare.

It could not be a coincidence that Hal had decided to pay him a visit now. If Jonathan had died today, his brother's sudden arrival could have appeared as him swooping in to save House Weldsmore. Jonathan chuckled to himself. He knew his brother would continue to try and wrest the business away, but he'd never believed Hal would try to kill him. Someone else was behind it. Besides, Elizabeth, Samuel, and Sampson could outmaneuver such an obvious power play.

His brother always had ulterior motives; Jonathan just needed to discover what they were before they became a problem.

4

Elizabeth tiptoed into the small dining area the family used for breakfast. A bright and sunny room with a view into the back garden, it had a tall ceiling with windows to match. Wallpaper with tiny pink roses on an ivory background gave the room a subtle elegance. A crystal vase filled with magenta lilies sat in the middle of a mahogany table covered with an intricate white lace cloth. Fine china with the Weldsmore crest was set along with a silver tea set and utensils.

She winced when she saw Samuel had already finished his coffee and was reading the *Boston Times*.

"Why didn't you wake me? Now I feel like a sloth."

He glanced up from his paper and smiled. "A sloth? I think I have to stop taking you to zoos. Besides, you needed to sleep."

"I love sloths." She pouted. "Don't make fun of them. Where's Father?"

"No idea, but I'm sure he's making plans to take over the world." Samuel folded the newspaper, placed it on the table, and stood up. He walked over and pulled out the chair for her. "He is one very driven man."

"That's the pot calling the kettle black." She raised her eyebrow at him.

"Where did you learn that phrase?" he asked, taken aback, as he returned to his seat.

"Never you mind. I'm hungry." Elizabeth was not about to tell him she heard it in a vision years ago and had grown to like it. That was a secret she'd keep to herself.

She reached for the servant's bell as an underbutler swept through the door carrying a fresh pot of tea. "Oh, thank you."

Mrs. Owen followed with a plate of scrambled eggs, bacon, and fruit.

Elizabeth frowned at her. "Mrs. Owen, you have more important things to do than to serve me breakfast."

"It's just for today, miss . . . Mrs. Hunter. I wanted to do it on your first morning back as a married woman. We are so proud of you."

"That I finally snagged a man?" Elizabeth teased.

Mrs. Owen put her hands on her hips and gave her the once over. "No, young lady, that you stood up to your father. That takes a bit of doing. Now, give me a kiss and we'll all get on with our day." The head housekeeper leaned over and presented her cheek. Elizabeth dutifully kissed it.

"I have a feeling this is not normal behavior in other Great Houses. Am I right, Mrs. Owen?" Samuel sat down in his chair again.

The older woman exited the room with a harrumph.

Elizabeth and Samuel burst out laughing. When she calmed herself down, Elizabeth reached across the table and took her husband's hand. He brought it up to his lips to kiss; she snatched it back before he could.

"What? You let Mrs. Owen kiss you."

"That's different. We are in my father's house now and I like certain things to remain . . . private."

"Which is why I want to move out."

"Samuel, we already came to an agreement."

He sighed. "No, you dictated terms, and your father and I capitulated."

Elizabeth frowned at him. "I offered a compromise that would allow us to get what we both want . . . in time."

Samuel gave her an incomprehensible look, then returned to reading the newspaper. "Your father is wrong. I think you are more than qualified to run the family business on your own."

"But I don't want to."

"And neither do I." He folded up the newspaper again and placed next to his plate. "I'm off."

"Where?" She mumbled while eating her eggs.

"The warehouse. There are some things I want to pick up."

"Let me come. I've never seen it, and it sounds very mysterious."

Samuel stood. "It's smelly and dirty and no place for a lady."

"But it's yours." She pouted.

"Don't do that."

"What?" Elizabeth batted her eyes.

"Fine. Finish your breakfast. I'll tell Sampson we're going out."

Elizabeth gobbled up her food in a most unladylike fashion.

***

Jonathan glanced out his upstairs library window to see Samuel leaving with Elizabeth sitting in the front passenger's seat. Another car with four of his guardsmen pulled out to follow them. He winced from the cut on his forehead as he watched Brendan pull up in a new car not long after.

He'd decided to spend the morning working from home. Mr. Evans had called and reported that the explosive device had been thrown rather than attached to the car. Jonathan was relieved to hear it, but he wasn't pleased when he was informed they had no leads on who was responsible.

As for his brother's arrival, Jonathan was confident that his executive assistant would do his usual efficient job of making his work office look functional, but with no important material lying around, just in case Hal showed up there first. All of this was incredibly annoying, but it would be imprudent to forbid his only brother from coming home. Though Hal had no real power or influence, he was married to the youngest daughter of Alfred Tillenghast, the most powerful Great House in the Midwest and the largest airship builder in the world. Often Hal would drop tidbits of useful information about his father-in-law, but there was always a price.

Sampson entered the study carrying a tray with his lunch.

"I presume everything is ready for my brother's arrival."

"Yes, sir. The entire staff will be sure to act surprised when he arrives." Sampson placed the tray at the end of the desk. "He'll know it's all a façade, of course."

"Naturally." Jonathan nodded. "But we must keep up with appearances." He glanced up at the house manager. "Where did Elizabeth and Samuel go?"

"Shopping and then to his family's warehouse. Mrs. Owen sent lunch with them as well as extra for the guards."

"Thank you."

"After what happened yesterday, I knew you'd want them to have extra protection. And I reminded Brendan that if anyone inquired, your injuries were due to a car accident."

Voices rising outside the study caught their attention. There was a shuffling noise, a shout, then one of the underbutlers scurried in.

"Mr. Weldsmore, sir. I'd like to inform you that—"

The underbutler's announcement was cut off by Hal Weldsmore stomping in to stand next to Sampson. He tried to imitate Sampson's rigid posture, but failed. "How do you do that, Sampson, old man?" Hal poked Sampson in the spine. "Do you have a piece of whatever new-fangled metal my brother is developing stashed up your drawers?"

"Thank you, Sampson. You may go." Jonathan reined in his anger at his brother's rudeness. He refused to let his brother goad him into saying something he'd use against him later.

As Sampson exited, Jonathan leaned forward to see if he could smell alcohol on his breath. He didn't, but he did notice Hal was losing his hair.

Hal peered at him. "What did your barber do to you? I hope you fired him."

Jonathan didn't bother to answer.

The brothers were the same height, but where Jonathan had maintained a regular exercise routine and was a fit for a man his age, Hal had developed a belly and hunched over. His skin looked waxy from indulging in fatty food and his nose had an almost bulbous quality to it. Jonathan suspected he was drinking too much.

"To what do we owe the pleasure of your unexpected company?" Jonathan forced a pleasant smile. "If you had informed me, we could have prepared a proper welcome."

"Really? You're actually going to pretend that you didn't know I was coming? Or have your spies gotten that bad?"

Jonathan shrugged. "Why are you here, Hal?"

"Can I sit?"

Jonathan stared at him, wishing he'd go away, but decided that was pointless and gestured for him to be seated.

"And what about him?" Hal jerked his head toward the door of the study.

In walked a sepia-toned Negro a few inches shorter than Hal, but broader across the chest and shoulders. His black curly hair was short and curved around his skull like a tight-fitting cap. He wore a long, obsidian-colored wool jacket that brushed his knees, with matching trousers, a copper-hued silk shirt, and black suede gloves. What surprised Jonathan was the gold and copper wire woven into his lapels and cuffs. Never in his life had he seen a Negro wearing the clothing of a man from a Great House. It meant only one thing: this was Thomas Rochester, head airship designer for House Tillenghast.

Jonathan took two strides forward and extended his hand. "Mr. Rochester. I apologize. I did not expect you."

"What he really means is that he knew I was bringing someone, he just didn't know it would be you." Hal smirked.

Thomas and Jonathan shook hands.

The Negro man's grip felt stronger and more solid than most men's. Jonathan wondered if he worked on the airship production line to assess quality control, but quickly dismissed that thought as being too menial for a man of Thomas's prominence.

"Please come in. The servants will bring refreshments in a few minutes."

Thomas gave him a polite nod. "Thank you, Mr. Weldsmore. I've looked forward to meeting you."

Hal waltzed farther into the study like he owned it. He wiped his hand on the newly polished desk and peered into every corner as if he had lost something. "You always were the fastidious one."

Jonathan escorted Thomas to one of the more plush chairs on the side of the room across from a glass-topped mahogany coffee table. Hal followed them over after he finished his quick inspection.

"I was sorry to hear about the death of your father. I understand he worked for Warrick right until the end." Jonathan commented.

Thomas nodded. "Yes. He loved working for Gwen after her father passed away. She was easy to work for. James, however, was a bit idiosyncratic."

"You know, I met your father once. When Lincoln honored him and Gwen for their service during the House Wars. He was a hero. I was surprised he didn't start his own company."

Thomas shook his head. "He was more interested in designing airship propulsion systems than running a business. Old Man Warrick was happy about that. He never handled competition well."

"I would have thought you'd go to work for Gwen. Though she doesn't come from a Great House, she runs a tight ship over there."

"I did for a while . . ." Thomas's voice trailed off. "But House Tillenghast offered me better opportunities."

Jonathan's eyes narrowed. "I can see that."

Hal slumped in his chair. "Refreshments?"

As if by magic, an underbutler arrived carrying a tray of tea, coffee, and cakes. He set it down on the table and picked up the teapot to serve them.

Jonathan waved him away. "We'll do this ourselves, Bernard."

"Sir." As he returned the teapot to the tray, the underbutler gave them each a quick bob of his head then left the room.

Hal went straight for the coffee then balanced three miniature cakes precariously on a cerulean-blue china plate.

Thomas, on the other hand, ignored the food.

Jonathan took this all in. He knew Hal was no stooge but merely playing a part. What role that was he had yet to figure out.

"How is Emily?" Jonathan inquired, hoping to take an indirect approach.

"Enlarging her doll collection since it appears we will remain childless." Hal munched on a cake. "But you don't really care, do you?"

Jonathan was about to make a rude retort when Thomas beat him to it.

"He's jealous of you, Mr. Weldsmore. And I don't think that will change anytime soon." Thomas sat up straight in his chair. "But I hope he will comport himself with a little more dignity from now on."

Hal shrugged as he brushed crumbs from his lips and reached for another cake.

"Why are you both here?" Jonathan demanded. "What do you want?"

Thomas took a deep breath. "To stop a war, Mr. Weldsmore."

5

The shadow of a passenger airship passed over Samuel and Elizabeth as they walked from their car over to the dock in the noonday sun. The sound of its propellers mixed with ship horns that echoed from the harbor, creating an orchestra out of the wind. As they approached a one-story brick warehouse, Samuel took a hefty key out of his pocket and inserted it into a padlock. He turned it, but the key mechanism jammed. He gave it a sharp twist; it opened with snap.

"You know I can buy you a new lock if you like," Elizabeth teased, cradling the lunch basket in her arms. "Consider it another wedding present."

"There you go trying to fix me." Samuel grinned as he slid the door to the warehouse back to reveal a dark, empty maw. The smell of dust, fish oil, and old leather drifted out.

"I don't want to fix you. I want to fix this place." She coughed and waved the dust out of her face. "There's no electricity, is there?"

"Not on this side of the harbor."

Samuel's parents had been ship chandlers who sold peacoats, lanyards, canvas trousers, rope, and hooks of every size and shape to seaman. His mother had managed the finances while his father handled sales and inventory. Well respected among the seafaring community, they were successful enough to send their only son to a good school in a better part of the Middle District. They'd hoped with his education he would expand the business. However, Samuel had had other plans.

Samuel felt around the wall until he found an oil lamp. He placed the lamp on his hip as he pulled up the glass globe. Steadying it with one hand, he reached into his pocket and produced one of the new automatic brass lighters they had bought while in Austria. With a quick flick of his thumb, the lighter ignited. He lit the wick, replaced the glass, then put away his lighter. He took hold of the handle and held the lamp out in front of him.

"Coming?"

"Can't we go sailing first? It's been too long." Elizabeth sighed, remembering a romantic time they'd had in a small boat right after they were married.

"Maybe tomorrow."

Elizabeth glanced longingly back at the indigo water before she gestured to Samuel to lead on.

Rats scurried about as they disturbed their lairs. Elizabeth tried not to flinch, but it was almost impossible. Samuel never noticed her discomfort as he was too busy pulling tarp off the windows to let in the sun.

The light revealed a modest-sized warehouse broken up into three sections by walls with a doorway through each one. A dark and inhospitable place, a person could barely see the inside of the building from one end to the other. Strewn across the floor were several broken crates; their contents long gone. Caught in the lamplight, spider webs glistened across the windows and most of the corners of the roof. A few shattered glass bottles dotted the floor. More oil lamps hung at regular intervals by each door as if expecting company. For a place once filled with love and activity, it was now a hollow reminder of what life had been for Samuel.

"What happened to the inventory?" Elizabeth asked.

"I sold it all after my parents passed away." He shoved a piece of crate with his foot. "This was their life, not mine." He turned down the wick in the lamp. "The office is this way."

"Father might be interested in leasing this from you. I've no doubt he has some secret project he could tuck in here."

Samuel shook his head. "No, this is mine. The only one I will share it with is you."

"I understand." She gave him a soft smile. "And thank you."

He stopped for a moment, turned, and kissed her. "We have to have something that is just ours."

"I agree."

"Here we are. Home sweet home." Samuel escorted her into a room off of what would have been the storefront. Inside sat a pine desk, a cot, two plain wooden chairs, a small cooking stove, and a lavatory tucked away in a closet.

"You lived here?" Elizabeth asked, choking at the dust.

"It's rather bleak, but I haven't spent much time here. Once I settled my parents' affairs, I found work as a bodyguard." He shrugged. "Most of the time I lived at my clients' homes. Usually in the servants' quarters."

Elizabeth shook her head in confusion. "I don't understand. You never lived at the house when father hired you."

"Actually, I did." He grimaced. "Sampson tucked me away into an unobtrusive spot as per your father's orders."

"He never told me! Why?"

"I think he didn't want you to feel like you were being watched all the time."

"But I was." Her voice lowered.

Samuel placed his hands on her shoulders. "It was my job. Please don't take it out on Sampson."

She pursed her lips in annoyance. "I would never blame Sampson. My father, on the other hand . . . Never mind. That's all in the past."

He grinned and jumped back. "So, I was thinking about turning this into a real office."

"You mean with file cabinets and better chairs?"

"Exactly."

Elizabeth watched in amusement as he got more excited.

"I'd need a sign, though. To hang out front."

"And what would this sign say, pray tell?"

He swung his hand in the air as if he was writing it himself. "*Samuel Hunter, Private Detective.*"

"You want to be a detective again? Why? I thought you were done with all that."

Samuel leaned against the desk. "I have to work, Elizabeth. And not for your father. Plus, I'm good at it and I can pick my own clients."

Elizabeth took off her gloves and reached into her purse. "But first you have to get them." She tapped one of the rickety chairs with the tip of her finger as if it would break apart at the slightest touch. "And they'll want to sit in here without fearing for their lives."

"You're no fun."

She took out a pencil and notepad and jotted down notes. "Let's see . . . new desk, chairs, file cabinet, proper stove, and heater."

Samuel crossed his arms, nodding in approval.

Elizabeth pranced out of the office and into the storerooms. She pointed at one of the interior walls. "Can we remove that? You may need more space."

"I'll have to check to see if it's a load-bearing wall. If not, then yes."

"You should have a nice but functional waiting room. Not too fancy. Subtle elegance so most everyone will be comfortable."

"Why not everyone?"

Elizabeth narrowed her eyes at him. "You'll never make everyone happy, Samuel. I suggest you become accustomed to that right now."

He nodded. "I'll need to get more equipment. A camera for starters."

"Or you could hire a photographer whenever you needed one. That might be more cost effective." Elizabeth stopped moving for a second, took a deep breath, then exhaled. "There's one more thing you'll need."

"What's that?"

"A partner."

Samuel's excitement evaporated. "Who did you have in mind?"

"Me."

"No." He stood up and shoved the desk back to the wall. "It's too dangerous."

"Samuel, even your father had a partner in your mother. Besides, who's going to manage the finances and invoicing for your services?" She took his arm. "And who knows, some of your clients may eventually come from respectable Middle District and Beacon Hill residences. And you'll need someone like me to make them feel more at ease."

Samuel shook his head. "No, I won't risk it. Besides, what will your—"

"—my father say?" She interrupted him. "He won't like it, but he'll agree. Besides, I want to be more than a society wife. I want to be useful."

"You don't understand. I may take on clients from the South Side or Liberty Row. Not exactly people you'd be comfortable with."

Elizabeth frowned. "I can learn."

"And there's the possibility that an irate client might show up. Or worse, the person I'm investigating." Samuel took her hands and held them to his chest. "I'm sorry. I can't let you do this."

She yanked them away, turned on her heel, and walked out.

***

Samuel decided it was best to leave. The day had definitely not turned out like he had planned. As he closed the warehouse door behind him, he thought he heard someone call his name. He stared into the vast darkness of the room. The air shimmered a bit, distorting the walls and ceiling. Samuel was about to go back in when he felt a touch on his arm.

"Are we going or not?" Elizabeth asked tersely as the touch became a light tug.

He blinked a few times as a wave of dizziness swept through him. Then it was gone. The shimmer undulated then disappeared. Thinking his eyes were playing tricks on him, he slammed the door and locked it.

As they drove away in silence, Samuel noticed the four men who had followed them from the house get back into their steam-powered car. They kept a decent distance behind them as they traveled through the narrow streets. He caught a glimpse of brass woven in the cuffs and lapels of their plain black woolen suits. Samuel was pretty sure they were Jonathan's men ordered to keep an eye on them. It annoyed him at first that his father-in-law didn't think he could protect his wife, but the Great Houses were vulnerable at certain levels, and kidnapping family members was not unheard of. Samuel decided that the unobtrusive guards took some pressure off of him. He would thank Jonathan for it later. It never hurt to tell one's father-in-law he was right every once in a while.

When they arrived back at the house, he noticed an unfamiliar car parked near the front entrance. A chauffer wearing a gold-embossed emblem of an airship on his cap leaned against a new silver Benz Motorwagen while he smoked a cigarette. One of the few cars that had enclosed seating, it was also a rare sight to see such an automobile in Boston. Based on the emblem that the chauffer wore, Samuel surmised a guest from House Tillenghast had arrived.

"My uncle is here." Elizabeth sighed.

"Now he shows up? Why couldn't he have come to the wedding?" Samuel asked.

She shrugged. "Be glad he didn't. Uncle Hal always tends to make a scene."

As Samuel stopped the car, one of the underbutlers opened the door for Elizabeth and helped her out while another attended to the driver's side. Samuel followed Elizabeth inside but was surprised when she headed straight for her father's study instead of upstairs. When he entered, he saw Jonathan sitting next to the coffee table while a Negro dressed as if he belonged to a Great House poured himself a drink. Slouched in a chair on the other side of the room was a man he assumed was Hal Weldsmore. Though there was a slight resemblance in the eyes and nose, he bore none of the dignity and self-confidence of his younger brother.

"Elizabeth! You look as lovely as usual. Marriage suits you." Hal launched himself out of his chair and stumbled over to her. It was clear he was going to manhandle his wife, so Samuel stepped in front of him and extended his hand.

"I'm Samuel Hunter. Elizabeth's husband."

Hal glanced at Samuel's proffered hand, shrugged, then shook it with just enough grip to be respectable. Afterward, he fled back to his chair.

"I'm afraid we have not been introduced," the Negro interjected as he walked toward Samuel. "I'm Thomas Rochester."

"Emmet Rochester's son!" Elizabeth exclaimed. "Father, you never told me you knew him."

"We just met, Mrs. Hunter. I'm traveling with your uncle." Thomas shook Samuel's hand then took Elizabeth's and gave her a little bow with his head. "It is a pleasure to meet both of you."

With the practiced eye of a detective, Samuel noticed Thomas's bearing and gait were a little off. His left foot struck the ground ball first instead of heel first, and his upper body leaned in front of his hips. Samuel wondered briefly if the man had broken his back at some point in his life and was wearing some sort of brace but was distracted by how charismatic Thomas was. Elizabeth beamed at his attention. That was very unlike her.

"Elizabeth, perhaps we should let your father continue on with his meeting," Samuel remarked a little too sharply.

"Nonsense," interjected Hal. "I haven't seen Elizabeth in ages."

His wife gave him an annoyed look. "Samuel, it isn't every day that you get to meet someone like Thomas Rochester."

Every nerve ending of Samuel's screamed that something of great importance was going on in this room. The sudden appearance of Hal Weldsmore accompanied by the son of one of the most famous Negro men in the country was more than a social call. Thomas's father had been on the crew that took down the metal-clad airship the *Ulric* at the start of the House Wars, though he later became a noted airship designer. Samuel vaguely recalled Thomas had followed in his father's footsteps, but he did not know where he'd ended up—until now.

"You work for House Tillenghast," Samuel remarked. "That must be challenging."

"That's a polite way of putting it." Thomas chuckled. "I understand you were a Pinkerton detective. You must have some interesting stories to tell."

"Sometimes a little too interesting," Samuel deflected.

Elizabeth patted his arm. "Pinkerton's loss was our gain. Wasn't it, Father?"

"I'm sure you're tired after your excursion down to the wharf and need to rest, Elizabeth," Jonathan said off-handedly as he reached over to pour himself more coffee. "Don't forget you are both attending the Gardners' salon and dinner tonight. Hal and Thomas will accompany you."

Samuel saw his wife's eyes narrow at the obvious dismissal, but then they brightened up. "Of course. I forgot. We had such a busy day planning our new business venture."

Jonathan stopped what he was doing and turned to face her. "What?"

"Samuel and I have decided to become private investigators," she announced. "Though truth be told, he'll be doing the investigating while I handle new business and finances."

It was if all the air had been sucked out of the room.

"Elizabeth, that is not—" Samuel started before he was cut off.

"Out of the question!" Jonathan roared. "I will not have my daughter gallivanting on the docks." He turned his venom on Samuel. "How could you agree to this?"

"I didn't," Samuel shot back. "But whether or not she becomes my partner is up to us, not you."

The two men stared each other down.

"What a wonderful idea." Hal spoke up, goading his brother. "Women should take a greater role in business. Just like Grandmother."

"We will discuss this later," Jonathan said, lowering his voice in an almost threatening tone.

"No." Samuel felt the bile rising in his throat. "There is nothing to discuss. Elizabeth will make an excellent partner. However . . ." He turned and stared at his wife. "Once we have children, she will focus her attention on them."

Elizabeth gave him her most charming smile. "Of course." She waltzed over and took her husband's arm. "Give us a few days to put together the business plan, Father. I'd love to have your thoughts."

"And if it makes you feel better, sir, you can post two of the guardsmen you sent to watch us today at the warehouse on a regular basis," Samuel offered.

"Wait? What?" Elizabeth stammered, caught off guard.

"Come, my dear." Samuel led her out of the room. "I'm hungry and I'm sure you'd like to get started on our 'business plan.'"

"Mr. and Mrs. Hunter, I wish you the best of luck on your new endeavor." Hal raised a small cake in salute. "And if I ever may be of assistance . . ." His voice trailed off.

"If they need assistance, House Weldsmore will give it to them, brother. Not House Tillenghast," Jonathan growled at him.

As Samuel exited the room, he realized that he had just watched Great House politics in play, and his wife had been a master at it.

***

A full five minutes of silence went by before anyone said anything after Samuel and Elizabeth had gone up the stairs to their suite of rooms.

"Has Alfred Tillenghast gone mad?" Jonathan leveled his gaze at Thomas. "He wants to start another House Wars?"

The young man shook his head. "Not here. In Europe. I've seen the airship orders come in and the new designs. He means to do this."

"Which could be misinformation." Jonathan glared at his brother. "It's not like we haven't seen that tactic before."

Jonathan referred to their grandmother, Beatrice. A woman known for her ruthless business acumen, she'd used any means necessary to take down her enemies, both real and perceived. Jonathan believed she could easily outmaneuver any Great House today, even Tillenghast.

"All I know is that Alfred Tillenghast brought me into his study, which is larger than yours by the way, and told me that if you and he formed an alliance, the Great States of America would be unstoppable on the world stage."

"That's a little grand, but possible if House Tillenghast is manipulating the European markets with the intent that it would ripple across the Great States and eventually Asia and South America," Jonathan remarked. "But they can't control all the markets."

"Nor do they want to," Hal replied. "They just want enough instability to make the Austria-Germanic Pact and the British nervous enough to beef up their navies, both in the air and on the sea."

"And if I join with House Tillenghast to monopolize the sales of both airships and sea-worthy vessels, our Houses would essentially control their ability to make war. And if Europe goes to war, we make more money." Jonathan frowned. "That would make sense if we were the only ones building ships, but we aren't."

Hal and Thomas gave each other a look.

Jonathan's gut twisted in a knot as he realized he was missing a crucial piece of information. "What is it?"

"We think there is another player who may be tasked with destroying our competition. One that some of the other Houses allied with Tillenghast fought against using, but lost." Thomas leaned forward and lowered his voice. "We believe House Tillenghast is using demons."

"That's ridiculous!" Jonathan retorted. "I can't accept Tillenghast would believe in such superstitious nonsense."

"My mother swore that an abolitionist saved her from one and died for his troubles." Thomas shrugged. "She may have been an illiterate slave woman, but she wasn't prone to making up stories. Especially about that time of her life."

"Nonsense. Utter nonsense." Jonathan tapped the table next to him with one finger as he thought. "Besides, Tillenghast and I would have to come to an agreement on who controls what and how much. Not an easy task."

Hal's demeanor shifted from dubious to hopeful. "Then you'll consider it?"

"I consider all proposals, Hal. You should understand that by now." Jonathan studied his brother. "But what do you get out of it?"

"A seat at the table, little brother."

6

The maid finished putting the final touches on Elizabeth's hair for the Gardner party. It was twisted up in a chignon with a silver wire fascinator woven to resemble a small bouquet. In the center of each flower sat a tiny emerald. Tonight, Elizabeth wore her long-sleeved steel-blue silk gown and a matching corset with silver wire laced through it in various star patterns. Her ankle boots were made of soft dark-indigo suede. As one of the younger members of the Boston Great Houses, she knew she set fashion trends throughout the northeast. Her influence was an accident of birth, but she enjoyed it and hoped she brought a little more common sense to clothing than previous generations.

Elizabeth stood up and examined herself in a long mirror while her maid checked the hemline. It would do, but it reminded her she needed more practical clothes for working in Samuel's new office.

"Sally?"

"Yes, miss." The red-haired girl with an Irish brogue brushed any lint from the back of the dress.

"Tell Mrs. Owen to make an appointment tomorrow with my dressmaker. After breakfast around eleven will do."

"Yes, miss."

"Will Tessa be here later to help me undress?"

"No, miss. Tessa has the evening off. We switched so she could go out with her beau." Sally looked worried. "You don't mind?"

Elizabeth shook her head. "Of course not. I'm thrilled to be back in such a well-organized house. You would not believe what we had to put up with on our travels." She leaned closer to the mirror to check her makeup. "As Samuel would say, you are all professionals."

"Because it's true." A deep voice declared behind her.

She turned to see her husband in his new finery.

Samuel wore a black woolen jacket that came down to his knees with a pair of matching pants and a white cotton shirt. Several threads

43

of copper wire were woven into the cuffs and lapels. It was just enough to make him look presentable in any Great House.

"If you tell me I resemble your father, I'm getting a divorce."

Elizabeth glided across the room and kissed him lightly on the lips. "You are far more handsome than my father."

He leaned in for a longer kiss, but Elizabeth stopped him by pulling away. "Thank you, Sally."

The maid bobbed a curtsy and exited, shutting the door behind her.

"Not even in front of the staff?" Samuel asked. "Or are you still pining after Thomas?"

"Don't be ridiculous. He's charming, which is a rarity in anyone associated with House Tillenghast." She poked him in the chest in irritation.

Samuel threw his arms up in surrender. "Fine. But he's a little too charming. Unlike your uncle. Now do I get to kiss my wife?"

"Not in front of the staff," Elizabeth replied. "They are loyal, but some tend to gossip."

"That we're married and we love each other? Oh, the scandal!" He mocked being horrified, then folded his arms across his chest. "And what will they say about what happened in your father's study this afternoon?"

She sighed. "I know. I'm sorry I manipulated you like that, but you were being unreasonable. There is absolutely no good reason why I can't help you."

"How about you have to learn more about running your father's shipping business. And that takes time."

Elizabeth was about to say something she'd regret when she remembered that Samuel had not grown up in a Great House—or, in particular, House Weldsmore. "After my mother died, Father used to bring me into his study and let me play with his prototype ships. Being a child, I had a million questions, and he answered all of them. When I was a teenager, I became the lady of the house, and I spent much of my time learning finances and my place in society. Among other things."

"Like what?"

"Keeping secrets," Elizabeth said, more somber than she intended.

Samuel cocked his head. "And what might those be?"

Elizabeth brushed off the question. "I already know a lot about the business."

"Then what is this really about?" Samuel asked.

Elizabeth took his hands. "I want something we build together. And not just children. Is that so wrong?"

He shook his head. "No, but it makes me wonder why we're still living here."

"Because my father would be lost without me." She held his hands to her chest. "This way he has time to get used to the fact I will be leaving. He's a lot more vulnerable than he appears."

Samuel frowned. "If that's true, then let's hope no one else realizes it."

***

They arrived at the Gardner mansion behind a row of other steam-powered vehicles. Samuel couldn't wait to get out of the car they shared with Hal and Thomas. The airship designer wasn't a problem; in fact, after Samuel got past the man's ability to charm every woman in the house, he decided he was interesting and a complete gentleman. Hal, on the other hand, stared at Elizabeth the entire time. Samuel felt the urge to punch him, but the repercussions of that were more than he wanted to deal with. And besides, the man wasn't worth the trouble.

As per Elizabeth's instructions, he waited for the Gardner footmen to open the doors, and he made sure he escorted his wife in before Hal and Thomas. Though both men were associated with Great Houses, Elizabeth took precedence since she was the heir to Jonathan's fortune. Great House protocol was almost as bad as what he'd had to deal with when meeting what he termed "so-called royalty" in Europe. He'd even considered packing two bags and bundling her off to his parents' warehouse for the duration of their honeymoon. However, in its current state of disrepair it would have been rather uncomfortable.

Samuel took Elizabeth's arm as they walked through a phalanx of Gardner guardsmen. Each bore the House emblem on their lapel of a pick and hammer on a shield. The Gardners owned most of the coal and iron mines on the eastern seaboard. As they approached the mansion, Samuel noticed it was much grander and more ostentatious than the Weldsmore House. Roman-style columns, oak doors two stories tall, and banners with the House emblem draped from the roof. Marble vases about six feet high were filled with trailing roses, and shaped olive trees flanked the steps leading to the front door. It was rather over-whelming, so Samuel ignored as much as possible and focused on his lovely wife.

They entered a hall lit with gold and crystal chandeliers hanging from a ceiling four stories tall. Small prisms of light reflected off the walls, giving the impression of a fairy land. A sweeping staircase with multiple landings took up one side of the room, which was lined with exotic flowers. Nearby, a row of guests waited to be greeted by their hosts.

"If I've got this right, Gordon and Esther Gardner have been married for forty-eight years. No children. Several nieces and nephews. No one is sure yet who they will pick to inherit, so there is a lot of jockeying around to see who wins the grand prize." Samuel ran through the basic information Elizabeth had told him about their hosts.

She nodded and smiled at a few guests as they followed them in. "It's not a prize, but a responsibility."

"That's your opinion." Samuel noticed a small group of young men huddled together on the other side of the room. Blond, blue eyed, and without a callous among them, he sensed they might be the nephews in question. "They, on the other hand, are only interested in the money."

Elizabeth glanced over at them. "I've no doubt you are correct. And it's shame. The Gardners may like to flaunt their money, but I under-stand that before the House Wars they aided escaped slaves."

"Really?"

"Don't look so surprised. Not all the Great Houses seek to crush everyone around them, including my father."

Elizabeth detached herself from him as they moved up in line to meet their hosts. She extended her hand to greet them. "Mr. and Mrs. Gard-ner, may I present my husband, Samuel Hunter."

Mrs. Gardner, a petite woman, wore a gold silk dress with a match-ing corset that had gold plates woven into it like a piece of armor. Her gray hair was bound up in a tight bun with more gold filaments braided into it. Samuel guessed her attire cost more than what the average Bostonian made in their lifetime. When she saw Elizabeth, she motioned for her to give her a kiss.

"Elizabeth, what a delight! I'm so glad you could make it." She smiled warmly at Samuel as she shook his hand. "Welcome, Mr. Hunter." Mrs. Gardner turned to her husband. "Gordon, come meet Elizabeth's new husband."

A foot and a half taller than his wife and with the girth of a small airship, Mr. Gardner looked down his nose at Samuel and squinted. "You used to be a Pinkerton man."

Samuel extended his hand. "Yes, sir."

Gordon Gardner stared at Samuel's hand and let it hang there. "What makes you think you're good enough for a Weldsmore?"

"Gordon!" His wife exclaimed. "Don't be rude."

Those nearest them stopped talking and watched the exchange, clearly hoping they would witness an upstart Middle District man being humiliated in public.

Samuel dropped his hand and looked Mr. Gardner straight in the eyes. "Because I am Samuel Hunter, sir."

Mr. Gardner pursed his lips and nodded. "Confidence. I like that." He extended his hand. "Welcome."

Samuel shook it as disappointed sighs echoed around them. Surprised to feel old calluses and scars on the older man's hands, he then remembered Elizabeth had told him Gordon Gardner's father had required all his sons to work the mines growing up. It was how he'd weeded out who was worthy and who wasn't. Gordon was the only one who had survived.

"My darling niece, you are holding up the line." Hal's voice piped up behind them. "I've no doubt that Gordon would love to meet Thomas Rochester."

Gordon leaned closer to Samuel and whispered, "Damned Tillenghast lackeys." Before he could respond, Mr. Gardner had turned his attention toward his wife's uncle. "Hal, to what do we owe the pleasure?"

Samuel took that as his cue to move on. He escorted Elizabeth into the crowded salon where waiters bustled about serving champagne and hors d'oeuvres. He plastered a congenial smile on his face as he navigated through a throng of people who felt they had to stop and engage his wife every few feet. They directed their conversation toward her, but watched him out of the corner of their eyes as if he were going to transform into something hideous. At one point, Samuel was tempted to say "Boo" just for his own amusement, but he knew his wife would take a dim view of that. Samuel thought most of the Beacon Hill elite tolerated him because of his marriage to Elizabeth, and most did, at least to his face. What surprised him were the subtle nasty looks he received from the servants. Apparently they did not approve of a Middle District man marrying above his station.

After the majority of the guests had arrived, Mrs. Gardner swooped in and took Elizabeth's arm.

"I'm absconding with your wife, Mr. Hunter. I must hear all the details of your honeymoon trip since I am not able to travel much anymore." Mrs. Gardner gave him a wink and whisked Elizabeth away.

While Samuel wondered how best to fit in without looking too obvious about it, a large hand landed on his shoulder. It took all his willpower not to throw it off and brace for a fight. His Pinkerton training dictated that he always be prepared, but it wouldn't do to assault what turned out to be his host, Mr. Gardner.

"Sir." Samuel gave Gordon a little nod of his head. "Thank you for inviting me. It's a lovely party."

"Don't let my wife hear you call this a party. It's a 'salon.'" Mr. Gardner rolled his eyes. "Music and/or readings are involved, but no dancing. I'm surprised Elizabeth hasn't taught you that yet."

"I must admit that I may have not listened to that particular lesson." Samuel grinned. "My head is still spinning from all the protocol we had to deal with in Europe."

"The Great Houses are worse." The older man chuckled. "You like whiskey?"

"Is that a trick question?"

Mr. Gardner slapped him on the back, almost knocking Samuel over. "I like you. Come on." The older man gestured toward a hallway on the other side of the room.

Samuel glanced over to where Elizabeth was beset by a group of women who fawned over her.

"She'll be fine. She's a Weldsmore." Mr. Gardner ushered him away.

As the two men wound their way through the crowd, Samuel watched as his host greeted people yet never allowed himself to be sidetracked. Samuel decided he needed Elizabeth to teach him that skill. Or better yet, the master of it himself—Gordon Gardner.

It took a few minutes, but Samuel eventually found himself in a library with a large empty space in the middle of the room surrounded by a number of stuffed armchairs and a bar. The maroon velvet curtains were drawn over three floor-to-ceiling windows with walnut bookshelves next to them. It was a more masculine room than what he had seen of the rest of the house. Samuel suspected that this was Mr. Gardner's hideaway.

The clink of glasses caught his attention; Gordon handed him a neat glass of whiskey.

"If you ask me to put water or ice in this, I'll have you thrown out of my house," the older man threatened.

"I wouldn't dream of it." Samuel lifted his glass to salute his host, then took a sip. He savored the taste on his tongue for a moment before he swallowed the smooth and earthy drink. It was the best whiskey he had ever tasted. "Excellent. Thank you. Now, maybe you can tell me why we're hiding in here."

Mr. Gardner almost choked on his drink, but recovered quickly. "I hate these salons, but I love my wife. Of all the people who might want to escape with me, I figured it'd be you. You see, I've done my homework on you, Samuel Hunter."

Samuel put his glass down on an end table. "Really. And what did you discover?"

"You're honest. Too honest." The older man poured himself another drink. "And you try to do the right thing. Even when it's hard. Even when it's impossible. And you're not one of us. Which is why I have a favor to ask."

Samuel crossed his arms across his chest and sighed. "You need an outsider."

"Yes. I will probably die before my wife, and she's a rather trusting soul. I need someone to watch over her. Protect her from my sniveling money-grubbing nephews."

"Why me and not Jonathan?" Samuel asked.

"You'll notice things others won't."

"I'd be happy to. Though I hope that won't be for many years to come."

Gordon walked over to the wall next to the bar, tapped a wooden slat until it popped open. Inside was a metal lever. "Stand back."

Samuel backed away from the middle of the room as Gordon pulled down the lever. A whirring sound shook the floor as two panels slide back to reveal a billiard table. Gears churned as it rose from the floor. Its legs were constructed of interlocking metal gears that slid into place when the table reached its full height.

Gordon nodded then pointed to the billiard table. "You play?"

"I most certainly do."

Without a word, both men picked out cue sticks. Samuel hoped that Elizabeth would not be too annoyed with him for disappearing with their host.

***

Elizabeth answered questions about her dress and their honeymoon with all the grace and decorum of a lady. Many of the young women wanted more salacious details about her Middle District husband, but she kept those to herself. Instead, she encouraged them to find suitable husbands outside the Great Houses. This caused one woman to flee in horror while the others entertained fantasies about what that would be like. Elizabeth almost burst out laughing. She realized that none of them would be allowed to marry outside their class. Not unless something exceptional happened, like it had between Samuel and herself.

Elizabeth thought she may have gone too far when she noticed silence had descended upon their little group and all eyes stared past her shoulder. Someone touched her arm. She looked over to see Thomas Rochester standing next to her.

He gave the women an elegant bow. "Good evening."

"Forgive me." Elizabeth's lips quivered in amusement. "May I introduce Thomas Rochester of House Tillenghast."

No one uttered a word until Thomas broke the silence. "In your own unique way, each of you ladies look remarkable tonight. You outmatch the women of the Midwest by far."

His rich baritone voice caused a few to giggle behind their hands.

"Now, if you don't mind, Mrs. Hunter promised to sit with me during the recital. And I want to make sure she gets the best seat." He dipped his head at them, then offered his arm to Elizabeth.

She took it, hiding her relief at being rescued. "Thank you, Mr. Rochester. I can't wait to hear Mr. Racine play." Elizabeth took his arm and allowed him to escort her away. She leaned a little closer to him. "Thank you, sir. That was well played. I guarantee you will be the topic of many conversations this evening."

"I do not know you well, Mrs. Hunter, but any woman from a Great House who marries a man like Samuel Hunter not only has my respect but my admiration. You did a brave thing by marrying him."

"Not really. I love him."

"That may be true, but often our familial and political ties do not allow us to follow our heart."

Elizabeth stopped and stared at him. "Mr. Rochester, I do believe you are a romantic."

"Let's keep that our secret." He gave her a warm smile.

"Tommy!" A male voice interrupted them.

Elizabeth turned to see a man in his mid-thirties, blond hair and green eyes, wearing a silk-blend black suit with gold filaments woven into his cuffs, lapels, and pockets. They were sewn in so expertly that they sparkled in the right lighting. She narrowed her eyes at the Tillenghast airship crest on his lapel.

"And who is this young lady, Tommy?" The man extended his hand toward Elizabeth. "I'm Leland Tillenghast. A minor cousin. Not one of the inner circle like Tommy."

Elizabeth stared at the proffered hand. When she did not take it, Leland withdrew it.

"Leland, may I introduce Mrs. Elizabeth Hunter. Formerly Miss Elizabeth Weldsmore. Mrs. Hunter, Leland Tillenghast."

She gave Leland a slight nod of her head.

"I wasn't aware that anyone else from House Tillenghast would be here. What brings you to Boston, Leland?" Thomas asked with a certain edge to his voice.

"I was bored. So I hopped on one of Uncle Alfred's airships, and here

I am." He threw his hands in the air. "But it appears I am too late. All the most beautiful women are taken." Leland extended his hand again. "It was a pleasure Mrs. Hunter, but I am off in search of greener pastures."

This time she took it in hopes it would be the last they saw of him. Instead of a cordial shake, Leland brought her hand to his lips. His kiss lingered a second longer than was necessary, and she snatched her hand away.

"You, sir, are not a gentleman," she exclaimed.

Leland gave her a seductive smile. "No, I'm not." He turned and walked away with a little jaunt in his step.

"My apologies, Mrs. Hunter." Thomas led her in the opposite direction of where Leland had gone. "As you can imagine, his family probably escorted him to the airship to avoid a scandal at home."

"Of that, I have no . . ." Elizabeth felt a wave of nausea worm its way up her stomach, changing to a sharp pain when it reached her head. She stopped and put her hand to her mouth.

"Are you all right?" Thomas asked.

"No. Could you please find my husband? I think I'd like to go home."

"Of course." He ushered her over to an empty chair, where she sat down. "I'll be right back."

She closed her eyes and took deep breaths to rid herself of the sudden headache. When she opened them, Elizabeth was met with Leland's piercing gaze from across the room. She looked away. Something about this feeling was familiar to her, like a forgotten memory. She was just about to remember when Samuel touched her arm.

"Let's go," he said as he took her hand. "Thomas will give the Gardners our apologies."

As Samuel escorted her out, Elizabeth glanced back to see if Leland was still there, but he had vanished.

7

A glass of port in his hand, Jonathan stared at the flames in the library's fireplace. They threw shadows on the walls as it crackled and popped. The house was quiet, as most of the staff had either gone to bed or were out for the evening. He loved this time of night. When he and Adaline were first married, they'd made a point of spending at least two evenings a week in front of the fire in this very room. Sometimes they talked, and, well, sometimes they did other things. The memories were not as fresh as they used to be, but the thought of her still filled him with warmth.

"Sir?" Sampson stood at the entryway. "Do you need anything else this evening?"

"Are they back yet?

"Mr. Hunter and Elizabeth returned early. She wasn't feeling well," Sampson replied.

Jonathan sat up straight. "Is she all right?"

"Mr. Hunter said she was a bit queasy. They've gone to bed."

Jonathan relaxed a little. "Good. Pour yourself a glass of port and sit down."

"I will happily take the port, but I will remain standing."

Jonathan watched as his house manager walked in and poured himself a drink. "You are the best, Sampson. I don't know what I'd do without you."

"Suffer someone stuffier than I am, I suppose," Sampson countered.

"Not possible." Jonathan gave the older man a sly grin. "You are the stuffiest and the most loyal."

"Yes, sir. If I might ask what your brother wants this time . . . ?" Sampson's voice trailed off.

"He's a messenger for House Tillenghast. They want me to join with them in monopolizing shipping and airship construction in Europe."

"And how do they plan on doing that? There are half a dozen on the

West Coast and at least a dozen small companies across the Atlantic as well as Asia and India. Does Tillenghast expect them to just kowtow to him?"

Jonathan sipped his port. "Thomas said he was using demons."

"Was he drunk?"

He shook his head. "Neither of them were."

"Aren't they merely Irish folktales used to scare children?" Sampson asked.

"Perhaps. Recent events have made me realize there is much we don't understand about the world." Jonathan scratched his chin. "But demons. No. If there are demons, then Tillenghast built them. It wouldn't be the first time that House tried to play God."

The house manager ignored his own rules and sat down. "There were rumors during the House Wars about such things. Maybe House Tillenghast is starting a propaganda war? Or sowing seeds of fear? But for what purpose?"

"Perhaps to take control of our government, as well manipulate those overseas." Jonathan put his glass down. "The long game is their forté."

"As is playing both sides. Just like you do, little brother." His hair and clothes disheveled, Hal stumbled in and leaned against the back of one of the chairs. "And why do you talk to a servant about such matters? It's . . . it's . . . it's so egalitarian of you."

Jonathan frowned. "You're drunk. Apologize to Sampson."

"Apologize to a servant? Have you gone mad?"

"I said, apologize."

Hal sniffed. "Fine. I apologize."

"Now go to bed before you embarrass yourself any more than you already have." Jonathan ordered.

"Why would I care what he thinks? I certainly don't care what you think."

"You'd better if you want this deal to go through with Tillenghast."

Hal dismissed his brother with a wave of his hand. "Bah! You'll never agree to work with him. They know it. I know it. Everyone knows it. Even Sampson knows it."

Jonathan stood up, walked over to Hal, and loomed over him like an ominous shadow. "Then why are you here, Hal? What is it you really want?"

Hal stood up straight, his upper lip quivering into a snarl, then backed off. "What I want, little brother, is to be far drunker than I am now," he said as if he hadn't a care in the world. He stumbled back, grabbed a carafe of bourbon, and lurched out of the library.

Jonathan gave Sampson a knowing look. The house manager put his glass down and followed the elder Weldsmore out of the room.

"Make sure he doesn't fall down the stairs again," Jonathan called after him. He then turned, crossed his arms, and stared into the fire again.

The Tillenghasts were using his brother, but to what end, he wondered. Hal had his own agenda, which might include taking control of House Weldsmore. Jonathan wasn't sure, but he assumed Tillenghast wanted to forge an alliance with him without the other Great Houses knowing about it. Tillenghast needed him to make his plan work, but why send Thomas and Hal? Why not a proper emissary? All of these machinations had to be a subterfuge for something else. Jonathan had to figure out what that was before Alfred Tillenghast started another war.

***

Elizabeth heard the faint sounds of a piano as she walked down a hallway in the Gardner mansion. The noise from the surrounding crowd was muffled, as if she had cotton in her ears, but the music from the piano grew sharper. Anxious that she was missing the performance, Elizabeth picked up her skirts so they wouldn't trip her as she hurried through what was now a throng of tightly packed people. She pushed and shoved her way through, not caring about decorum. When she got to the edge of the crowd, she lurched forward and found herself staring at a blank wall. She reached out to touch it. The wall was warm, soothing even. The heat wound its way up her arm and circled around her neck, soothing her. It touched the base of her skull, probing, then without warning pierced her brain. Elizabeth screamed.

She opened her eyes to find herself staring at a dilapidated brick wall. Droplets of water trickled through the mold ridden cracks. The dank smell of an unventilated room assaulted her nose. An old bed spring dug into her shoulder, and whoever's body she inhabited turned over.

Rage and disappointment overwhelmed her. She was having another vision.

The nature of her gift allowed her to inhabit the body of someone in the near or far future. How far, she was never certain. However, by the style of the clothing and the condition of the building, Elizabeth guessed she was somewhere in the South Side. Her visions never took her outside of Boston. It had not occurred to her before that proximity might be an important factor, but perhaps she should consider that.

Elizabeth wished she had the ability to control the bodies she 'visited.' Helpless, all she could do was wait and attempt to figure out why her psyche was drawn not only to this person, but to this time and place. Where in time, she wasn't sure, but her gut told her it was in the near future.

Her host's eyes were open, so she could confirm the hands she stared at belonged to a girl, perhaps a teenager. Calloused and scarred from some sort of menial labor, the newer cuts were healing. The girl gazed across the room, which allowed Elizabeth to see she was not alone. A number of cots were set up, and people wearing the same type of russet brown-colored clothing were sleeping or muttering to themselves, some curled up in a ball rocking. Elizabeth first presumed she was inside an insane asylum, but there were no orderlies or guards, nor were there bars on any of the four windows or the solid-looking door. She had never been inside such an institution but knew they kept the inmates locked up and supervised. Here no one seemed too interested in doing much of anything.

Footsteps caught the girl's attention. They came from beyond the door. Anxious, she sat up. Elizabeth felt her heart race and skin perspire. The girl was afraid.

Elizabeth hoped whoever was coming might provide her with some answers, but instead something strange happened. The footsteps stopped in front of the door, and an orange-reddish glow began to emanate around the doorframe. It was if a single sun rose behind it. The girl's heart beat faster, as she raised her fists and beat herself on the head.

"Get out! Get out!" the girl screamed. She dug into her scalp trying to tear out her hair.

Did the girl sense Elizabeth's presence, or was it something else? Elizabeth winced inwardly at every stroke as if she was assaulting herself. She cried out to the girl, "Stop it! Stop hurting yourself!" even though she knew the girl could not hear her. She tried to force herself to wake up so the girl would stop torturing herself, but it was no use. Something was holding her back. It felt like another presence, but how could that be?

Through the girl's tears, Elizabeth noticed the door opening. The glare of the light blinded her as a blast of heat washed over her body. A tear streamed down her face it was so intense, but she forced herself to try to see what lay beyond the door. The outline of a person formed in its aurora; its features were fuzzy and indistinct. She was trying to make out who or what it was when someone or something tugged at her.

"Let me go!" Elizabeth shrieked.

"Elizabeth!" Samuel yelled. "Wake up!"

She opened her eyes to see her husband sitting on top of her and holding her arms down. "Samuel?"

The fear and worry on his face told her what had happened. Not only were her visions back, but they were obviously stronger and even more visceral than before.

"Thank God!" He hugged her to him like he was never going to let her go. When he finally did, the detective part of him took over. "What happened? What's wrong?"

"I'm so sorry, Samuel." She shuddered. "I thought the visions had stopped."

"It's not your fault." He got off of her and held her in his arms. "But there must be a reason you had one now. Tell me what you saw."

Elizabeth took a deep breath and told him about what she'd thought was at first a dream about being at the Gardner party, then how it switched into a vision and how she'd had the sensation that the girl may have sensed her presence.

"Is that even possible?" he asked.

She shook her head. "I have no idea."

"Too many questions that neither of us can answer, I'm afraid." He kissed the top of her head. "We need to go to someone who can."

"My father will never allow it."

"It's not up to him, Elizabeth," Samuel declared. "You have to learn how to handle your gift, and the only people I know who can do that are the South Side Irish."

She shook her head as she pulled away from him.

"We don't need to tell him. Not everything we do is your father's business."

"Yes, it is." Elizabeth sighed. "I'm heir to House Weldsmore. Everything I do is his business. You must accept that. Besides, I'm not going to lie to Father. Not anymore."

"There's something else." He handed her a glass of water.

Elizabeth took it as she sat up on the edge of their bed. "What?"

"Look in the mirror."

She stood up and faced her full-length mirror. She did not notice when she dropped her water glass. All of her exposed skin was sunburned. Not badly, but pink enough to give the impression she had been out in the sun a touch too long. She approached the mirror and reached up and touched her cheek with one finger, pressing on it to see the skin turn white then pink again.

"How can this be?"

Samuel walked up behind her, putting his hands on her shoulders. "We have to find out."

She nodded then turned to hug him. "Let me tell him. It will be better that way."

***

Jonathan ate his breakfast quickly the next morning and headed to his study. Sampson had already delivered the telegrams that had come in overnight and hovered over Jonathan waiting for the various responses that had to be sent out as soon as possible.

"Will Mr. Evans be coming to the house today, sir?" Sampson asked.

"No, he has too much to do at the office, but I'll go in later." Jonathan wrote a series of missives and handed them to Sampson. "Send these out now."

Like most Great Houses, they had their own telegraph machine, and other than Jonathan, only Sampson and one other underbutler were trained on how to use it. However, the house manager was tasked to handle the more sensitive messages. It was a habit Jonathan had started not long after his grandmother had died and he had taken over the business.

"Another one came in." Sampson handed him the telegram but didn't immediately let go of it.

Jonathan frowned. "What is it?"

"The shipping yards in Glasgow and Brest have been destroyed. And a small workshop in Aumund, Germany."

"What?" Jonathan yanked the telegram out of his hand and read it several times before putting it down. "Tillenghast didn't waste any time, did he? Even creating rumors that there was something supernatural about the attacks."

"You can't really believe that demons had anything to do with it?" Sampson asked.

"Rumors and innuendos followed by violence will distract people from figuring out what House Tillenghast is really doing." Jonathan gathered up his briefcase and the rest of the telegrams. "Tell Brendan to bring the car around and get my guardsmen in here. I want security doubled at the house and the shipping yards."

Sampson gave him a slight bow and passed Samuel and Elizabeth as he hurried out.

Jonathan noticed them as he stood up to leave. "Whatever you need, it'll have to wait until later."

"No, Father. We have to talk now." Elizabeth raised her hand and motioned to the guardsmen to close the massive doors to her father's study.

Stunned, the guardsmen did not react until Jonathan yelled at them. "Close it!"

Jonathan said nothing else until the heavy doors shut with a heavy thud. "This had better be important." He put his briefcase down and crossed his arms across his chest. He only then realized Elizabeth was sunburnt. "What's happened?"

She took a deep breath, then spoke. "My visions are back."

"Last night?"

"Yes."

Jonathan uncrossed his arms and sat down in his chair. "You were there?" he asked, staring at Samuel.

His son-in-law nodded. "It took me five minutes to wake her up."

"Are you sure it wasn't just a nightmare?"

Elizabeth thrust her sunburnt arms forward. "I certainly didn't get this at the Gardner party."

"How is this even possible?"

"I don't know, which is why I need help in understanding this 'gift' I have." Elizabeth squeezed her husband's hand. "Samuel knows people among the Irish who can teach me how to deal with it."

Jonathan shook his head. "No. I forbid it."

"Look at her!" Samuel yelled. "This has gone far beyond what she has ever experienced before. It affected her directly. What if next time it does her even more harm?"

"Father." Elizabeth's voice was slow and steady. "I'm going to do this whether you approve of it or not. I refuse to wallow in ignorance."

Jonathan sat lost in thought. He could feel Samuel and Elizabeth's eyes on him as he weighed what to do. Finally, he spoke. "All right. But you must have my guardsmen with you at all times."

Samuel shook his head. "That will never work. They'd be spotted instantly on the South Side."

"That's the point," Jonathan snapped at him. "They are a deterrent."

His son-in-law sneered at him. "If I show up with two Great House henchmen at my back, anyone who might help us will disappear like that." Samuel snapped his fingers.

Jonathan grimaced. "Point taken." He leaned back in his chair, pondering what to do. "Can you guarantee her safety?"

Elizabeth stepped between Samuel and Jonathan. "No one can do that, Father. Especially since my visions have changed. I need to do this. For myself and House Weldsmore."

"Very well." Jonathan pressed the button on the desk to signal his guardsmen to open the doors. "But don't take any unnecessary chances."

"As if I would allow that to happen," Samuel said as he offered his arm to his wife. The two of them walked out of the study as soon as the doors were wide enough.

As Jonathan watched them leave, the sorrow of Adaline's death encased him like an invisible cocoon. He had hoped that Elizabeth's joy in her new marriage would let him break free, but it hadn't. He was afraid. Jonathan realized Samuel was more than capable of protecting his daughter, but he hated feeling helpless. Or worse—irrelevant.

Now he had no choice but to hand over the one thing that brought him happiness to a man he barely trusted.

8

It took Samuel a few days to reach his contacts on the South Side. In the meantime, he and Elizabeth continued planning out the details for their office on the wharf. Elizabeth dove into organizing their new business endeavor with such ferociousness he had to remind her to eat. It was obvious she was trying to shove her vision, and all its implications, out of her mind. He wasn't sure how to cheer her up other than to support her efforts to redesign the interior of the warehouse. It turned out to be fun, and she had a flare for it. Samuel had been working on his own for so long he had forgotten how nice it was to have a partner.

After three days, he received a note from an old informant telling him he had found a medium willing to meet with them. When he told Elizabeth, she bit her lip then nodded.

"When do we leave?" she asked.

"This evening. Right before sundown. You'll need to wear something less . . . opulent." Samuel informed her. "In fact. You should dress as a Middle District lady. Not only there, but when we go to the warehouse as well. They come and go on the South Side with more frequency than, say, Elizabeth Weldsmore Hunter of House Weldsmore. And it'll be easier not to constantly hide from the house staff when we go there."

"Mrs. Owen should be able to help me find appropriate attire," Elizabeth remarked.

Samuel frowned. "I know you love her dearly, but can you trust her not to talk about it?"

"Absolutely. There is no way she'd endanger my life. But . . ." Elizabeth pondered for a moment. "I'll need to send Sally on an errand. She's a good girl, but might accidentally say something."

"While you deal with that, I'll inform your father."

Elizabeth leaned in and kissed him. "That's for luck."

Though Jonathan had agreed to their plan earlier, Samuel knew he would change his mind—and he did.

"I don't like it." His father-in-law paced behind his desk in the study. "I want guards with you."

Samuel shook his head. "They'd be spotted. I have a better idea. Let me hire some local talent on the South Side to use as bodyguards. I won't tell them who Elizabeth is, but say a lady needs to call upon one of their own and is nervous about being there. It wouldn't be the first time a Middle District woman went to the South Side to have her fortune read or get a love charm."

Jonathan stopped pacing and looked shocked. "Are you serious? Middle District women do such idiotic things?"

Samuel shrugged. "I imagine some of the ladies, and a few gentlemen, who attended the Gardner party, have indulged themselves."

Jonathan dismissed Samuel with a wave of his hand. "Fine. Take care of it. I'll tell Sampson to keep the staff preoccupied later. No need anyone seeing Elizabeth not dressed in her usual attire."

"Elizabeth and I have already done that."

Annoyed at Samuel for thinking ahead of him, Jonathan scowled.

"Aren't you forgetting something, sir?" A voice boomed behind him. "Something Mr. Hunter should be aware of?"

Startled, Samuel whirled around to see the house manager standing nearby. "My God, Sampson, how do you do that?"

"One learns how to tread lightly in the household of Beatrice Weldsmore." The house manager gave him a slight but knowing smile.

"What am I forgetting?" Jonathan asked, not wanting to know the answer.

"The . . . 'car accident,' sir."

Samuel's face changed from puzzlement to realization. "It was an assassination attempt."

"A failed one."

"That's why you've been hypervigilant." Samuel marched over to Jonathan, so close to him that he could smell his breath. "Do not ever withhold vital information that could affect my wife's safety again. Are we clear?"

Jonathan took a step back, nodded. "Perfectly."

***

Sampson waited until Samuel had left the room before he spoke again. "You must trust in him, sir."

"It seems I don't I have a choice. Elizabeth is as stubborn and as smart as her mother was. She's going to do this thing whether I like it or not." Jonathan sat down. "I still worry that whoever is behind the assassination attempt will come after her."

Sampson shook his head. "Even Alfred Tillenghast would not cross that line. Besides, Mr. Hunter wouldn't have survived this long without knowing how to deal with unsavory characters." Sampson stepped closer to the desk. "If I might be so bold?"

Jonathan peered at the older man. "You usually aren't so reticent about voicing your opinions in private, Sampson. Why do it now?"

Sampson held a special position within the Weldsmore household, but he also knew it was possible to overstep his bounds. He had known Jonathan Weldsmore since he was a boy, and the man felt things very deeply even if he did not acknowledge it anymore. Sampson took a deep breath. "You must learn how to let her go, sir. She's a grown woman and married."

"I know that, Sampson."

"Yes, sir. In your head, but not your heart."

Jonathan stared blank faced at him. Sampson wondered if he had gone too far.

"Thank you, Sampson. I will take your advice under consideration."

With that, the house manager knew he had been dismissed.

***

Elizabeth frowned as she adjusted her plain brown hat with two threads of copper wire running through the brim. Accustomed to wearing fascinators, she had a hard time fitting it to her satisfaction. Exasperated, she finally yanked it off and threw it on the bed.

"Now, miss, there's no sense having a fit over it." Mrs. Owen picked it up and plopped it back on her head again. "Wear it like so. No one will be the wiser down at the docks."

The hat matched her tawny dress, which had two copper wires woven into the hem and the collar and lapel of her long jacket. Mrs. Owen had convinced her to put on a plain white cotton blouse instead of her usual corsets, claiming working Middle District women found them too constricting.

Samuel poked his head in the room. "You look ready. Are you?"

Elizabeth pursed her lips. "It's ugly, but comfortable."

"See? You might have something to learn from Middle District women after all," Mrs. Owen commented as she brushed lint off the back of Elizabeth's jacket.

"The dress is perfect. Where did you find it on such short notice?" Samuel asked.

Mrs. Owen guffawed. "Housekeepers have secrets too." She backed up two steps and gave Elizabeth the once over. "You're done."

Elizabeth took a good look at herself in the floor-length mirror. She didn't recognize the woman who reached up to tuck a lock of hair up under the hat. It was as if she was seeing a vision of herself in another life.

"Elizabeth," Samuel called out to her. "We need to go."

She adjusted the jacket one more time before she took an old leather purse from Mrs. Owen's hands.

The older woman smiled. "You'll do fine, miss."

***

Elizabeth sat on a lumpy cloth seat in the back of a horse carriage. Samuel had insisted on using a carriage instead of the steam-powered car, saying it would make them less obvious. The last time she had done that was in Europe with some baroness or another. Though the baroness's mode of travel had been much more well appointed, with fine leather seats and lace curtains, it was still a horse carriage and not a car. It still puzzled her why the so-called European royalty held on to such vestiges of the past.

She drew back the curtains to take a peek outside. They were passing through the section called the Middle District in Boston. Every major city in the Great States of America had one or something similar. It was a neighborhood that bordered Beacon Hill and the South Side and encompassed Liberty Row. The Middle District itself was divided between those who lived a lifestyle closer to Beacon Hill, those on the other side of the economic spectrum, and everyone in between. The people who resided here were tradesmen, shopkeepers, bureaucrats, and well-educated servants. In short, these were the people who worked for and supported the Great Houses in various capacities.

The carriage's wheels rumbled as they ran over uneven cobblestone. They were getting closer to the South Side. Elizabeth felt almost ashamed that she had never been to this part of Boston where the poor Irish lived, but being the heir to House Weldsmore limited her movements more than people understood—not that she ever complained. Elizabeth knew full well her life was one of extraordinary privilege, and she hoped that with the help of her husband she could use it to do some good. That is if she could get her visions under control.

Samuel touched her hand. "Elizabeth, we're almost there."

She let go of the curtain and sat back. The carriage came to a stop. Samuel opened the door and stepped out, closing it behind him. The vehicle rocked as one of the hired guards climbed down from the driver's perch. After a minute, Samuel opened the door again and offered her his hand to help her out. She took it and stepped into a world she had only read about.

Coal dust embedded every crack and crevice on the street and the brick tenement buildings. The dirt-encrusted windows on the local shops made it impossible to see their wares though the locals who strolled by seemed not to notice. The men and women dressed in plain brown and black woolen clothing without a hint of metal. Elizabeth was not surprised at this, as anyone outside their social class wearing copper or even brass in their clothing would face harassment if not outright jail. Though there was no law forbidding the lower classes from wearing metal, it simply wasn't done nor encouraged.

And then there was the smell.

The odor of rotting garbage and sewage made her gag. As she dug into her purse for a handkerchief to cover her nose, several children, their faces covered in soot and their clothing two sizes too small, scurried over and begged her for coins. Clutching the purse to her chest, Elizabeth backed up against the carriage, not knowing what to do.

One of the Irishmen Samuel had hired stomped over and shooed them away. They yelled at him for interfering as ran off.

"Elizabeth, they won't hurt you."

"I know. I just didn't expect . . ." Her voice trailed off.

Samuel took her elbow. "Let's go." He gestured toward a door next to a shop that sold leather goods. It opened up to a four-story walk-up. Elizabeth followed her husband up the creaking wooden stairs for two flights. The Irishman who'd chased away the children stayed at the bottom of the stairwell. She was sure his looming presence would dissuade anyone from bothering them.

Samuel stopped on the final small landing and knocked on the door. There was shuffling inside, then it jerked open. A tiny, wizened old woman with pewter-colored hair and cataract-ridden eyes stared out.

"You be him to come see my Rachel?" she asked.

"Yes, ma'am," he replied. "Myself and my wife."

The old woman inhaled sharply.

Worried that she might not be well, Elizabeth stepped in front of Samuel and smiled. "Are you all right? May we come in?"

The old woman ignored her and turned to walk back into the apartment, leaving the door open. Samuel shrugged then gestured for Elizabeth to go inside.

She walked into a clean but dilapidated room with dark-blue linen curtains, a moth-eaten wool rug with an unrecognizable pattern, and two couches with blankets thrown over them to hide the holes. An ancient wood-burning cookstove took up one corner and vented up through the ceiling. The old woman disappeared into an adjoining room. They followed.

Smaller than the first, Elizabeth suspected that the space used to be a bedroom, but now it was furnished with a wooden table that sat four and was covered with a lovely ivory lace tablecloth and a single large candle. Four wooden chairs surrounded it, and the window was blocked by a solid sheet of black cloth. But the most interesting part of the room was the woman who sat at the table and the man who stood next to her.

Elizabeth guessed the woman was in her forties, with the gray streaks that riddled what she surmised was once striking red hair. Her eyes were green with a hint of white as she had undoubtedly inherited cataracts from the older woman, whom Elizabeth assumed was her mother. She wore a pewter wedding band on her left hand and a matching necklace of three intertwining hollow leaves that formed a triangle. To her surprise, Elizabeth remembered it was called a trinity knot. Elizabeth also sensed that whoever the woman's husband was, he was long gone. It might be why deep furrows lined her face, as if each had been won in a hard-fought battle. Time had not been kind to her.

The man standing next to her was a little older and his hair was completely gray. His face had a kinder and calmer aspect than the woman. He looked somewhat familiar to her, but she couldn't quite place him. The idea that she had met him before seemed far fetched, but she thought he recognized her too. It took a moment for Elizabeth to realize that they were assessing her in the same way she was assessing them. She wondered what they saw when they looked at her.

Then the unexpected happened. Both of them turned their attention to Samuel. The woman peered at him as if searching for a hidden clue while the man's face took on an almost overwhelming look of sadness. Elizabeth wanted to reach out and comfort him, but that instinct was swept away when a blinding headache and nausea hit her.

"Samuel." Elizabeth reached out and grabbed his arm.

He pulled out a chair. "Sit."

"Ah, I should have known she'd be reacting like this," the woman commented, her Irish accent soft and lilting. "Sometimes mediums feel sick whenever they're around others of their kind. It be like two balls bouncing into each other unexpectedly. Whenever you ever feel that way, sing a tune in your head. It might help."

"Seriously?" Samuel guffawed.

Elizabeth thought the idea was silly, but tried to think of the last song she had heard. A little ditty bounced around inside her head and the pain eased.

Samuel pointed to the Irishman next to Rachel. "Why is he here? I thought we agreed that it was just to be the three of us. No outsiders."

The woman smiled, her eyes lighting up in amusement. "Aye. I'm sorry. Andrew be so much a part of what I do I often forget he's here."

Andrew sighed. "And here I thought you be appreciating me," he quipped in a thick Irish brogue.

"Still . . ." Samuel did not look happy.

"It be fine, Mr. Hunter. This be Andrew O'Sullivan. A medium and spirit photographer. He be my anchor when . . ." Her hand spun around in the air. "When I be in the minds of other folk. Not unlike what the missus can do from what you told me."

The pain in Elizabeth's head subsided enough for her to remember her manners. She extended her hand. "I'm Elizabeth Hunter. Thank you for seeing me."

"Rachel Callahan." She stared at Elizabeth's hand. "It not be wise to take another medium's hand without an invitation. It could lead you into even more trouble if you're not ready."

Elizabeth dropped it. "I'm sorry. I didn't know."

Rachel leaned back in her chair and peered at her. "I'm thinking there be a whole parcel you need to learn."

"You don't have to be rude," Elizabeth shot back. She wiped her brow with her handkerchief. "Are you going to help me or not? Otherwise, there are other places I'd rather be."

Rachel laughed. "I say this, Mr. Hunter, the missus has some fight in her." She leaned forward on the table, hands clasped in front of her. "I want ten thousand dollars. Five by next week and five in six months, as I reckon that's how long it will take for the lady to learn enough not to hurt herself or anyone else."

"That's outrageous!" Elizabeth seethed. "Samuel, this is extortion."

"Did you think I be doing this out of some sort of bond between the likes of us?" Rachel asked.

"I'd assumed you'd be doing this out of a sense of responsibility."

Rachel tapped her fingers on the table. "Responsibility. Well, then, let's see . . . I'm responsible for those you and your kind cast aside." She gestured toward the ceiling. "For those with nothing. Not even a roof over their heads."

Samuel put his hand on hers. "Elizabeth, you have to learn how to control your visions. Mrs. Callahan knows how to do this."

"You're on her side?"

"Elizabeth, I will always be on your side. That's why we're here."

Elizabeth's eyes narrowed as she stared down Rachel. "What are you going to do with that kind of money?"

"Buy food, clothing, find lodging for those with none."

"Fine, but we're doing it my way." Elizabeth yanked her hat off and plopped it on the table. "You say you need the money for food, clothes, yes."

"Aye."

"I will buy them," Elizabeth declared.

"What? No!" Samuel protested.

Both Rachel and Andrew gaped at her in astonishment.

Rachel recovered first. "You? You're going to waltz into one of our shops and order clothes and food for the likes of us? I don't think so."

"You're right. I can't do that. But I can negotiate bulk quantities through my family's business contacts and have them delivered through those gentlemen my husband hired to escort me here. And I can get a far better price than you can. It would make the money go much farther. Plus, it'll help cut down on the skimming."

Andrew burst out laughing. "The lassie's got you, Rachel."

"Do I have anything to say about this plan?" Samuel asked.

"No," both women replied.

Rachel offered her hand. "It be a deal, Mrs. Hunter."

Elizabeth eyed the medium's hand suspiciously.

"It be fine, since I be the one doing the offering." Rachel reassured her.

"Thank you, Mrs. Callahan." Elizabeth reached across the table and grasped the older woman's hand. This was the first real business deal she'd ever made, and she was determined to make it work.

***

Elizabeth spent the next hour listening to Rachel explain that not all mediums have the same abilities. Some were able to commune with the dead while others sensed ghosts or demons. Some could see the future or the past. A rare few could reach into the minds of others. Those with that kind of power either used it to heal or to do harm. Rachel revealed that she had a small talent for reading tarot cards, but was also one of those like Elizabeth who could inhabit the minds of others, but only in the present. Though she was able to enter a mind at will, she had never been able to take physical control over the person in question. When Elizabeth described what had happened to her, she saw Rachel's face tense up in alarm then relax just as quickly, as if she were trying to hide her concern.

Rachel told her that Andrew's abilities were quite different from hers, but because they had both been trained by his uncle when they were children they had formed a strong and trusting bond, like a brother and sister. She used him as her anchor whenever she journeyed into someone else's mind; he was her link back in case she got lost. Rachel said she hoped Elizabeth would feel comfortable enough with Andrew to use him as her own anchor once she had a better grasp on her abilities.

The first thing Rachel wanted to do was to enter Elizabeth's mind to get a sense of how strong a medium she was.

"You want to do what?" Elizabeth's voice went up a notch. "No." She shook her head. "I don't want anyone roaming around inside my head."

"Lassie, she's not going to pick up on any secrets unless you want her to," Andrew chimed in.

"And how can I stop her?"

Both Rachel and Andrew chuckled.

"Every mind has its own defenses. I suspect yours be strong, but I'll teach you a few tricks," Rachel chided her.

Elizabeth turned to Samuel, incredulous. "And you're all right with this?"

"I want you to be in control of your visions. You are in too powerful a position to allow anyone else to have influence over you." He took her hand and squeezed it. "Besides, I'll be here the whole time."

"I don't like it." Elizabeth scowled.

"This is the way it'll be, Mrs. Hunter." Rachel sat up straight in her chair. "I'll help you relax and enter a place we call *spiorad pasáiste*. A kind of spirit passageway. From there I will lead you to a vision. If you practice entering this passageway first, it will help you control when you have your visions. Then, with Andrew's help, I'll enter your mind. And I be hoping you take a walk in some nice person's head."

Elizabeth tapped her foot as she considered her proposal. "Fine. But I still don't like it."

Rachel reached around her neck and took off the trinity knot necklace. She held it about two feet in front of Elizabeth's face and let it swing back and forth like a pendulum. "Watch the charm. Get all that clutter and worry out of your head. This be a safe place."

Elizabeth watched the charm sway. Her mind refused to let go of all the turmoil in her life. Images of Samuel, her father, and her vision kept surging around in a whirlwind. She closed her eyes and focused on relaxing her body then her mind. Elizabeth had no idea how long it took, but she finally quieted it.

She imagined floating, and when she opened her eyes, there was nothing but darkness—a dead void of nothingness. Elizabeth gasped, panicking in this dark abyss. Her arms and legs flailed, trying to find purchase, but there was nothing to grab on to. She thought she was lost . . . until a woman's whisper calmed her down. Rachel was with her. A speck of light far away twinkled as if to call her. She willed her mind to follow it. Soon the vision began.

In an instant a sea breeze swirled around her, brushing a stray lock of hair across her cheek. An airship soaring over the bay from Dorchester filled the sky. It dwarfed the sailboats that cruised by.

Whoever's body Elizabeth inhabited took off running and waving their arms. The person shouted at someone. That's when she realized her vision had brought her into the mind of a young girl. She glanced down long enough for Elizabeth to see she wore ill-fitting and tattered woolen clothing. From what she could tell, she was still on the South Side shoreline off the old Bay.

Something pinged in the back of her mind. She suspected that was Rachel now traveling with her. It gave her a sense of confidence she'd never had before and she decided to enjoy the sea breeze that whisked though her hair as the girl ran, then hopped, skipped, and jumped. It was a joyous moment of freedom.

The girl rushed over to three other children—two boys and another girl—as they dug for clams in the hard-packed and ash-ridden sand. One boy looked up, his freckled face sunburnt.

"About time," he remarked with a hint of annoyance in his voice.

"Where be Abigail?" she asked. "I thought she was bringing more buckets."

He shrugged. "Her Ma said she never came home last night."

"Did you go look for her?"

"Nah. Not my business. Here." He handed her a small shovel. "I can't do it all myself."

As the girl took the shovel, dizziness overwhelmed her. "Gabriel!" The girl staggered and fell to the ground, her eyes closed.

Elizabeth saw only blackness, but heard the boy she had called Gabriel crying out in alarm. Soon she felt nothing but her own heartbeat or that of the girl's. She wasn't sure. It was then Elizabeth realized that she wasn't alone.

"Mrs. Callahan," she called out in her mind, but her voice echoed back at her. "Rachel!"

As she stared into the blackness, Elizabeth sensed rather than saw movement. To her surprise it didn't frighten her. Could it be Rachel? Or could it be someone else?

Curious, she reached her mind out, only to have it snap back. In a moment the vision was gone.

Elizabeth opened her eyes to see Samuel sitting on the edge of his chair ready to leap up and Rachel studying her from the other side of the table.

"A girl is missing," Elizabeth announced.

"Aye, a lot of girls go missing on the South Side," Rachel replied. "Most leave in search of something better. As for you, Mrs. Hunter, ever heard the saying about how curiosity killed the cat?"

Elizabeth nodded, pursing her lips.

"We do this a step at a time. Don't you go chasing after things you don't understand."

"But that was you, wasn't it? I sensed you."

"Aye, but . . ." Rachel gestured that they were moving on. "You need to go now. Start ordering clothes and things like you promised. We can meet again in two days."

Samuel stood up. "We'll be back." He held out his hand to Elizabeth, and she took it, but not before she stopped and picked up the trinity knot necklace Rachel had left on the table.

"Do all mediums have this?"

Rachel reached out and took the trinket from Elizabeth's hand. "All mediums use something to focus on. You'll figure out what yours be in time."

9

From his warehouse office Jonathan stared at the flurry of activity on his new ship while waiting news that Samuel and Elizabeth had returned home safely. The thought of her on the South Side with only two Irish henchmen for protection made him crazy, but there was nothing he could do. Even the scion of a Great House had limitations. Besides, the Abyssinian envoy was due to arrive at any minute.

He remembered what Sampson often said to him whenever he was overwhelmed. *"One thing at a time, sir. One thing at a time."* Jonathan smiled to himself and wondered what he would do when Sampson retired. It added to his already burdened mind, so he banished it from his thoughts.

The hiss of welding and the clanking of metal being moved into place got louder. Mr. Evans had opened the door.

"Mr. Weldsmore, your guest has arrived," his assistant announced.

Jonathan turned to face a man who was his exact height, but who boasted a more muscular build and who carried himself like an officer: straight backed and focused. His skin was much darker than most American Negroes he had seen, and he had a triangular face and a broader nose. He shifted his brown woolen suit, trying to make it more comfortable. Jonathan suspected he did not succeed. Though only two copper filaments were woven into his cuffs and lapel, his bearing gave one the sense he should be dressed as a person from a Great House.

"Please, come in." Jonathan gestured for him to enter as Mr. Evans closed the door behind him. "And thank you for the gift. The workmanship was exquisite."

"It was blessed by one of our priests to ward off all evil," the man replied in a clipped accent Jonathan couldn't quite place. "If you believe in such things."

Jonathan gestured to one of the wooden chairs. "Would you like to sit? Please excuse the lack of refinement and comfort."

75

The man ignored his question as he turned to stare out the office window overlooking the construction of the new ship. "Is that it?"

"Yes. As per the agreed upon design with Mr. Abdul. And how should I address you?"

"Mekonnen," he responded. "It is a title bestowed by his majesty to his top emissaries."

"I was surprised when I heard Mr. Abdul would not be returning. I presumed His Majesty likes consistency."

A hint of a smile crossed Mekonnen's face. "You Americans presume much. Mr. Abdul was what you would call a 'numbers man.' I am a seaman and a shipbuilder here to inspect what you are creating for us."

"Excellent. We can start with the blueprints, and then, when the workers are on break, I will give you the tour."

Mekonnen's nose shifted as if an unpleasant odor permeated the office. "No. I want to see the men work. Their attitude is important for the finished product. But you already know that, don't you, Mr. Weldsmore? The real reason is that you do not wish to have to explain why you are giving an African man a tour of this facility."

"Mr. Mekonnen, I do not have to—" Jonathan attempted to reply before the Abyssinian envoy cut him off.

"Just, Mekonnen. Adding the 'mister' is superfluous."

Furious at being treated like a servant, Jonathan took a deep breath before he continued, not wanting to add to the already increasing tension in the room. "I thought His Majesty wanted to keep our association a secret. Waltzing around the floor with you would be a bit obvious."

"Oh, I realize the contract is secure. You did a most admirable job of leaking misinformation about a new project with an unnamed House. However, it is widely known that you have been courting various foreign nations for business." Mekonnen leaned closer to the window and studied the men working below.

"That's how I obtain and expand our market share."

Mekonnen glanced back at him over his shoulder. "Even to the point of destroying shipping yards?"

"I had nothing to do with Glasgow and Brest." Jonathan seethed, barely keeping his anger in check.

The envoy turned and examined him. Jonathan almost flinched under the stare of those dark and intelligent eyes.

"That is obvious." Mekonnen relaxed. "You are an obstinate yet honorable man. Which is why His Majesty agreed to do business with you."

"Then why insult me?"

"I was curious as to how you would react." The envoy shrugged. "Are you a superstitious man, Mr. Weldsmore?"

"No."

"Good."

"Why would you ask that?" Jonathan walked over to the window to stand next to him.

"You have heard the rumors about how the shipping yards were destroyed?" Mekonnen tapped the glass with one finger.

"Demons?" Jonathan spat out the word. "Rumors to stoke fear. That's all. The whole idea is ridiculous."

"I am glad to hear you speak that way. I prefer to deal with a rational man in an irrational world. Too many of my people, and yours, are steeped in ignorance. It is only our innate superiority that allows us to overcome what others fear."

Jonathan said nothing. The last thing he would discuss was his daughter's ability to see the future.

"Ah, I spoke too quickly. It appears others like myself are welcome among your men." Mekonnen gestured down to the work floor.

Jonathan frowned and glanced out the window. To his dismay, Hal and Thomas were wandering about with two Weldsmore guardsmen trailing behind them. "If you'll excuse me." He exited the room and walked down the stairwell with enough speed to show off his athleticism, but slow enough to appear unbothered by their unexpected appearance.

Thomas smiled at him as Hal talked it up with the foreman. "Mr. Weldsmore, please forgive our unannounced arrival, but Hal insisted the best time to see your new ship was before lunch."

"I'd have been happy to give you a tour, but I'm busy at the moment," Jonathan said in a measured tone, trying to hide his annoyance at being interrupted. "Tomorrow afternoon would be better." He cringed at Hal's boisterous laughter then continued. "We could even have lunch here."

"That would be perfect. And once again, I apologize . . ." Thomas glanced over Jonathan's shoulder. ". . . for interrupting your meeting with . . . ?"

The envoy extended his hand as he walked over and stood next to his host. "Mekonnen."

Thomas shook it while inspecting the Abyssinian. The young man took in every aspect of the foreigner's bearing and clothing. It made Jonathan wonder who the real spy was from House Tillenghast, Hal or Thomas. Or perhaps both?

"It's a pleasure, Mr. Mekonnen," Thomas replied. "You are from one of the African states. Correct?"

"Yes. I am a shipbuilder in my own country and Mr. Weldsmore graciously offered to demonstrate some of his innovative techniques while I am here visiting relatives."

Jonathan noticed Mekonnen did not correct Thomas on how to address him, nor did he divulge where he was from.

"Jonathan being gracious? Bah!" Hal stomped over and barged into the conversation. "What did you pay him?"

Mekonnen's face changed from friendly to stoic in a flash. Jonathan wasn't sure how the Abyssinian would respond to such an insult and prepared himself for what he assumed would be a tirade of proportions befitting the envoy of a monarch who took ostentatiousness to newer and greater heights. When raucous laughter came out of Mekonnen's mouth, he was stunned.

"It is nice see that someone in your family has a sense of humor." Mekonnen's laughter eased down to a chuckle. "When it is quite clear that you do not."

"That's Hal's job," Jonathan grumbled. "I'm too busy building ships."

"A long time ago you had one, little brother," Hal said with more warmth than he probably intended. The warm and caring brother Jonathan had once known leaked out then was promptly stoppered back up.

He missed that brother.

Hal covered up his slip by laughing again. Thomas joined him, though with less exuberance.

"Since we're all here, why don't you show us around now?" Hal suggested. "Save yourself some time."

Jonathan shook his head. "I promised Mekonnen a private tour. And I keep my promises."

"I'm sure Mr. Mekonnen won't mind if we join him," Hal responded.

"Ah, I'm afraid I must hold Mr. Weldsmore to his promise." The envoy gave both Thomas and Hal an ingratiating smile. "My time is limited, and I have very specific questions that I'm sure will bore you."

Jonathan laughed to himself. Here he'd thought he'd have to think of a way to brush off his brother, and Mekonnen did it for him. He was starting to like the man.

Before Hal could reply, Thomas jumped into the conversation. "We understand. Hal, we should go and leave your brother to his guest."

With a harrumph, Hal made a beeline for the office stairwell. "Then we'll just wait in the office. You still keep the good bourbon up there, don't you?"

"I've had Mr. Evans lock up all the files, Hal. You might as well return to the house or to the club," Jonathan called out after him.

Thwarted from his obvious attempt to snoop, Hal turned on his heel and walked away. "Come, Thomas. We're obviously not welcome here."

"If you'll excuse me, gentlemen." Thomas gave them both a quick nod of his head and followed Hal out the side door.

The noise from the room had quieted. Jonathan cranked his neck around to see his men watching the scene like it was a stage play. Whether they deemed it a comedy or a drama, Jonathan couldn't tell. He motioned to his foremen.

Without wasting a beat, the foreman whistled and yelled, "Get back to it!" Soon the sounds of welding and metalwork once again filled the vast space.

Jonathan spent the next two hours showing and discussing the new design with Mekonnen, who proved as knowledgeable about shipbuilding as he claimed. Jonathan had forgotten how much he loved to 'talk shop.' His time was consumed with running the business, Great House politics, and now Elizabeth's visions. The envoy seemed pleased at their progress on his nation's first advanced military vessel. Jonathan was certain it would give the Austria-Germanic alliance pause before they considered colonizing another African nation. He had no love of their imperialist tendencies and thought a nation's people should be governed by their own, no matter how corrupt or inept.

"Do you need my car to take you to your hotel?" Jonathan asked when they were finished with the tour.

Mekonnen shook his head. "No, thank you. My man is waiting. I will tell His Majesty what I have seen. I look forward to the sea trials." The two men walked together toward the door. "I do fear you might anger some of your own allies when they discover our business dealings. I hope you are prepared for that."

"You needn't worry about them."

With a polite nod, Mekonnen exited.

Jonathan waited until the door closed before he checked his silver pocket watch. He couldn't allow Mekonnen to see him rush out of the office. He might get the wrong impression. So Jonathan watched the miniature internal gears as the minute hand move once then twice around the dial. After three minutes he bolted up the stairwell where Mr. Evans waited, holding his briefcase.

"Mr. Owen has the car running, sir." The secretary handed him the leather satchel. "And be careful going down the stairs, Mr. Weldsmore."

"Has Sampson called?"

"No, sir."

Jonathan hurried back down as fast as he could without breaking his neck. The last thing he needed was to give Hal an excuse to ransack his office. With the Abyssinian envoy pleased with their progress, he could now focus on Elizabeth. Although he had to, he hated trusting Samuel. Samuel was Elizabeth's husband and would look out for her best interests, but not necessarily the interests of House Weldsmore. It disturbed him that there was even a possibility that the needs of his daughter and that of the House might be diametrically opposed.

As he leapt into the car, he couldn't help but wonder why Elizabeth's visions had started again after lying dormant for a year. Was it the house? Old memories? Jonathan didn't know, but something in his gut told him he needed to find out. Right now, the only thing that mattered was Samuel would do anything to ensure her safety.

***

Sampson stood by the front door waiting for Elizabeth and Samuel to return. Mr. Weldsmore had instructed him to call his office as soon as they arrived back at the house. He would never admit it to anyone, but he was just as worried about Elizabeth as her father was. She was the daughter he had never had, having devoted himself to this family his entire life. It hurt him that Mr. Weldsmore had not taken him into his confidence with regard to Elizabeth, but their secrets were his secrets, and he would take them to his grave.

He had known about Elizabeth's visions since she was a girl. Though it was Mrs. Owen who held her after she woke in terror, crying in the middle of the night, she'd always thought the girl was having nightmares due to her mother passing at such a young age. Her own Irish ways made her blind to the fact that someone other than one of her own could possess such an ability. It wasn't until Elizabeth mentioned a trolley accident that didn't occur until three days later that he wondered if she was a medium. His suspicions were confirmed when she begged him to not send one of the underbutlers on an errand. Later, the carriage he would have been driving broke an axle and would probably have killed him.

Sampson had the impression she had not had the visions during her honeymoon but for some reason they had started again. He would have to be watchful and make sure none of the other staff gossiped about it.

His reverie was cut short when he saw the horse-drawn carriage Samuel had rented drive up to the entrance. One of the underbutlers tried to get to the door before Samuel opened it but failed. Sampson sighed. For all his skills as a detective, Samuel Hunter failed to notice that his actions upset the staff. He would have to correct that.

He opened the front door as Elizabeth and Samuel approached.

"I hope you had a pleasurable day, Mr. and Mrs. Hunter," he spoke in a casual tone.

"Fine. Thank you, Sampson," Samuel replied, not taking his eyes off his wife.

Elizabeth gave him a wan smile as Samuel escorted her inside. Her drab clothing made her face appear pale, but based on Samuel's upbeat demeanor, he assumed their excursion had gone well. He suspected it had something to do with her visions, but thought better than to ask. Instead, Sampson did his duty and headed toward Mr. Weldsmore's study to call him and let him know they had returned.

Before had walked two steps, he heard Mr. Weldsmore's car returning. Both Elizabeth and Samuel did as well and waited for him at the bottom of the staircase. Sampson watched as Jonathan swept in and gestured for both of them to follow him. He saw Jonathan hug his daughter with more joy than he had seen a long time. Sampson smiled to himself, pleased that his employer could still show love. Maybe, just maybe, this would become a happy house again.

10

The tugboat horns distracted Samuel from his wife's discussions with the deliveryman about the placement of the furniture. Even after everything she had been through the last two days, she had contacted a local clothing and food wholesaler and arranged for the new office furnishings. Samuel saw the tiredness set around her eyes and mouth, but it made him proud that she was so determined to not only do a good job setting up their detective agency but keep her promise to Rachel as well. He wondered if her self-imposed busyness disguised her anxiety over her upcoming session with the medium. The brusque Irishwoman was not one to be trifled with, but Elizabeth had dealt with her better than he had expected.

Her work on the warehouse was paying off. She had hired three Irish women to clean, and they had dug into it with a vengeance—but only after they had complained loudly at the poor state it was in. Now the warehouse was almost dust and dirt free. Sunlight poured through the windows, banishing the shadows that lurked in the most unlikely places.

"Bring the desk and the wooden chairs into the back office and the rest of the upholstered chairs into the front room." Dressed in a somewhat dowdy Middle District skirt and blouse, Elizabeth instructed the deliveryman as she checked items off a clipboard. "I want our clients to be comfortable. And be sure to bring the ice box next time."

"They be more comfortable than they rightly deserve, miss." The man chuckled, his thick Irish brogue twisted across his tongue. "What about the foodstuffs and clothes?"

She gestured to Samuel. "Mr. Hunter will give you the final instructions for the food and extra clothing. But I want them brought here first so I can inspect them."

"Yes, miss." He gave her a tip of his hat. On his way out, he leaned toward Samuel and whispered, "The lass looks a wee bit knackered, sir. You might want to be taking her on home soon."

"Thank you for your concern. If you can convince her to do that, I'd be much obliged."

The delivery man threw up his hands as he stomped out the door. "Gah! Women!"

Preoccupied with her list, Elizabeth didn't notice the man's feigned outrage.

"Elizabeth," Samuel called out to her.

She frowned, ignoring him as she tapped her pencil against her cheek three times then flipped through more pages of her notes.

"Elizabeth," he said a little louder.

Her head shot up. "Hum?"

"We don't have to see Rachel today. You're tired. Let's put it off until tomorrow. I'm sure it'll be fine."

"No. I gave her my word, and I want to give her an update on the first delivery."

Samuel walked over and put his arm around her, leading her to one of the new upholstered chairs. "Then at least sit down."

As they both sat next to each other, he took her hand. "You know, you need to let me do something. You can't do all this on your own."

Her shoulders drooped. "I'm sorry. I'm sort of taking over everything, aren't I?"

"Just a little . . . not that I mind." Samuel paused and backpedaled. "Although I did have certain ideas about how my office would look and—"

"You were too polite to say anything." She sighed. "It's the upholstered chairs, isn't it? They're too much."

Samuel held up his thumb and index finger so they were an inch a part. "Maybe." He bounced up and down in the chair. "They are comfy, though."

Elizabeth bounced on her chair as well. "Oh, my. You're right."

They both laughed as they bounced like two ten-year-olds until someone's throat clearing caught their attention. Much to Samuel's embarrassment, Mr. Owen stood at the front door and gaped at them in astonishment. It was obvious he had never seen someone of Elizabeth's class behave in such a manner. When he realized they were both staring back at him, he snatched his hat off his head and clutched it to his chest, muttering apologies.

Elizabeth jerked up, sending her clipboard clattering to the ground. "Mr. Owen. We didn't expect you."

"No, no, miss. It's my fault." He scrambled to pick up the clipboard then handed it to her, keeping his eyes down during the whole process.

"May we help you?" Elizabeth asked.

Still clutching his hat, Mr. Owen got enough courage to look up at the both of them. "I overheard you were looking to be a detective again, with Mrs. Hunter helping."

Elizabeth pursed her lips in annoyance but said nothing.

He shuffled his feet. "I don't have much money, but maybe we can do something in trade, being that you're just setting up shop."

"Mr. Owen, have you lost something?" Samuel pressed him.

"Aye. My sister. To start."

"To start?" Elizabeth and Samuel said in unison. They both gave each other a stunned look.

Elizabeth gestured for him to sit. "Please, Mr. Owen."

"No, Mrs. Hunter. Not on those." Horrified, he backed away from them as though the mere touch of an upholstered chair would burn him.

Samuel grabbed one of the remaining old beat-up chairs from the other room and plopped it down in front of the elderly Irishman. "How about this?"

"That'll do just fine, sir." Mr. Owen sat on the edge of the plain oak chair.

Samuel retrieved two more chairs for himself and Elizabeth. They sat across from the chauffeur, who clutched and unclutched his hat. Samuel realized he was waiting for them to start the conversation.

"How old is your sister?" Samuel asked.

"Mary be forty-two, sir. Lost her husband near four years ago in the coal-mine blast. Never been quite right in the head since. Sometimes she wanders off for a few hours, but not this long. My cousin looks in on her."

"How long has she been gone?"

"Be three weeks this Sunday. I be searching high and low, and no one has seen her."

"Couldn't she have gone to a friend's or another relative?" Elizabeth asked.

"Only my cousin and myself be her kin since Patrick passed on. And she stays close to the house. Only going out to shop or run a few errands."

"This is what you were upset about when you picked us up at the harbor, isn't it?" Samuel asked.

Mr. Owen nodded. "Aye. And I'm sorry about that."

"There's no need," Elizabeth responded, a gentle smile on her face.

"I don't mean to be cruel, but it is possible that she's . . . dead," Samuel said as kindly as possible.

"Aye, I know. But I just have this feeling in my gut that tells me she's still alive. And if she be, then the others might be too."

"And you've informed the police," Elizabeth asked.

"Aye, Mrs. Hunter. But they don't care about the likes of us on the South Side if we go missing. If there be murders, they'll give it a go, but otherwise . . ." The chauffeur shrugged.

"You said there were others?" Samuel pressed him.

Mr. Owen nodded, tears welling in his eyes. "There be some children too."

"How many?" Samuel asked, fearing what the answer might be.

The Irishman's brow furrowed. "Five or six. Jennie was the last one and before her was Abigail and Daniel. But there have been a few around my Mary's age, both men and women."

Elizabeth gasped; he turned to see her face had drained of color. "Elizabeth, what's wrong?"

"Did you say Abigail?" Elizabeth asked Mr. Owen in a very controlled and measured voice.

"Aye, she be about ten. She never came home one night. Then Jennie disappeared after she'd gone clamming."

"Samuel?" She turned to him, trembling.

"Elizabeth, what's going on?" Samuel demanded, his voice dropping an octave.

"I . . . I . . ." Elizabeth put her hand to her forehead.

Mr. Owen's face twisted in alarm. "Oh, Mrs. Hunter, I'm so sorry to have troubled you. Please don't tell Mr. Weldsmore that I came."

"No, no. Of course not. It's fine. I'm just a bit tired. Don't worry yourself." The color returned to her face.

Samuel focused his attention back on Mr. Owen. "I'm not going to lie to you. I don't know if we can help you or not, but we will try."

"I don't have any way to pay you out right, but I can run errands whenever Mr. Weldsmore doesn't have need of me." Mr. Owen replied. "And please don't tell the missus I've asked you to help. She'll think I've overstepped."

Elizabeth smiled and patted his hand. "Not a word. Can you tell us any more?"

Samuel listened to Mr. Owen while Elizabeth took copious notes. He knew it paid to listen to everything a client said, even the off-handed comments, because they often gave him details that someone might otherwise overlook. They sat for over an hour and learned the disappearances had begun a month before they returned from their honeymoon. What piqued his interest more was that even though the victims ran the gamut in age and were both male and female, each of them was special in some way: slow, very bright, or not quite right in the head, like Mr. Owen's sister.

After the chauffeur left, Elizabeth told him more about the vision she'd had at Rachel's. A boy named Gabriel in her vision had talked about Abigail disappearing, and Elizabeth feared they were somehow linked. Samuel made a note to find Gabriel and talk to him or his family.

They both had tea and the lunch Sampson had sent over. When they were done, Samuel slid two of the upholstered chairs together and insisted Elizabeth nap before they headed over to the South Side. He suspected the sessions with Rachel were going to become more draining, and he wanted to make sure she was prepared for it. He did not doubt she could master her gift, but what worried him the most was how she would react if they never found Mr. Owen's sister and the missing children.

***

The short nap at the new office had refreshed Elizabeth, but she was anxious to meet Rachel again. For the first time in her life she felt like she had a purpose. No longer was she just the heir to House Weldsmore but a woman who had the ability to help others in a much more personal way. She knew Samuel did not approve of her working at the dock, but he was warming up to the idea faster than she had anticipated. It made her happier than she'd ever thought possible.

The horse carriage jerked over the rough and pitted cobblestone road as they entered the South Side once again. On the way over, she and Samuel put together a list of the people they would interview. Samuel had told her it was a shame they had only found out about the missing people now as he knew the longer they were gone, the less likely they would be able to find them. Elizabeth hoped that if she could control her abilities, she could remedy that.

"Whoa!" a voice from outside called.

The carriage stopped and the same man Samuel had hired before opened the door. He had arranged for the Irishmen to deliver the food and clothing she promised Rachel. Samuel negotiated their cut, but Elizabeth had pre-approved the amount beforehand. It galled her that these men would not negotiate with her because she was a woman. It was absurd, especially after her grandmother, Beatrice, had run the family business for decades. She would have to change that if she was going to take control of House Weldsmore.

This time she was prepared when the children swarmed the carriage and had a single coin ready for each of them. Samuel did not approve, but after seeing the squalor and despair on her first trip, she had to do something. Elizabeth suspected Samuel was right when he said that now the children would expect it every time she arrived and that when she was tired of doling out money they would resent her. She hoped the food and clothing would help deter that, but even that was a brief respite from the poverty most of these people lived in. A few made it out, like Mr. and Mrs. Owen, but the rest eked out a living working here or for a Middle District family or their business. It was a problem rooted in the Great Houses. What she could do about it, she had yet to figure out.

After climbing the stairs to Rachel's apartment, she knocked on the door and waited. Andrew opened it and smiled as he greeted both her and Samuel.

"Punctual. Rachel be liking that." He escorted them into through the front room. "How you be feeling, lassie? Any nightmares or visions since the night before last?"

"No." Elizabeth shook her head. "Have you heard about the children that have gone missing as well as Sean Owen's sister, Mary?"

"Aye," Andrew replied. "I even set about to do a bit of looking myself, but those bairns be gone. And for Mary . . ." He sighed. "I fear she be dead."

"Samuel and I are looking into it for him. Perhaps if you know of anyone who might have seen her before she disappeared, you could introduce us?" Elizabeth gave him her most beguiling smile.

Andrew's laughter rumbled out of his chest. "Oh, lassie. You don't need to get all girlie on me. You already have me wrapped around your pinky finger."

"And here I thought you were immune to my wife's charms, Mr. O'Sullivan." Samuel joked.

"Call me Andrew, laddie. It sounds odd having a gentlemen talk to me in such a fashion."

"I'm just a mere Middle District man like my father and grandfather."

"Everyone knows that." Andrew's eyes twinkled in mirth. "You be one of the few men who married into a Great House."

Samuel stood back and gave Andrew the once over. "Is there anything you don't know about us?"

"You and the missus stand in the spotlight while the rest of us linger in the shadows." Andrew took on a serious tone as he addressed Samuel. "Though I be thinking you've spent some time there."

Elizabeth's eyebrows furrowed. "What do you mean, Andrew?"

"He means nothing," Rachel interrupted as she pulled the curtain away from the doorway where she stood. "It be time we start our lessons, Mrs. Hunter."

Andrew led the way into the now familiar room as Elizabeth sat down in a chair across the table from Rachel. Samuel leaned by the curtained window out of her field of view.

"I appreciate you keeping your word," Rachel remarked. "The South Side will have an easier winter this year."

"Isn't there something else I can do?" Elizabeth asked. "It seems if your people were better educated they would find better jobs. What are your schools teaching?"

Rachel chuckled. "Exactly what the Great Houses want them to learn. Only about being servants and the like." The older woman shook head. "Most of our people live in ignorance, but I fear it be you who are truly the ignorant one."

Elizabeth sat up straight, not sure if she should be angry or not. "Then perhaps you will educate me."

"Only about being a medium. The rest you be learnin' on your own." Rachel reached her hands out toward Elizabeth. "It's time. Take my hands and focus on the trinity knot around my neck. And let's see if you can enter the passageway and call a vision without me helping. Andrew?"

The Irishman put his hand on Rachel's shoulder.

Elizabeth nodded and stared at the necklace around Rachel's neck. After what seemed like fifteen minutes of trying to find her way through, she released Rachel's hands and sat back in defeat. "I can't do it."

Rachel sighed. "Try again."

Elizabeth composed herself, took Rachel's hands again, and fixated on the trinity knot. Again, nothing happened. "What am I doing wrong?"

"You be trying too hard. Let your mind relax and let go of this world."

"But I don't want to!" Elizabeth exclaimed.

Everyone, including Samuel laughed at that.

"Lassie, find a memory that be special," Andrew offered.

"Then let it wash over you like a wave of warmth," Rachel added.

"All right." Elizabeth settled down again and focused on the necklace, imagining she was wearing it. It gave her a sense of joy and sadness at the same time. That's when she realized there were emotions attached to it. Rachel's emotions.

And just like that, once again she floated in the blackness. Her mind imagined a door. Behind it would be her next vision, but this time Elizabeth had a choice about whether to open it or not. Happy with her modicum of control, she willed it to open.

Elizabeth stood in the middle of a cobblestone road. Horses and carriages clomped past. Street vendors hawked their wares as the South Side bustled with activity on the rare bright and clear day. Giggling echoed behind her, and she turned to see two kids pointing at her then running away. Another boy about twelve years old with dark-red hair and soot on his face dashed by and struck her in the head with his hand.

"Abigail, get on with ye before Ma gets angry and blames me for why you be late."

The girl stuck her tongue out at him as he ran on. "I hate you!" she yelled at his back. "You be a meanie!" Satisfied that her response had the desired effect, she turned to the right and stared into a candy-shop window. Pink and blue taffy hung on simple wooden stands while other colorful sugar delights sat in varnished wood trays. Saliva filled her mouth as she put her hand up on the window, pressing her fingers into it.

The girl glanced up, and Elizabeth saw the reflection of a ten-year-old with stringy dark reddish hair that looked like it hadn't been washed in weeks. Her brown woolen shift fell to her ankles while the sleeves were way too long and covered her hands. Patches were sewn onto the elbows and under armpits. It must have been a hand-me-down from an older relative. And she itched.

"I want you . . . and you . . . and you," Abigail said as she pointed at each of the treats she yearned for.

While the girl contemplated the candy, it occurred to Elizabeth that this was a time from before Abigail had disappeared. She knew she had to find out more and reached out with her mind to Rachel, hoping for guidance. Elizabeth sensed the older woman's presence, but no help was forthcoming that she could tell. Perhaps she wasn't strong enough yet or didn't understand the signs if Rachel was communicating to her. Either way, she wasn't going to waste this opportunity; she needed to discover where Abigail was going.

The girl looked up again, and Elizabeth noticed a stray lock of hair had fallen across her face. She thought about brushing it out of the way—and to her surprise, the girl did it. Puzzled, Abigail stared at her hand. When Elizabeth realized what she had done, she decided to try something else. She reached up, put one finger on the glass, and slid it down. The girl watched in horror as her hand moved on its own accord.

The result was predictable as Abigail took off screaming down the street. Loose and jagged cobblestones gouged the girl's feet through the thin leather soles of her shoes. She knocked into passersby as she ran, earning her sharp words and a strike across the back of her head. It sent her tumbling to the ground; her nose slammed into the gravel-and-ash ridden street. Pain radiated up her cheek, and when she looked down, blood poured down onto her torn and dirty dress. Elizabeth ached to comfort the child but realized anything she did would only frighten her more. She decided to let the girl handle it herself and lead her to some clue as to where she had gone.

Still panting, Abigail struggled to get up, but a pair of boys running by knocked her down again. Her emotions welled up, and Elizabeth sensed every one of them: fear, anger, humiliation. Soon, warm tears coursed down her face. Elizabeth resisted the urge to wipe them away, but Abigail did it herself. This time when Abigail attempted to stand, a large hand took her by the arm to help her up. The girl flinched at the touch, but when a blow did not follow, she relaxed a little. Curious to see who was helping her, Elizabeth turned Abigail's head to see a man's hand, uncalloused and clean. The cuffs of his jacket were well made and unfrayed. This was no South Sider.

As Abigail's eyes glanced up, a crippling pain shot through Elizabeth's head as though she had been electrocuted. Her vision went black, and without warning she fell back into the abyss.

"Rachel!" she cried out.

Terrified, her arms flailed for any kind of purchase, but there was nothing. Nothing but darkness. And then . . . A whisper drifted past her ear, calling her name. It was faint, but Elizabeth used every ounce of her concentration to focus on that voice. "Rachel?" she called out. "Is that you?"

Something in the dark flashed by her. It sped by so quickly she couldn't make out what it was. It zipped past her again, closer this time.

Determined to figure out what it was in hopes it could lead her home, Elizabeth listened very closely, and the next time it whizzed by, she reached out and grabbed it.

The thing pulsated light through her clenched fist. It reminded her of a firefly, and she wondered if this was Rachel's way of leading her back. "I do hope it's you, Rachel." She opened her hand with great care. Inside sat a flaming pebble with Rachel's trinity knot etched in the middle.

Elizabeth smiled to herself as her body floated in nothingness. She clenched her fist around the pebble again and thrust it in front of her—or what she thought was her front. "Take me home."

At the command, her hand lurched forward and pulled her toward who knew where. Elizabeth had to trust in Rachel and Andrew to bring her mind back to her body.

Up ahead in the inky blackness, she saw the image of a large oak door not unlike the one at the Weldsmore mansion. It opened. A blaze of light blinded her, and she gasped for breath as if all the air had been sucked out of wherever she was. Desperately trying not to panic, she reached her mind out to Rachel. A familiar warmth coursed through her. It was the medium.

And yet, as her mind slipped away from the blackness and through the door, Elizabeth felt a tug on her boot. It was as if something was trying to drag her back. Suddenly frightened, she kicked at it then threw herself forward—

Elizabeth wasn't even sure she was still breathing until a set of hands placed themselves on her shoulders and shoved her into a chair. She opened her eyes to see sweat dripping down Rachel's brow and her breathing labored.

"What the hell just happened?" Samuel demanded, his face pale and anxious with worry.

Elizabeth glanced up to see Andrew's hands on her shoulders. "Thank you."

Andrew smiled and nodded. "It be nothing, lassie." But the tiredness and strain in his eyes told her another story.

"I thought we lost you," Rachel took a sip of water. "You didn't panic. That be good. But you be doing dangerous things with that girl."

"I didn't mean to take control of her. It just happened!" Elizabeth protested.

"What?" Samuel bellowed.

"I saw Abigail. One of the missing children and I . . ." Elizabeth took a deep breath. "I accidentally took control of her body."

The medium glared at her. "Accidentally? You did it on purpose. I be there too. Remember?"

Samuel paced around the room. "Wait a minute. You can do that? You told me that wasn't possible."

"I didn't think it was." Elizabeth trembled, the shock of the experience settling in.

"Lassie, you rest a bit before you be heading home." Andrew scooted the chair back to help her. As she stood up, the chair leg caught on an uneven edge of the floorboard. He leaned over to adjust it—and stopped cold. "Your boot."

"What?" Elizabeth asked. "Is something wrong with it?" She peered down.

"Missy, there be a handprint burnt into the side of it."

11

Jonathan woke up angry. He knew Samuel and Elizabeth had not told him the whole truth last night about her latest encounter with the medium. He hated even acknowledging the word *medium*. That such people like this woman existed was contrary to every rational bone in his body, and now Elizabeth was one of them. She was no longer just the daughter of a Great House, the wife of a former Pinkerton detective, and heir to a legacy he hoped would live far beyond him. Elizabeth Weldsmore Hunter was a medium. A psychic with powers she had yet to understand.

And it scared him. Scared him more than anything he had ever dealt with in his entire life.

When Elizabeth had returned late yesterday afternoon, she'd looked more drained and vulnerable than before. Samuel had appeared shaken, something Jonathan had never thought possible. But what alarmed him most was that Elizabeth carried herself as if there was more to this than she was telling her husband. To describe Samuel as observant was an understatement, but he had a blind spot when it came to his wife.

Jonathan needed to keep better tabs on Elizabeth himself. It was his duty as her father, after all. Perhaps he should put a stop to her visits to the medium. But that might put Elizabeth in more danger. He could hire a detective to watch her, but that would mean someone else would know about his daughter's excursions to the South Side, and that was too risky. Besides, Samuel would most likely catch the tail and confront Jonathan.

And then there was Hal, Thomas, and the Abyssinian contract to deal with. Jonathan sighed. He was stretched too thin. This whole thing was spinning out of his control, and there seemed to be nothing he could do about it without alienating his daughter and son-in-law.

A knock sounded at his bedroom door. Sampson opened it and entered carrying a breakfast tray.

"I'll eat downstairs, Sampson, like I always do," Jonathan said, eyeing his house manager. "And why are you bringing it up anyway and not Joshua?"

"My apologies, sir, but Mr. Mekonnen has arrived without an appointment," Sampson announced.

"What?" Jonathan shoved the covers off and flew out of bed. "Draw a quick bath for me, and I'll shave myself. Did he say why?"

Sampson lifted an eyebrow at him.

"Never mind." Jonathan headed toward the bathroom while pulling off his nightshirt. "Where are Hal and Thomas?"

"Mr. Rochester left early this morning to inspect the Tillenghast airships in Charleston, and your brother is still in bed. Sleeping off last night's entertainment, I presume." Sampson set down the tray on a small, circular mahogany table with a star pattern inlaid in the center. "And Mr. Hunter and Miss Elizabeth are having breakfast in their room."

"Humm." Jonathan frowned as he halted in front of the bathroom door. "Hal didn't bring home a 'guest,' did he?"

"No, sir. After last time, I believe he learned his lesson."

"Good." He shoved the memory of the prostitute who'd redecorated Hal's bedroom by lighting it on fire out of his mind. "I assume Mrs. Owen has offered Mekonnen breakfast?"

"Yes," Sampson replied. "He politely refused, but after some cajoling and a whiff of her muffins, he ceded to her demands."

"I should have her negotiate all my contracts. It would make my life a lot easier," Jonathan yelled from inside the bathroom.

"Yes, sir."

Jonathan poked his head out the door. "Did you just agree that Mrs. Owen should negotiate all my contracts?"

Sampson smiled and shrugged.

"I thought so." Jonathan, looking mildly annoyed, motioned for Sampson to leave. Sampson nodded and exited the room.

As Jonathan shaved, he pondered all the possible reasons that the Abyssinian envoy would drop in unannounced. Even with that distraction, he made sure not to cut himself. The last thing he needed to do was look sloppy in front of a client.

***

Mekonnen must have been on his third muffin and a second plate of Mrs. Owen's poached eggs by the time Jonathan made it down. The envoy gave him a nod in greeting as he shoveled a forkful of egg into his mouth. As Jonathan sat down, one of the underbutlers poured him a cup of coffee then left.

Jonathan and Mekonnen were alone.

A satiated Mekonnen wiped his mouth with a cloth napkin, put it on the table, and grinned. "Why are you not fat, Mr. Weldsmore? Your staff serves most excellent food."

"It's called discipline."

Mekonnen leaned back and laughed. "I like you, Mr. Weldsmore. Oh, and congratulations on the marriage of your daughter. A glorious event, yes?"

Jonathan peered at him. "Of course."

"Is she happy in her new life with a man of whom you do not approve?" the envoy asked.

"It seems an odd question to ask."

Mekonnen shook his head. "Not at all. I'm simply gauging how you deal with disappointment."

Jonathan sat back and chuckled under his breath. "Why are you here? I thought our business was concluded."

"Whether they like it or not, the world knows American ship-builders are the best. Perhaps that is why Brest and Glasgow were destroyed. They were simply inferior. Unworthy."

"Whether or not they were 'unworthy' does not justify the death of so many good men," Jonathan retorted.

"Why would you care about them, Mr. Weldsmore? They are beneath you," Mekonnen commented.

"Because it's a waste of manpower and skill."

The envoy nodded as he sipped his coffee. "True, true."

"You haven't answered my question, sir."

"His Majesty would like to hire a team to come to our country and build ships for us there."

"What?" Jonathan almost spilled his coffee as he set it down. "When did he say this?"

"It is something we discussed before I left. He gave me permission to arrange for this if I saw your men were worth the expense. And they are. You have exceptional workers."

"I'm surprised that you're letting me have the advantage in this negotiation, knowing you are willing to pay pretty much whatever I ask." Jonathan grinned at him. "I'm not sure His Majesty would be pleased."

Mekonnen sighed. "I will be blunt. His Majesty is more interested in staying alive than haggling over a trifle such as this." The envoy leaned forward. "War is coming, Mr. Weldsmore. We both know it. And I, and His Majesty, refuse to allow our country fall to any European nation. Will you help us?"

Jonathan tapped his fingers on the table while he pondered. "Let me think on this, but offhand I'd say this was doable, but only with men who volunteer. Preferably single men with no family ties since they'd be gone for several years."

"And how much will this benevolence cost?" Mekonnen asked, not bothering to hide the sarcasm in his voice.

"How much do you have?"

Mekonnen smiled, his white teeth gleaming against his dark skin. "Enough."

***

Time flew by as Jonathan and Mekonnen hammered out a preliminary deal over the breakfast table. The staff must have been apoplectic since they were unable to clean up before lunch. A loud knock finally startled both of them, and Mekonnen was not pleased when Sampson entered. Jonathan thought the envoy would burst a blood vessel at the interruption.

"Sir, would you like lunch brought in for you and your guest?"

"No, thank you, Sampson. We are done for now." Jonathan stood up, but Mekonnen waited until Sampson walked over and helped him with his chair.

"Mr. Mekonnen, would you like Mrs. Owen to wrap up a few muffins to take with you?" Sampson asked.

The envoy's demeanor swung back to utter joy at the suggestion. "Yes, I would."

"I will see to it." Sampson hustled out of the room.

"I may want to take your cook back to Abyssinia," Mekonnen quipped.

"That will never happen." Jonathan escorted him to the door. "There are some additional factors I need to consider before I have my lawyers draw up a contract. Give me a few days. Are you still staying at the Astoria Hotel?"

The man shook his head. "No. I am at our consulate. You may contact me there."

An underbutler entered the room to escort Mekonnen to his car. "This way, sir," he said, handing over a packet that appeared to contain a goodly number of Mrs. Owen's muffins.

Jonathan had walked over to the table to grab a drink of water when movement caught his eye. Hal was standing at the doorway.

"You're awake." Jonathan commented.

"It's one o'clock. Even I have to get up to eat at some point," his brother retorted. "And since when do you have foreign shipbuilders over for breakfast?"

"That's none of your business. If you'll excuse me, I have work to do." Jonathan headed toward the door.

"Jonathan," Hal called after him. "Whatever you're planning, don't do it. If it's one thing I've learned about House Tillenghast, if you're not working with them, then you'd better damn well not be working against them."

Jonathan looked over his shoulder at Hal. "All of my business dealings benefit House Weldsmore and the Great States of America. Therefore, by extension it benefits every House. And I would never broker a deal where I did not have control over production. Tillenghast knows that." His allowed his voice to ooze contempt. "Even you're smart enough to figure that out."

"You're splitting hairs, dear brother. And everyone knows you have a weakness."

Jonathan whirled around and faced off with Hal so quickly his older brother almost lost his balance. "They wouldn't dare touch Elizabeth," Jonathan sneered.

Hal gulped and backed off. "Not directly, no. They will come at you in ways you could never imagine."

"Is that why they sent you to betray me?"

"Me? No. I'd be too obvious. I figure I'm just a distraction. For what, I don't know."

"And Thomas?"

Hal shrugged. "I suspect he has his own agenda."

"Why are you really here, Hal?"

Jonathan watched as his older brother collapsed into a chair next to the table and proceeded to wipe out a used water glass with a napkin and pour himself some orange juice. When three maids entered to clean up, Jonathan motioned for them to leave. They scattered like leaves on a sharp cold wind.

"Which answer do you want? The one where I'm running away from my crazy wife whom I actually love or the one where I'm doing the bidding of my father-in-law?"

Jonathan pulled up a chair facing Hal and sat down. "What does Alfred Tillenghast really want?"

"All I know is what I told you before. He wants you to join him in monopolizing the industry. And now that Brest and Glasgow have been destroyed, I'm sure more shipping yards will follow. Joining him may be inevitable."

"I haven't said no yet."

"You will." Hal swigged down some orange juice.

"There has to be something more."

"Of course there is. How would Grandmother handle another House who refused a request like this?"

Jonathan looked grim. "She would destroy them."

Hal raised the empty glass in salute. "There's your answer."

***

Samuel, already dressed for the day, sat on the bed while Elizabeth showered.

The burnt hand mark on her boot had shaken him to his core. Rachel and Andrew attributed it to a psychic echo from a spirit long past, but that answer did not satisfy him. The event had triggered something inside him that he did not understand. All the despair he had been able to push aside after marrying Elizabeth bellowed like a wounded beast. His struggle to contain it threatened not only his marriage but his sanity.

Samuel knew where his melancholy came from and had hoped those days were past, but he was wrong. He did his best to conceal his feelings, but he suspected Andrew and Rachel saw right though him. However, that didn't matter. Samuel had to master the beast in his heart for Elizabeth's sake.

It didn't help that Rachel was upset over Elizabeth having taken control over someone else's body. She'd castigated his wife for being too willful and disrespectful. The medium even accused Elizabeth of exercising the privilege of her class without considering how her actions affected others. A humbled Elizabeth had promised never to do it again unless instructed by Rachel. Through all of it, Andrew had remained silent, but a worried look had remained on his face, as if he knew there might be something else. Samuel made a mental note to talk to Andrew alone later.

Samuel was more alarmed that Elizabeth wasn't bothered by it all. She had found and inhabited one of the missing girls and had beaten back what she now referred to as a spectral assailant. In fact, she'd felt so confident in her abilities she wanted to have another vision right then and there to see if she could find any of the other children. Rachel had refused and instructed Elizabeth to go home and rest. They would meet again in a couple of days. Samuel suspected the medium needed time to digest what had occurred and confer with Andrew.

Samuel glanced up. Still in her robe, Elizabeth stared at him.

"Are you all right?" she asked.

He pointed to the breakfast tray on the nightstand. "You'd better eat or there will be hell to pay from Mrs. Owen."

"Fine." Elizabeth grabbed a piece of toast, slathered jam all over it, and gobbled it down.

"I guess walking around in other people's bodies makes you hungry."

"Stop it." She scowled at him as she poured herself some tea. "This whole experience is amazing. I bet I can find out where all those people disappeared to. I wonder what else I'm able to do."

"Not so fast. You have a lot to learn from Rachel. Remember you kind of got lost there for a bit."

"But Rachel found me and brought me home. What I have to do is leave a trail behind me. Like psychic bread crumbs."

"Isn't that what she uses Andrew for?" Samuel asked.

"But what if I could learn to do it without an anchor?" Elizabeth said as she headed toward her closet. "Wouldn't that be exciting?"

Samuel put his head in his hands and took long, deep breaths. "One thing at a time. One thing at a time," he muttered to himself.

***

Samuel was surprised Elizabeth was dressed in her Middle District outfit within forty-five minutes and ready to head out to interview the relatives of the people who had gone missing. Andrew had provided a more complete list after getting the word out that Mr. Owen had hired a detective to find his sister. Over thirty were missing and about a third were children. It boggled Samuel's mind that the Boston police were not involved. Andrew said a few sympathetic local cops had made inquiries, but it had led nowhere. Otherwise, no one cared. They were, after all, only Irish.

Elizabeth wanted to say goodbye to her father on the way down, but Sampson informed her he was busy in his study after having a guest and didn't want to be disturbed.

Samul had sent word out earlier for the horse carriage to be ready around noon, and the two Irishmen were prompt. It appeared they liked this work and the cut of food and clothing they were getting from Elizabeth. Their enthusiasm was such that when she walked out the front door, they shoved the underbutler out of the way to open the carriage for her themselves.

Samuel decided he liked that.

When they entered the South Side this time, Elizabeth had the curtains pulled back so she could use the light to read the partial list of addresses in her journal that Andrew and Mr. Owen had given them. They hoped talking to these families would lead them to others with missing relatives. Samuel expected this endeavor would distract Elizabeth from delving into her ability any more than was necessary to learn how to control the visions.

The carriage stopped. The larger of the two Irishman opened the door and extended his hand to help Elizabeth out. Samuel sighed as once again almost everyone who met his wife treated her like royalty.

Oblivious, she glanced down at her list as Samuel followed her out and on to the street. "1201 Sanger Street. This is where the Shannons live. Mr. Owen said their son, Seamus, never came back from his job at the tanner's." She marched over to a weather-beaten door whose dark blue paint had been blasted off by the wind and rain over the years. Samuel escorted her in, leaving Eddie to stand guard outside. He trailed his wife up three flights of stairs until they reached apartment number seven.

Elizabeth knocked on the door. A woman a few inches shorter than Elizabeth with broad hips and graying reddish hair opened it. Her woolen dress was frumpy and stained. Samuel guessed she was about his wife's age, but the harsh life on the South Side aged her faster.

She gave Elizabeth and Samuel the once-over before she spoke. "You be the ones looking for Seamus and the others?"

"Yes," Elizabeth replied. "You must be Mrs. Shannon. I'm Elizabeth Hunter, and this is my husband, Samuel. He used to be with Pinkertons."

Samuel saw the woman flinch.

"I hear about what the likes of you did in Pennsylvania. Why should I trust you?"

Much to the woman's surprise, Elizabeth took her hand. "We're here to help. My husband is a good man."

Samuel turned his head away in case Elizabeth or the woman caught his expression of shame and remorse. This was not the time or place to display his guilt.

"May we come in?" Elizabeth asked.

Mrs. Shannon nodded. Elizabeth let go of her hand as they were led into a much smaller and dingier apartment than Rachel's. The Irish woman gestured to a small table with three chairs around it.

"I'd offer you tea, but I have to be back at work in a half hour."

Samuel pulled up a chair across from Mrs. Shannon while Elizabeth sat next to her.

"When did Seamus disappear?" Samuel asked.

"Two weeks this Sunday. He was supposed to bring back bread from the O'Malleys, but they never saw him."

"We understand he was twelve years old. May I ask why he wasn't in school?" Elizabeth looked puzzled.

Mrs. Shannon guffawed. "School? He be apprenticed to the MacGuires. That's enough schooling for any man. Though he be smarter than other boys. Good with numbers and the like."

As Elizabeth jotted notes in her journal, Mrs. Shannon leaned over to take a look at what she was writing.

"You not be writin' anything bad about my Seamus, would you?" Her voice took on a hostile tone.

"No, Mrs. Shannon. I'm writing that your son was very smart. What does your husband do?"

"Coal miner. He be smart too. Taught Seamus his numbers and his letters. Me, I don't see so good. Don't need to read or write in a laundry."

Samuel cleared his throat. "Mrs. Shannon, did anything odd or different happen right before your son disappeared? It could be something as insignificant as a new coworker, an odd conversation, an off-hand comment. Anything you can think of?"

Mrs. Shannon sat back in her chair and crossed her arms over her chest, blinking a few times as she stared at the table. She nodded. "Once he talked about a dream he had. Seamus usually keeps such things to himself, being that age when boys' dreams lead to well . . ." Mrs. Shannon gave them a wink. "What men do."

Elizabeth blushed at the comment, which made Mrs. Shannon laugh.

"You be a bit divvy, being a married woman and all."

"Mrs. Shannon, what did he dream about? Did he tell you?" Samuel interjected to save his wife from any more embarrassment.

"A man stepping out of a fire or a blazing sun. I feared he saw the devil coming out of the mouth of hell, but Seamus seemed sure it wasn't. Claimed he didn't feel evil." Mrs. Shannon chuckled. "But nothing about the devil ever does until it's too late."

***

Samuel and Elizabeth spent another ten minutes with Mrs. Shannon before she had to leave for work. Neither made a comment about Seamus's dream until they got back into the carriage. Samuel noticed Elizabeth looking a little wan.

"Are you all right?" he asked her as the carriage trundled down the road.

"Um, yes." She buried her head in her journal.

"Do you need to eat?"

"No, no. These people have been missing too long. We have to visit as many families as we can today," she insisted.

Samuel nodded. "Fine. But promise to let me know when you get tired. You had a big day yesterday."

Elizabeth slammed her journal shut with a resounding thump. "Stop it."

"Stop what?"

"Don't coddle me like my father." She glared at him. "I'm not some flighty woman who faints at the slightest cause. For God's sake, Samuel, I'm a Weldsmore."

He grinned. "Now you're a Hunter."

"No, now I am both. Which makes me a double threat. It's time you start treating me like an equal."

"My equal? Elizabeth, you rank far above me!"

"You know what I mean." She frowned at him. "We're partners in this business, correct?"

"Yes."

"Then treat me like you would treat a male partner," she instructed him. "Would you ask a man how he feels every other hour? If he needs to rest? Have lunch? Would you be constantly watching him to see if he was going to embarrass you?"

"You never embarrass me," he insisted. "But you have had a rough couple of days. I have a right to be concerned."

"Of course you do. But you don't have to remind me every hour."

He matched her stern gaze. "As my partner, I need to be sure you have my back. If you are ill or injured, then it affects me and how well we do our job."

Elizabeth blinked. "Oh." she replied after a moment.

"The only difference is if you were a man, I wouldn't use such delicate language. I'd simply order you to rest and not return to work until you were ready. Sometimes it can mean life or death."

"So you're treating me like a real partner?"

Samuel put his hands in his coat pockets. "Yes. Albeit the most attractive one I've ever had."

Elizabeth leaned over and kissed him on the cheek. "Thank you. But I'll let you know when I get tired." She opened her journal again. "Now, the next stop is on Colebrook, then up to Sixth."

The following hours were frustrating and enlightening. As before, the victims were either very bright, a bit dim, or plain odd. No one was just average. Most had friends, but a few did not. What was unusual was that all of them were very trusting, much more so than one would think given their station in life. However, no one had a clue where they had gone or who had taken them. A few had told the police like Andrew had mentioned, but that had gotten them nowhere. The most likely answer was they were dead or kidnapped to be used as slaves in some of the more unsavory factories in the Midwest and on the East Coast. They had disappeared without a trace, and no one cared but their friends and relatives.

Samuel had spent a fair amount of time in the South Side, so he knew not everyone was miserable. In fact, there was what Elizabeth described as small gardens of happiness sprouting up in the most unlikely places. There were musicians playing on the street with children dancing around while adults clapped their hands, an elderly woman telling stories to old and young alike on the stoop of her tenement, and the usual happy drunken messes in the local bars. However, Samuel couldn't help but wonder if it was all to mask an underlying dissatisfaction with life. Everyone put on a smiling face because otherwise, their lives were too painful.

As they left their last stop for the day, a hard reality sunk in. Though they had gotten more details on who was missing, all of their substantial leads had come from Elizabeth's visions. Every protective bone in his body ached with the thought that his wife was part of this ugly business, but it might be time to admit that if they wanted to find the missing people, Elizabeth might be their only hope in bringing them home.

12

Four men sat across from Jonathan at his office on the wharf: the foremen, his two sub-foremen, and the chief engineer. All of them had an expression of disbelief on their faces.

"Is he really going to pay us that much?" his foreman, Nicholas Abney, spoke as if he just witnessed an angel coming down from heaven.

Jonathan nodded. "Yes. With bonuses for early completion. I have a feeling more will be forthcoming depending on how he gauges the quality of your work."

"We're the best, Mr. Weldsmore, sir," Jeffrey, one of the sub-foremen, piped up.

"Here is the preliminary contract. It won't be official until we have enough volunteers. And I can't tell you where you'll be going until everything has been signed." He handed each of them a small stack of paper. "Read it over before you leave tonight and return them when you're done. If you agree, it will mean you'll have to delay your wedding for two years, Jeffrey."

"Sarah'll wait when she sees how much I'll be able to put away," the younger man grinned. "She's no fool."

"Then why is she marrying you?" Nicholas teased.

The men laughed and joked around, but when they saw Jonathan stand up, they jumped to their feet in attention. "If you have questions about the contract, make an appointment with Mr. Evans. I don't want any of you going unless you understand what is required."

"Yes, sir," they said almost in unison.

As the men filed out, Jonathan noticed Mr. Evans standing by the door motioning that he should look out his office window and onto the floor. Two of his guardsmen were preventing Thomas from entering the building while he tried to talk himself in. Jonathan walked back to his desk and picked up the internal phone line.

"Escort him to the office, Mr. Fowler."

He put the phone down and cleared paperwork off his desk. Just as he finished, Thomas arrived with the burly guardsmen right behind him.

"Thank you, Mr. Fowler."

The smaller of the two guards nodded before they both turned and left.

As Thomas gave the room a quick once over, he straightened his coat. "You certainly keep a tidy office, Mr. Weldsmore."

"What can I do for you, Thomas?"

"I wanted to talk."

"We could have done that at the house."

"Alone."

"All right, but where is Hal now?"

"I dropped him off at the bank. He thinks I went to the tailor to have another suit made."

"He'll notice when a new one doesn't show up."

"Oh, I ordered it before I left Chicago. It should arrive at the house tomorrow."

Jonathan studied him long enough to realize this might be important. "Sit."

As Thomas sat down in front of his desk, Jonathan noticed that he carried himself oddly. "Are you all right?"

Thomas grimaced. "An old injury. Nothing to worry about."

Mr. Evans entered carrying a tray of coffee, tea, and small cakes. He set them on a table not far from Jonathan and left without saying a word.

"What did you want to speak about?" Jonathan sat down.

"I don't know what Hal has told you in private, but I'm guessing it's only a half truth."

"I'm fully aware of that."

"He wants to take control of House Weldsmore, but Alfred Tillenghast will only help him do that if he convinces you to ally with him in controlling all air and sea travel to Europe."

"Why would Tillenghast care about Hal if he already got what he wanted?"

"Because he would have a patsy as the head of your House," Thomas replied.

"Then he would have to kill me and Elizabeth. That would start another House War. Even he isn't that insane."

"Not if he made it appear like an accident, illness. Or something not . . . obvious." Thomas stared at his hands. "The other Houses would not be happy with your alliance with Tillenghast, but they would respect it. If Hal tried to do it, they would remove him and find some distant relative to prop up House Weldsmore just for appearance and stability."

"Why are you telling me this? And don't give me some claptrap about how you like me and my daughter."

"Actually I do, but that's not why." Thomas drummed his fingers on the arm of his chair. "Though my talent for airship design is well known, sadly, my business acumen does not match it."

"Ah . . . How much are you in debt for?"

"A little over four hundred thousand dollars."

Jonathan blinked a few times, trying not to gasp. "Gambling? Investments?"

"Aren't they the same?" Thomas shrugged.

"Declare bankruptcy and start over. Go work for Warrick down in Philadelphia. I'm sure he'll give you a job."

Thomas shook his head. "I can't do that."

"You have too much pride, Thomas."

"Won't you even consider a loan? Especially after what I just told you?" Thomas clenched his fists, though his left hand didn't quite close.

"None of this is news to me. My brother has tried wresting House Weldsmore from me before. It didn't work then, it won't work now."

Thomas stood up and walked back over to the window, studying the workers below. "Tillenghast will push you to the edge, Mr. Weldsmore. Be sure you don't fall off."

Without even acknowledging his host, Thomas marched toward the door and left.

Jonathan took two deep breaths before he reached for the phone. It was apparent that Hal and Thomas were working him from multiple sides. No doubt some of what they told him was lies, but there was truth buried in there somewhere. He needed someone outside of his usual contacts to investigate this. Jonathan considered his collection of spies and inside informants might be compromised. It was time he used a person none of them would suspect—Samuel Hunter.

***

Elizabeth was relieved that Hal and Thomas were not present at dinner. It made for a rather civil and pleasant meal with just herself, Samuel, and her father. Afterward, she told them she was going to take a walk in the garden before it got too chilly. Neither of them wanted to join her, so she took it upon herself to have Sampson order an under-butler to light the oil lamps. They hadn't run electricity out to the garden area yet, but she liked the nice amber hue the lights gave off even if they also gave off a smelly odor.

She grabbed a shawl and headed outside while the two men sat at the dinner table discussing weaponry. Samuel preferred the newer multi-barrel handguns he had used as a Pinkerton and later as a bodyguard while her father discussed the merits of the compound bow. When Samuel expressed an honest interest in what he had to say, she made a hasty exit. She wanted them to have time to get to know each other better without her being around. It was important to her that they should have at least a modicum of respect for one another.

Elizabeth opened the French doors that led out to the back garden. Elegant and refined, the space reminded her of the gardens at Hidcote Manor Garden in Gloucestershire, though much smaller in scope and size. The lamps cast shadows over the roses, the hornbeams, and the black pines as their nettles twisted in the moonlit sky. Italian marble benches sat ten feet apart on a walkway made of polished, iridescent dark-blue granite. It was like strolling through a starscape, but it wasn't her intended destination.

She walked twenty paces, took a hard left turn through a small opening in the trellis that held up the hornbeams, and entered a tiny alcove bursting with wildflowers and shrubs. No staid roses here except for fuchsia-colored ones climbing the trellises at the north side. The rest were a mix of purple trillium, geraniums, blue hepaticas, and many more. Three lanterns about head high lighted her path as she settled into a bamboo swinging chair suspended from two black pine trees.

This place did not have the rigid organization of the larger garden, and it was planned that way. Her mother, Adaline, had insisted that the family have a space in the garden to call their own and not share with any guests unless invited. It was one of Elizabeth's best memories of her mother.

The chair swung gently as she tucked her legs underneath her skirt and wrapped her shawl around her shoulders. France and Italy were beautiful, but neither of them held the memories and the warmth of this place. There had been some romantic moments here with Samuel as well. She stared up at the night sky as she listened to the faint noises of the cars and carriages traveling down the street. The sounds were soothing, and she felt her body relax like it had at Rachel's.

Elizabeth wondered if she could summon a vision without Rachel or falling asleep. From what she'd learned so far, she needed to clear her mind and focus on something. So she closed her eyes and willed the world to be silent other than the sounds of the surrounding garden. Soon all she heard was the sound of water dripping. It intrigued her. She concentrated on each drop, imagining she was a single tear falling from the sky and that right before it hit the earth she leapt onto the next one like playing leap frog. She did this a number of times, enjoying the pleasure of being free, but when she reached for another drop, it wasn't there. Instead she fell farther and farther into a watery abyss.

Worried, Elizabeth forced open her eyes and realized she was no longer in the garden. She was back in the room where she had first seen the blinding light that had burned her. Once again, she was lying down on a cot, but this time she faced a boy who slept across from her. That she had slipped into a vision without Rachel's help or being asleep astounded her. Giddy with excitement, she wanted to leap out of the bed and jump for joy. The thrill of being in control was a heady experience.

Not wanting to alarm whoever she inhabited, however, she moved only her eyes to find out what was around her. She saw several boys sleeping on nearby cots. Testing her abilities, she moved one finger then another in front of her face. It looked like a boy's finger, maybe around ten or eleven, and fortunately he did not react to her intrusion. She reached into his mind and to her surprise found he was asleep.

Hoping whatever she did would not wake him, she pushed herself up with great care so she could get a better look at her surroundings.

Cots filled the majority of the room, with tables set up at the front by the door. Utensils and plates were stacked on the tables, so she assumed that was where they received food and water. People of all ages slept in the cots, which appeared to be evenly divided between men and women, or boys and girls. No matter the gender, all wore beige linen smocks over brown woolen pants, even though there was a stack of regular clothing piled next to one of the walls.

The basement windows were high, narrow, and barred. Elizabeth strained her neck to see if she could spot the girl she'd inhabited before, but that cot was empty. Perhaps she hadn't been kidnapped yet.

A sleepy occupant stumbled out of one of the two privies at the end of the room. A key in the lock of the only door in and out startled her. She lay back down again, closed her eyes, and pretended to sleep.

The heavy footfalls of two men walked in. She heard a tapping sound, then a shoe skidding on what she could only presume was a wet surface.

"Damn floor." A clipped and educated younger man's voice complained. "Any problems?"

The tapping stopped and a tired older man with a heavy Irish brogue responded. "Nah. They sleep sounder than death."

"Good. It's working." The younger man sniffed. "Has anyone else been here since I left? Something's changed."

"Not that I've heard."

Elizabeth had to find out who these men were and where they were holding all these people. She opened her eyes to sneak a peek but only got a glimpse of the older man. Stooped, gray bearded, and wearing a frayed brown woolen coat and pants, his eyes were pure white. He was blind. The younger man was not in her field of vision. She closed her eyes again.

"She's here."

Who's here? Elizabeth wondered. *Another kidnapper? Someone he's working with?* She tried to relax into the boy's body, but his knee jerked. Elizabeth didn't notice the younger man had moved closer to her. It was only when she felt his breath on her cheek that the boy's knee stopped moving. The intruder's breath moved up her cheek and to her ear. A sensual gesture, the heat from it excited her, and to her surprise a shock of pleasure shot up her spine.

"Gotcha."

Terrified at the encounter and her feelings, Elizabeth pulled her mind from the boy's with such force that hers wandered in blackness. Lost in a sea of nothingness, she flailed about trying to make sense out of what had just happened and where she now was, but nothing worked. All she knew was that she had to get back to Samuel and the garden. Grasping on to that fact, the image of her husband took shape in her thoughts. She held on to it and focused on the garden and what it meant to her. The sights and scents of the living, green place flooded her senses . . .

Gasping, Elizabeth's eyes flew open to see she was back in her mother's garden. Flushed and perspiring, her head whipped around searching for whoever had spoken to her in case he'd been able to follow her back. Once she calmed down, she realized that was impossible. He was in another time and place.

Or was he?

Disturbed by the incident, Elizabeth hugged her shawl around her, fled the garden, and rushed into the house. As she hurried through the parlor and neared her father's study, she overheard Samuel and her father still talking. Both were engrossed in something concerning her uncle and Thomas Rochester. Torn between wanting to share her success at entering her visions on her own, and feeling ashamed at the excitement she'd felt, she stopped before she reached the entryway. The one thing Elizabeth desired most in the world was to make her husband and her father proud of her. However, the ability to keep secrets was at the heart of every powerful House. Both her mother and father had taught her this.

Elizabeth decided she would tell Samuel and her father once she had a better grasp on what she'd seen and how she could enter her visions at will. One way to accomplish that was by controlling her abilities. If she were successful, she reasoned, then she could find the missing Irish. It was also the one thing in her life that was uniquely hers. She could not share it or give it away, nor would she want to. For the first time,

Elizabeth possessed a sense of freedom over her own destiny and, quite possibly, the ability to shape the future of House Weldsmore.

***

Jonathan pointed to one of the compound bows on his office wall while holding a glass of port in the other. "I took down a two-hun-dred-pound buck in a single shot with that one."

"I don't doubt it. That bow must pack a lot of power," Samuel remarked. "I'd love to give it a try sometime. If you don't mind."

"Do you think you could handle it?" Jonathan quipped.

"I think I can handle much more than you give me credit for," Samuel replied.

The two men stared at each other for a moment until Jonathan gave him a brief nod. "Touché."

"I assume this banter of ours is leading up to something," Samuel walked over and sat down.

"Hal and Thomas."

"Ah, that makes more sense."

Instead of sitting behind his desk, Jonathan pulled up one of the guest chairs across from Samuel. "I need you to find out if Thomas has any debts. And if yes, to whom and what for."

Samuel raised his eyebrows. "Why me? I thought you had enough resources of your own."

"Normally I would use them, but I'm concerned that my network is becoming sloppy or compromised."

Samuel scratched his chin. "I'm curious. Why do you think Thomas has money problems?"

"He told me he did, but I want to be sure."

Samuel was obviously taken aback. "You think he'd lie about being broke? Why?"

"I never take anything at face value."

"I presume this is to protect Elizabeth's interests."

"Yes."

"I'd be happy to, but then I might not have time to escort her to her lessons on the South Side."

Jonathan pondered this. He did not like the idea of Elizabeth going to the South Side without Samuel, yet there was really no one else he could trust.

"Are you satisfied with the men you hired to guard her?" he asked.

Samuel nodded. "They practically worship her. She seems to have that effect on almost everyone she meets."

"Her mother did as well. I've sometimes found it inconvenient that I do not possess the same qualities."

"I have previously had informants at a few of the larger banks, but if Thomas is hiding money somewhere, it will probably be in one of the Negro-owned ones in Liberty Row. They'll be harder to obtain information from. And I'll need cash to get into some of the more high-end gambling establishments he may frequent," Samuel remarked. "However, since I'm no longer with the Pinkertons, I might not be able to find out if he's got bank accounts overseas. Or if he's hiding from his creditors and anyone else, for that matter. You might have better luck than I."

Jonathan reached into a drawer. Inside was a small combination safe, which he opened. He pulled out five thousand dollars in twenties and handed it to Samuel. "Here. I think this should take care of any bribes or other expenses."

Samuel counted it. "Do you need me to sign a note?"

"No. Whatever you don't use, spend it on Elizabeth."

"I'll get this information to you as soon as possible." Samuel tucked the money away in his inside jacket pocket. "And thank you, Jonathan, for trusting me with this."

"It hasn't been easy. Learning to trust you with my daughter."

"I understand. Let me check on her." Samuel nodded then got up and left.

Jonathan reached over and shut the safe and the drawer. When he looked back up, Sampson stood by the chair that Samuel had vacated, holding a silver tray with a steaming cup of hot mint tea. He placed the tray on the desk next to Jonathan.

"As per Mrs. Owen's instructions. She insists you'll sleep better drinking this with all 'the ruckus' going on. Is there anything else you'll need this evening, sir?"

"No. Thank you, Sampson."

Sampson sighed. "You really should take him hunting, sir. A holiday outside the city will be good for both of you."

"Perhaps after this thing with Thomas and Hal is over."

"Yes, sir." Sampson gave him a slight bow of his head and left.

Jonathan leaned over and sipped the tea; its fresh and yet biting flavor relaxed him. As he stared into the opaque green liquid it occurred to him that whatever was going on with Hal would never be over—not until one of them was dead.

13

By the time Samuel got to bed that night, he thought Elizabeth was fast asleep. He tried to be as quiet as possible, but when he crawled in she turned and snuggled up to him. She stroked his cheek and leaned in to kiss him. He responded and, feeling their passion rise, took her in his arms as she slipped out of her nightgown. For the first time, Elizabeth took the lead in their lovemaking and Samuel, though surprised, found that he didn't mind.

The next morning he told her about the task Jonathan wanted him to take care of.

"I'm very disappointed in Thomas," Elizabeth remarked as she adjusted her Middle District dress. "It seems he's more like my uncle than I hoped."

"Even good men make mistakes." Samuel sat on the edge of the bed and tied his shoe. "But yes, I know what you mean." He stood up. "So you have the interview list?"

Elizabeth pointed to her notebook. "In there. When I'm done with that, I'll stop by Rachel's and check up on the food and clothing distribution. We can go over my notes after dinner tonight unless you'll be back sooner."

He shook his head. "I doubt it."

Samuel left right after breakfast and drove one of the Weldsmore cars downtown. He did not want to use his contacts at the Pinkertons unless he needed to. They had a habit of calling in their markers for any favors they handled, and he worried about what they would ask him to do whenever that happened. Plus, just being anywhere near other Pinkerton agents set his teeth on edge. They liked having power over others too much.

On his way to Liberty Row, Samuel thought about where Thomas might be hiding money, if in fact he was. Thomas would have had difficulty obtaining a bank account in Beacon Hill and the Middle District even though he was associated with a Great House of the size and influence of Tillenghast. A Negro man would be required to produce a letter of introduction from his employer if he wanted to open a bank account in those neighborhoods. If Thomas was squirreling away money without anyone in Boston, or elsewhere, knowing about it, Liberty Row was the logical choice.

The corner of Beach Street and Harrison was the unofficial dividing line between the white and Negro sides of the Middle District in Boston. Locals called the Negro neighborhood Liberty Row even though it took up eight square blocks and stood a few blocks north of the channel. The same brownstones, window boxes, and flowers were on one side as the other. The white families who lived across from Liberty Row were much like their neighbors; most were skilled workers or owned their own businesses. Neither side displayed family emblems nor had guards or doormen at the entrances like the Great Houses in Beacon Hill. Horses and steam-powered buggies shared the road, though there were more horses here than in Beacon Hill, which was many blocks and a large park away.

As he drove down Harrison, he noticed the easy flow of Negros crossing the invisible border. Many of the residents worked all over Boston but found living here more hospitable. He had sailed with a few Negro tradesmen while on a merchant ship when he was younger. A few had even served as sailors. Impressed by their professionalism, he knew his opinion was irrelevant to most of them. They lived their lives, and he lived his. It was simply the way it was.

He caught a whiff of the smoke that drifted across the channel from the coal-fired power plants on the South Side where most of the Irish worked. They spewed a horrific combination of soot laced with chemicals that, if it landed in your eyes, burned for hours. For most of the Middle District and those on Beacon Hill, the ocean breeze forced the acidic air out to sea. However, if the wind shifted, those who lived closer to the South Side closed their windows and brought their children inside to play. The Irish bore the brunt of it, but Liberty Row wasn't exempt.

Samuel parked the car down the block from the four banks located in the area. Both were family owned and had been established right after the House Wars. He suspected the locals didn't deposit their money in white-owned banks, and he couldn't blame them. Most of the inhabitants were descended from former slaves. Why would they trust anyone outside of their own community?

His first stop was the First Liberty Bank, a simple three-story brick building with a brass sign with its name engraved on it. He entered behind several other gentlemen, one of whom was white. The lobby ceiling soared up all three stories with balconies circling the room on the second and third floors. Open-air offices took up most of the space, with two closed-in ones toward the middle. On the right-hand side of the first floor were the teller stations. All the way to the back, past two locked iron gates and four Negro guards, stood the bank vault.

Samuel's plan was to open an account with some of the money Jonathan had given him. It would ingratiate him with the manager and enable him to ask questions about the bank's clientele. However, he needed to spend time inside just listening to conversations without it looking suspicious. He often found eavesdropping could garner a wealth of information.

One of the white men who'd entered ahead of him asked a teller for a Mr. Larsen, but was told he was in a meeting and asked if he would mind waiting. He did and left in a huff. If a white man was requesting someone in particular in a Negro-owned bank, it meant that this Mr. Larsen handled more delicate transactions. Samuel took that as his cue and approached the teller. A short young Negro man with a short haircut and plain tan woolen suit, he smiled politely as Samuel walked up.

"I'm looking for Mr. Larsen. I believe he's one of your account managers. Is he in?" Samuel asked.

"No, sir. He's currently at a meeting outside the bank. Mr. Mason can assist you if you like?" the young man responded.

Samuel pretended to look annoyed. "No. I was referred to Mr. Larsen. Will he be long?"

"About a half hour."

That was plenty of time to get a sense of what type of customers the bank had.

"Fine." He sighed. "Where can I wait?"

The young teller pointed to a group of upholstered chairs off to the side by an oak coffee table holding a pitcher of water with glasses and several newspapers.

"Thank you." Samuel replied and headed over. He sat in the chair closest to the door so he could overhear anything being said as people walked in and out. He grabbed a newspaper, opened it, and feigned reading, turning the pages from time to time. This kind of detective work was boring and not terribly glamourous, but could be very effective. In the first fifteen minutes, he learned one of the account managers was having an affair with his secretary, the young teller he spoke to was an up-and-coming employee, and another secretary was training to be a teller. As for the clients who wandered in and out, most talked about the weather, how busy they were, and that they needed to get back to work. The majority of them were employed either in the Middle District or had businesses of their own in Liberty Row.

As he sat there for over an hour, he learned something even more important: Mr. Larsen was held in high regard for his discretion.

A man clearing his throat caught his attention. "Sir. I'm Mr. Larsen."

Samuel looked up and saw a lean Negro man about five feet eight inches tall with short black hair that was graying at the temples. His skin was jet black and matched his black woolen jacket and pants, which had a single copper thread running through the cuffs and lapels. Samuel guessed by his clothes and his age he was more than just a mere account manager.

Samuel stood and offered his hand. "Yes. I need to open an account for my . . . sister."

Mr. Larsen shook his hand. "Of course. We can handle that for you."

The account manager turned and led him up two flights of wrought-iron stairs to the third floor. Two of the four enclosed offices were labeled *President* and *Vice President* on the glass doors. The other two were left blank. Mr. Larsen escorted him into one of the latter and gestured for him to sit while he shut the door.

"What can I do for you, Mister . . . ?" Mr. Larsen inquired.

"Sampson. Mr. Sampson." Samuel thought the house manager wouldn't mind as long as he never knew anything about it.

Mr. Larsen sat behind an unassuming walnut desk with a small eggshell-colored porcelain vase of flowers sitting on the corner. He studied Samuel for a moment before he reached into a drawer and pulled out several forms, placed them on the desk, then picked up a pencil.

"What is the name of your . . . sister?"

"Elizabeth."

"And will anyone else need access to the account besides yourself?"

"Yes. A Mr. Thomas Rochester."

Mr. Larsen paused, then continued writing.

Assuming that Thomas had an account here, Samuel ventured to push Mr. Larsen for more information. "I believe you already have Mr. Rochester's signature on file. Or do you need him to come in as well as?"

Mr. Larsen broke into a smile meant to instill confidence and security. "That won't be necessary. Once I fill out the forms and you make your deposit, we'll arrange an appointment for your sister to come in at her convenience." He stopped writing and glanced up. "How much will you be depositing today?"

"A thousand dollars."

"Very good." He slid the paperwork across the desk. "Will there be anything else?"

The rest of the conversation consisted of pleasantries as the account manager ushered Samuel to the front door and held it open for him after wishing him a good day. Samuel headed out to the next bank.

His *modus operandi* was the same at the next bank, though it took more time to sniff out a manager who wasn't already there so he could eavesdrop in the lobby. After a brief conversation while opening an account, Samuel could tell that the account manager had never heard of Thomas Rochester other than that he was the son of Emmet Rochester. It was clear he was in awe of both men and asked if it were possible to get an introduction. Samuel told him he would ask. The man gushed with joy as he escorted him back to his car.

It would be impossible for Samuel to find out how much money Thomas had in Liberty Bank without either a warrant or a certain amount of subterfuge; he wasn't willing to take that risk quite yet. He knew with the information he had Jonathan might ferret out how much Thomas had deposited. It was as simple as Jonathan calling Liberty Bank and claiming Thomas was doing business with him. Liberty Bank wouldn't hesitate to give him any information he needed, being he was the head of House Weldsmore. In fact, Jonathan would probably even open an account there as a sign of gratitude for their help.

The real question was why Thomas would hide money in a Negro bank in Boston. There were plenty of banks in Chicago, and Samuel had no doubt Tillenghast paid him well. If he had gambling debts, then why would he be squirreling away money and not paying them off? The risk to his reputation was too great. However, he might be secreting it for another purpose. Samuel considered contacting his former Pinkerton informants to find out what they could come up with. He no longer had any in the Chicago area to keep an eye on House Tillenghast, so he didn't have much choice. In the meantime, he had hired two men to trail Hal and Thomas during the day. He planned to meet with one of them later this afternoon to get his first report.

Samuel also decided to follow up on the information Elizabeth had gleaned from her visions. After visiting the other banks and learning nothing more, he left Liberty Row and headed for the bay off the South Side where she had seen the children clamming. He knew the area and hoped the locals would talk to him. Then he would stop at the candy store. If he was lucky, perhaps the proprietor would remember something about the little girl. It might not lead to anything, but it was worth a try.

As he drove the car through the bustling streets, Samuel relaxed. He was enjoying his foray back into detective work, no matter how minor. It pushed the worry he had about Elizabeth and his own dark thoughts far away so they only nibbled at his consciousness. He found it a relief to feel almost normal again. Though he worried, he resisted the urge to turn and head over to the South Side and check up on Elizabeth. She had to be done with her interviews by now and was visiting the medium. His wife had been pampered and catered to her entire life; it was time he let Elizabeth take control of her future even if she could see it from time to time.

***

Elizabeth walked out of another three-story walk-up with an aching head and heart. The stories these families told her were familiar now—a loved one gone to work or to run an errand, never to be seen again. A few came from troubled homes, some harsh enough to run away from. One parent insisted that was what had happened and that their son was working on a merchant ship out of North Carolina. They had no proof, but Elizabeth thought it was worth investigating. As before, the missing were either slow or very intelligent, but ran the gamut of age. One women's eighty-year-old grandmother had disappeared in the last two weeks, but they believed she might have fallen into the bay after wandering off on her own.

Elizabeth instructed her guards to take her to Rachel's as she organized her notes in the carriage. She tried to decide if she should tell Rachel about what had happened in the garden. She was proud of the fact she had entered her vision and returned without help, but she also wondered if it was a fluke. If it was, then they needed to discuss it. That way they could work together to hone her skills. Rachel might be angry, but it was the wisest course of action.

Whoever this man was, he had to be a medium himself, otherwise how could he have known she inhabited the boy. By the looks of his hands and his speech, he was not only an educated man but one of some wealth. Elizabeth was positive he'd known she was there. The whole experience thrilled and scared her, but not enough to not want to try again. Something about the way those people had acted led her to think they might be drugged. But why kidnap them? And why keep them there? And who was that man?

The carriage rumbled to a stop. They had arrived at Rachel's. She climbed out and into a waiting group of children clamoring for more coins. Chagrined that Samuel was right, she gestured to one of her Irish guardsmen to hand out the shoes she had tucked away for this very reason. That distracted them long enough for her to enter the building without being accosted again.

By the time she got to Rachel's door, Andrew had already opened it. His eyes lit up when he saw her.

"You be a fine sight, lassie."

She put her hand on his arm. "And you be quite the charmer, Mr. O'Sullivan."

"And when are you going to call me Andrew?"

"Never." Elizabeth flounced into the room with exaggerated grace. "It wouldn't be proper."

He chuckled at that. "Have a sit. Rachel be running a bit late. There be an accident at the power plant, and she be patching a few of the boys up."

"Are they all right?" Elizabeth frowned in worry. "Do they need a doctor?"

"They'll be fine. She be doing it all the time."

"Oh, so she's a nurse too?"

Andrew struggled not to be disrespectful. "Lassie, there be no doctors or nurses here. We take care of our own. Now, why don't you have a sit. I'll get us some water."

They walked into the adjoining room where they had met before. Elizabeth sat down while Andrew poured them each a glass. When he handed one to her, she noticed sediment settling at the bottom. Not wanting to be rude, she took a sip then set it down, making a mental note to talk to her father about the condition of the pipes in the South Side. She was sure she could convince him to do something about it once he was aware. Such things could lead to disease and illness. And since the Irish did so much labor in the power plants and in the city, it was in everyone's interest to have them healthy.

After that, Elizabeth considered how she could improve the education in the South Side. However, change did not come easily to the Great Houses, and she would have to convince them and her father, which would be quite a task.

"You know, lassie, we've met before," Andrew remarked.

Startled out of her train of thought, Elizabeth glanced up. "What? When? I don't remember."

"I be working for a murder detective by the name of O'Malley then. We were on our way to a case in Beacon Hill when you passed by with your governess."

Nausea and a dull, thudding pain crept up from her stomach to her throat.

Andrew put his hand on her shoulder when he noticed her distress. "I'm sorry, lassie. I didn't mean to upset you."

Elizabeth took a deep breath and calmed herself. She remembered now. "It was at House Bridgeworth. I walked past, and you were in the alley."

"Aye."

"A servant girl was murdered along with her beau," Elizabeth recollected. "I overheard our servants talking about it. You and the detective solved it?"

He nodded. "Aye. We did." Andrew winked at her then turned when he heard the door open. Rachel had returned.

"My apologies." The woman dropped a battered, stain-ridden leather case the size of two loaves of bread on to the floor. Then she took off her coat and threw it onto a chair in the front room as she marched over to where Elizabeth sat. "More men needed tending than I thought." Rachel spied the water on the table. "Though that might kill you faster than a mine blowout."

"I'm sure it's fine," Elizabeth remarked. "Once you've settled, I have something to tell you."

Andrew and Rachel sat down across from her, and she spent the next half hour telling them about her experience in the garden, more details on the room, and the man who appeared to know she was there. Rachel clasped and unclasped her hands numerous times as she spoke while Andrew's face darkened with worry. Neither interrupted her. A palpable tension had filled the air by the time Elizabeth finished. By the amount of stress on the medium's face, it occurred to her that Rachel might be afraid.

"What you did was dangerous." Rachel's accent became heavier, almost guttural. "It be showin' great progress, but you be needin' more control. You cannot be falling in and out of your visions willy-nilly. And be writin' down everything. Especially if that truly be the place where all the missing are being hid."

Elizabeth pulled out her notebook. "I do."

"Good." Rachel leaned back in her chair. "Today, I need you to think about how you felt in the garden. What did the air smell like? Were you cold? Hot? A breeze? You said you were gazing at the stars. Let's begin there."

"I want to search for Abigail. The girl in the candy-store window," Elizabeth replied. "If I can find her, then I know I've found where the missing people have gone. Then perhaps I can discover where they are being hidden."

"That be most admirable, but you still be too new at this," Rachel warned her.

"I have to." Elizabeth's voice cracked. "Samuel and I haven't found much in the way of clues as to where they have disappeared to or why. I have to find out more, and this may be our only hope of solving this case."

"First things first. I want you to be learnin' how to protect yourself."

"I don't understand. How can anyone hurt me in the spirit passage-way or in a vision?" Elizabeth asked.

"Not your body, but your mind." The medium extended her hand. "Take it. We do this, then we go look for the missin'."

Elizabeth sighed. "Fine."

For the next hour Elizabeth and Rachel practiced building a meta-physical wall brick by brick in the passageway. Unlike before, Eliz-abeth was much more aware of Rachel's presence as the medium instructed her on how not only to build but to destroy the wall she had built. When all she could do was throw the equivalent of mental darts, she watched as Rachel's physic energy blasted a hole through it. Eliza-beth resolved to do a better job after that.

After a brief tea, Rachel agreed to assist her in trying to reach one of the missing, though her presence would not be so apparent.

"I will be there like a fly on the wall and help you back if need be."

Elizabeth took Rachel's hand, closed her eyes, quieted her mind, and entered the passageway again. Not wanting to linger in that dark abyss, she pretended she was back in the garden gazing up at the stars. Her gaze shifted from star to star until one that sparkled blue and green caught her attention. Taking a cue from Rachel, she imagined leaving tiny trinity knots in her wake to help her find her way back. Once she did that Elizabeth focused on the star. As she did, her mind sensed a gentle tugging. She allowed herself to be pulled along, getting closer and closer to the star. It flared, blinding her for a brief moment. When she regained her vision, Elizabeth was once again back in the room filled with the missing people.

A clanking sound distracted her. Two men in work clothes carried a large iron pot over to a spigot and a drain and washed it out. Another man cleaned up the table where the plates and utensils had lain. The smell of food wafted through the air. A meal had been served, though it appeared most everyone had finished and had returned to their cots. Without thinking, she forced the hands of the person she inhabited out in front of her to get a better look at them. Elizabeth heard a gasp.

The hands were of a middle-aged woman, calloused, scar ridden, and with large veins crisscrossing the top of the thin skin. She sat on a cot like the others, but although this time they were awake, no one talked to each other. A few mumbled, but Elizabeth couldn't quite hear what they were saying.

Elizabeth berated herself for being thoughtless and let go of her control over the woman's body. She was startled when the woman stood up and walked over to a trough of water about six feet long with three spigots sticking out of the brick wall over it. The woman leaned over and stared at her reflection. It was as if they were both getting a good look at each other.

Elizabeth's first guess was correct. The woman was in her forties with graying dark-red hair and pale green eyes. Crow's feet had already formed around her eyes, and the skin around her jaw sagged. She wore the same smock as everyone else, but it covered a heavy-set body that hunched over from too much menial labor. Elizabeth wondered why she had been kidnapped. Her answer came faster than she expected.

The woman mouthed the words, "I see you."

14

The car rocked as it hit a pothole. In the back seat, Jonathan glanced up at the rearview mirror to see the chauffeur's eyes tense up then relax.

"Sorry, Mr. Weldsmore." Brendan apologized for something that was not his fault. "Roadwork."

Jonathan studied the final Abyssinian employment and trade agreements. No assassination attempt today. "Can you detour using Franklin?"

"I'll give it a try, sir." The car made a left turn and settled into traffic.

The contracts were generous, and Jonathan knew he'd be making a lot of money over the next few years unless someone sabotaged the deal. The income would be enough to support House Weldsmore and its employees for years to come. It was more important than ever to educate Elizabeth and Samuel on the business in case House Tillenghast assassinated him. It wouldn't be the first time a Great House had done it. His grandmother, Beatrice, had arranged the accidental death of Emily Tillenghast's late husband in order for Hal to marry her. As her former husband was an abusive man, neither Alfred Tillenghast nor Emily had seemed to mind his sudden passing.

The few times he had met Alfred Tillenghast Jonathan had been impressed by his business acumen, though in his opinion the man's desire to control everything around him was a weakness. If one hired competent managers and delegated, then a company ran more efficiently and effectively. That didn't mean there shouldn't be a strong hand at the helm, but one confident enough not to be threatened by change.

Jonathan didn't think Tillenghast would assassinate him, but it could happen. However, Hal wasn't lying when he said Tillenghast might try to destroy him but not House Weldsmore. Keeping the infrastructure of the House intact would allow for a smooth—or rather smoother—transition of power to someone of Tillenghast's choosing.

Though Hal didn't know about the Abyssinian deal yet, Jonathan knew Tillenghast would eventually learn about it one way or another. Whether Tillenghast would consider it a threat, he wasn't sure. But the clock was ticking. Jonathan needed to do something that House Tillenghast and the other Great Houses would not expect, something to throw them off balance. Jonathan smiled to himself. He knew just the thing, but the risk and possible public fallout would be great. He decided it was worth it.

Jonathan closed the file in his lap.

"Mr. Owen?"

"Yes, Mr. Weldsmore."

"Take me to the office of the *Boston Times*."

Jonathan saw Mr. Owen's expression of shock in the rearview mirror.

"The newspaper, sir? Wouldn't you rather they come to the house?"

"No, I want this to be a surprise."

***

If one could feel shock while inhabiting the body of someone else, Elizabeth did. As she attempted to get her bearings, her initial reaction was to take control of the woman and flee. However, Elizabeth resisted the urge and instead tried to communicate to her.

To her delight, the woman pointed to her chest and mouthed the word, "Mary."

Her name was Mary.

Elizabeth's excitement grew. This must be Mr. Owen's sister. She had to find out more and hoped to God that Mary could read. Spying sludge at the bottom of the trough, she took control of the women's arm and thrust it into the water. She dragged her finger across the bottom to write the word *Beth*. Elizabeth saw Mary grin in the reflection.

She took control of Mary's arm again and wrote *Where?*

Mary shook her head and wrote back *The bay? Smell fish.*

That didn't help much. The bay all around Boston reeked like a fish market. She wrote another message in the sludge. *Look out window.* The woman nodded and took her arm out of the water.

Elizabeth hoped Rachel was seeing all of this.

Mary's cot was located across the room from the windows, so she had to walk through the maze of cots to reach the other side. Elizabeth took control of her head so she could move it back and forth and get a good look at who was there and anything that might give her a clue as to where they were. She scanned the room until a tangled mop of red hair on a young girl caught her eye. Elizabeth nudged Mary in that direction. The older woman complied. As they maneuvered toward the girl, Elizabeth wished she could thank Mary for being so cooperative. It must be an odd feeling communicating with someone else in your head.

About halfway there, however, Mary stopped.

"Mary, love. What you be doing walkin' about?" a man with a thick Irish brogue called out to her. He put his hand on her shoulder. "Let me get you back before he sees you."

Mary turned, and Elizabeth saw it was one of the men who'd helped clean the food pot. He put his hand on Mary elbow and led her to her cot, but not before the girl with the unruly hair turned to face them. It was Abigail.

Elizabeth fumed inside as Mary sat back down and the man returned to his duties. They had to try again. Elizabeth tried to force Mary to stand, but the older woman shook her head, refusing to budge. Elizabeth nudged a foot forward, but Mary still refused to move. She took control of Mary's finger and wrote out the word *Why?* on her smock.

Mary whispered, "He's coming."

They both heard a key in the lock and the door open.

Elizabeth tried to get Mary to turn her head again so she could see who entered, but the woman fought her. Defeated, Elizabeth sulked and decided to wait it out. Soft footsteps and quiet words drifted across the room. Elizabeth focused all her energy on trying to hear what was being said, but something gnawed at the back of her mind, as though she'd forgotten something. The footsteps moved away.

Thinking the feeling bothering her must be Rachel trying to get her attention, Elizabeth released her hold on Mary. She almost resented vacating Mary's mind. Inhabiting someone made her mind tingle like a mild wave of electricity flowed over it. Before she'd married, her visions had left her off balance and unsure of herself. It was different now. Each time she entered someone's mind it increased her confidence and her sense of worth. She was in control, and she liked it.

Floating in darkness, Elizabeth found the tiny trinity knots she had left behind. Silver and glistening as if moonlight reflected on them, she followed their path only to see a mist in the shape of a hand pluck them out of the inky blackness, leaving her alone and directionless.

"Rachel!" she cried. "Rachel, where are you?" Terrified, Elizabeth floundered for what seemed like an eternity until she saw a turquoise-blue light pulsating in the dark. It was Andrew; she could feel it. He had sent a psychic signal flare. Now it was her job to reach it.

She concentrated on the light, but something tugged at her as if it had latched on to her clothing and wouldn't let go. Whatever it was it dragged behind her like an anchor.

Elizabeth struggled toward the light. It grew in size until it appeared to become a door. She presumed that whatever had attached itself to her wanted to keep her here, lost in this limbo. But . . . the tension on her dress never changed. She wasn't being pulled back.

That's when she realized whatever it was didn't want her to stay, it wanted to come with her. Alarmed, she imagined her hand tearing at the back of her dress, ripping off the piece it held on to. It took some doing, but she did it. When she felt the drag release, Elizabeth thrust herself into the light. She opened her eyes to a breathless and pale Rachel and Andrew.

Elizabeth grabbed the glass of dirty water and gulped it down. "Did you see it? Did you see what grabbed hold of my dress?" She stood up and scoured the skirt for any tears. When she didn't find any, she sat down in relief.

Rachel shook her head. "No. I saw my sigil disappear, so I used Andrew's spirit to help guide you back." She frowned. "Something had a hold of you? Like before?"

Elizabeth nodded and related her story—first of Mary and then how Rachel's sigils had vanished just before something or someone joined her.

Both Andrew and Rachel said nothing until she finished.

"It be good that Mary be alive," Andrew remarked. "And the bairn as well. But I worry over this thing that seems to be tracking you."

"Aye." Rachel swept back a lock of hair that had fallen in her face. "Could it be this man that spoke to you?"

"It could be. It seems the most likely answer."

"You might be wantin' to tell Mr. Hunter about this, lassie. He being a detective, he might have some thoughts on the matter. Be able to help."

Elizabeth chirped in her excitement. "Yes. Of course you're right. I'll do that tonight. But isn't this wonderful? I found Mary. I definitely have to go back tomorrow and find out where they are."

Andrew and Rachel exchanged a worried glance.

"First you be getting some rest. And no more trying to enter your visions on your own," Rachel admonished her.

"I promise."

As Elizabeth stood up, she noticed a jagged tear in the petticoat under her dress, but in her eagerness thought nothing of it.

***

The visit to the South Side clamming area confirmed what Samuel already suspected. Abigail used to dig for clams there with her brother and friends until her disappearance. No one knew where she had gone or why. Her brother said she was prone to fits, something her parents had failed to mention when he and Elizabeth interviewed them. They never told anyone, the brother explained, fearing the church would label her possessed and take her away. But since she was gone, he saw no reason not to talk about it.

Other theories about ghosts, perverts, and white slavers were rampant, but no one had any solid proof.

A child named Aiden described a man with blond hair and odd clothing watching them from afar. The older boys had run him off, but they had seen him again later, lurking about. When Samuel asked him what was odd about the man's clothing, the boy responded by saying they fit him like they were borrowed. Samuel considered this a good observation and noted that the mystery man could have been from the Middle District and was masquerading as a South Sider. He also could be a newbie private detective trying to blend in for whatever reason.

Samuel found that being himself yielded better results. However, he was impressed with the boy and took his name down for future reference.

His next stop was the candy store where Elizabeth had seen Abigail's reflection in the store window. The owner was a tall thin man whose skin was so pale and translucent you could see his veins running up and down inside his arms. He sized up Samuel with a simple glance.

"You be the one asking about the missing people," he stated matter-of-factly.

"Yes." Samuel grimaced. "Bad news travels fast."

"No, sir. Not bad. Good to know someone cares." The man squinted at him. "Of course, it all depends on what you get out of it."

"A chance to do something about it," Samuel blurted out, surprised he had spoken the truth.

"To make up for some bad?" The candy-store owner offered Samuel a sample of his sweets.

Samuel shook his head. "No, thank you. You heard about Abigail, then?"

"Aye. Gave her taffy now and again until she had some sort of fit. About scared me to death."

"What did you do?"

"Nothing. Her brother bundled her off and begged me not to tell their people," he replied. "The girl was touched. Surprised they didn't send her away."

"Did you ever see a blond man in ill-fitting clothing loitering nearby? Or anyone who seemed odd?"

"You mean like you?" The candy-store owner chuckled at Samuel's expense then shook his head. "No. Wait. Maybe. I don't leave the store much, and I live upstairs."

"Please contact me if you think of anything that might help." Samuel handed him his card, thanked him, and left.

It was past noon and he was hungry, so he parked the car and headed for a bar down the road from the candy store in question. A few of the South Siders who passed him gave him a side glance then continued on their way. Sometimes his presence wasn't always welcome.

He trudged up the muddy sidewalk that, depending on the diligence of the shop owners, was swept free of trash or debris ridden. Children whispered behind their hands when they saw him. Word had spread that a man was asking questions about the missing people. A few followed him to the bar then scattered when the apparent owner barged out and yelled at them. He held the door open for Samuel.

The bar had emptied out as most of the men had returned to work. Samuel took a small table toward the back so as not to frighten off customers. The man whom Samuel assumed was the owner lumbered over to take his order. Rotund with beefy arms and an attitude to match, the few fringes of gray hair that remained on his head acted like they would fall off at any moment. He grunted after Samuel ordered whatever stew was leftover and a stout.

A few customers slept with their heads on the tables. Samuel wasn't sure if they were drunk or catching some shuteye before the next shift. Ignoring them, he wrote a few notes in his journal before the food was served. He dived in to find it soupy, but not bad. The stout was bitter, but it tasted good after such a long morning.

He had finished eating when a man walked up to his table and pulled out a chair to sit. It was Andrew.

Alarmed, Samuel stood, but Andrew motioned him to sit back down.

"It be fine, laddie. The missus be on her way home," Andrew informed him.

"How did you know I was here?" Samuel asked.

Andrew's face dropped in disbelief. "You truly be asking that question? I thought you be a bit brighter than that, Samuel Hunter." He grinned; his eyes twinkling with mischievousness. "Besides, I have a wee bit of experience working with detectives."

"Really? Who?"

"A murder detective named Mallory. You and he . . ." Andrew sat down across from him. ". . . would have hated each other."

"Hah! I'm glad to see even mediums have a sense of humor," Samuel replied as he motioned the bar owner over. "Could we have two more stouts?"

The man grunted again and shuffled away.

"Are you sure you want to be doing that, laddie? This not be the fine drink of a Great House."

"Which I'm still not used to yet." Samuel tapped his finger on the empty glass. "I miss places like this."

"How often?"

"Not too often."

Both men laughed.

The drinks arrived, and they settled in.

"How did Elizabeth do? Any progress?" Samuel inquired.

"More than I care to admit." Andrew frowned.

"Is she all right?"

"Aye, but she pushes hard. She be on her way to being a powerful medium, but I'd like it if she takes it a wee bit slower."

Samuel sat up straighter. "What happened today?"

"I think I be lettin' the missus tell you herself. It'd be more proper." Andrew stared into his stout, plucked out a fly, then took a sip. "When I heard you be talking to a few of the locals, I figured I'd stroll over and pay you a visit."

"A visit? Seriously?" Samuel wiped foam off his upper lip. "I knew you had a reason as soon as you pulled out that chair."

"Aye, you would at that." The older man leaned back, crossed his arms over his chest, and studied Samuel.

Employing Pinkerton tactics, Samuel patiently waited for the older man to speak, but when Andrew said nothing, he decided he needed to prod him along. "Do I have to guess? Remember, I'm not a medium. No psychic powers here."

Andrew unfolded his arms and leaned forward, his voice just above a whisper. "No, but something be haunting you. You pretend like you be plain sailing, but deep water surrounds your ship."

Taken aback by Andrew's insight, the screams Samuel had buried into the depths of his mind surged forward. He heard the voices of men begging for their lives and then the sound of gunfire. His chest locked up and he couldn't breathe—

A splash of lukewarm stout cascaded down his face. Andrew had thrown his drink at him. He gasped and breathed again.

"Laddie, maybe you better be telling me what's been eatin' at you."

Unfazed by the commotion, the bar owner threw a dirty towel at Samuel, who used it to dry off his face.

"I . . . don't . . . know if I can," Samuel stammered. "I've never discussed it with anyone."

"Aye. I guessed that." Andrew sighed.

Samuel ran the towel over his face one more time, then set it on the table. He wondered if talking to Andrew might help keep the darkness at bay.

"Maybe talking to Rachel be a better idea?" Andrew ventured. "Sometimes it be easier talkin' to women folk."

Samuel shook his head. "No. You'll do." He forced a smile.

"Whenever you're ready, laddie."

Samuel clenched his hands into fists then released them, placing them flat on the table.

"I was assigned to lead a group of Pinkertons to break the strike at the Homestead Steel Works in Pennsylvania. The workers had valid grievances, but that wasn't my job. I was there to get the scabs to work by any means necessary." Samuel flinched as a flood of memories washed over him. "The strikers were strong and determined. You had to admire them. The owners negotiated and the workers listened until it became obvious that everything House Carnegie promised was a lie. They weren't going to increase their pay, decrease their workload, nothing."

Samuel twisted the beer glass in his hand. "The strikers were angry. More than angry. Incensed. We were ordered to beat them back with bully clubs, but a few of my men were itching to pull their guns. I ordered them not to fire unless fired upon, but they panicked when the strikers broke through our line and headed toward me and Carnegie's son-in-law, who handled the so-called negotiations. It was chaos."

Samuel put the beer glass down. "I reloaded my Colt five times."

Andrew's eyes never wavered from Samuel's face the whole time he spoke. "I'm sorry, laddie."

"I don't know how many I killed that day, but I do remember one." Samuel's voice cracked. "He was about your age though a little shorter and broader across the shoulders. He looked so surprised when I shot him. He collapsed in my arms. I felt him die. One minute he was there. The next he was gone. I held a dead man while the men around me cheered. How could they cheer?"

Samuel wiped his eyes. "Then I heard it."

"What?"

"That whisper. I couldn't quite make out the words at first." Samuel closed his eyes. "Sometimes if I'm quiet and still enough, I can hear what it was trying to say to me."

"What?" Andrew's asked, his voice tinged with alarm.

Samuel felt himself go cold. "I think it said, 'You're the one.'"

***

Returning to his car, Jonathan reflected on how the newsroom of the *Boston Times* had erupted into a flurry of action when he arrived. This was the first time the head of a Great House had taken it upon himself to visit the newspaper unannounced. The editor-in-chief had been at a lunch meeting, so the managing editor pranced around trying to keep Jonathan entertained while he waited. The only one who showed any sense of professionalism had been the female reporter who covered home and family life. She'd led him to her boss's office and ordered tea, coffee, and snacks.

The office had three upholstered chairs and a large walnut desk. On the other side of the room sat a small circular conference table with six chairs surrounding it. Several wooden file cabinets took up two of the four corners in the office while a square wool rug with a diamond pattern in various shades of blue lay on the floor. Jonathan sat down in one of the chairs and made himself comfortable while the female reporter held her colleagues at bay. She wanted him all to herself—not in a personal way, but professionally. Her astute knowledge of Great House protocol and his family history kept him entertained until her boss ran in smoothing his hair down, trying to appear unruffled.

Jerrod Gordon, editor-in-chief of the *Boston Times*, had gotten his position by political maneuvering and doing favors for the Great Houses. Freedom of speech was considered a quaint notion and rarely applied to anyone except those in power. The *Boston Times* employed a few investigative reporters, but they were there to ferret out corruption everywhere but in the ruling class. Nepotism and backroom deals were the order of the day. So when Jonathan Weldsmore arrived on their doorstep it was uncomfortable for everyone on the staff except for the female reporter who refused to leave Mr. Gordon's office after he arrived. Jonathan suspected she sensed she was sitting on the biggest story they had seen in a long time. She was right.

"Mr. Weldsmore, what a pleasure." Mr. Gordon stuck out his hand; Jonathan shook it. "I see Miss Price has seen to your comfort." He motioned to the female reporter.

"Yes, she has," Jonathan replied. "Her attention to detail reminds me of my daughter."

"How is Miss Weldsmore?" he asked.

"Mrs. Hunter," Miss Price interjected.

"What?" The editor-in-chief's eyes registered confusion.

"She's married now," she replied.

"I knew that!"

Jonathan sighed as Miss Price rolled her eyes.

Annoyed at making himself look stupid, Mr. Gordon brushed it off. "I'm sure she is very happy being married." He gave Miss Price a pointed look. "That will be all, Veronica."

"I prefer to have Miss Price stay." Jonathan made the request an order. "She has a unique grasp on House Weldsmore that I believe would benefit the article."

"If you wish, sir." Mr. Gordon buried his irritation and moved on. "Miss Price. Have a seat and take notes."

She smiled at Jonathan as she pulled one of the wooden chairs over from the conference table and sat across from him.

Mr. Gordon remained standing, unsure what else to do. "What can we do for you, Mr. Weldsmore?"

"I have a story I would like you to run. It's about a foreign contract I have with the Abyssinian government."

Jonathan watched as Mr. Gordon's neck tilted to the side. "What? You do? Is Congress aware?"

That question was code for "Do the other Great Houses know?"

Jonathan shook his head. "No. It didn't seem wise at the time to inform them. But since the contracts are complete and are also broadening in scope, I thought it best to keep the public apprised before news leaks out and the deal is misconstrued or misunderstood."

"I see. Miss Price, are you getting all this?" Mr. Gordon asked, without taking his eyes off of Jonathan.

"Yes, sir."

"And what would you like us to say in this article, Mr. Weldsmore?"

Jonathan took the next hour describing his original contract to His Majesty, the king of Abyssinia, without going into any details about the new design or the new alloys they were using. He also discussed how His Majesty was paying a premium wage for his men to go to his country and build three ships for their navy over the next five years. It wasn't the first time a Great House had had foreign contracts, but the first where an American company was building a military warship for a foreign country. To some it would be deemed traitorous, but for Jonathan it served several purposes: it would make him a lot of money and it annoyed those who would seek to control him and others like him. Mekonnen may be African, but he had the same social standing in his nation as Jonathan did in his, which meant they were equals after a fashion.

Mr. Gordon had sat down after the first half hour, overwhelmed by Jonathan's financial and political exploits. Miss Price forgot to take a notes, she was so mesmerized.

"What I don't understand is why decide to reveal this now?" Mr. Gordon scratched his head. "It would have eventually come out, but by then there would be nothing anyone could do about it except complain."

Jonathan shrugged. "I deemed this to be the most appropriate time. Besides, our citizens should know that we are part of a worldwide economy."

"So you think we are too isolated?" Miss Price asked. It got her a harsh look from her boss, but she ignored it.

"Actually, I believe the Great States of America may have too much influence," Jonathan replied.

Miss Price opened her mouth to ask another question, but Mr. Gordon cut her off.

"Thank you, Mr. Weldsmore, for coming to us instead of the *Boston Globe*." The editor-in-chief wiped his brow with a handkerchief. "Why did you?"

Jonathan glanced over at Miss Price, who already had the answer.

"Mr. Weldsmore and Mr. Pulitzer's son went to school together. He would naturally want to give his House the first crack at this story," Miss Price answered with just a touch of condescension in her voice.

Mr. Gordon scowled. "Miss Price, please hand over your notes to Mr. Stevens. He'll be writing this story."

"But, Mr. Gordon . . . ," she protested.

"He is the senior financial reporter." He gave her a look that told her not to argue.

Jonathan decided to make Mr. Gordon's day more awkward. "I want Miss Price to write this story."

"What?"

"She's obviously qualified, and she understands the families involved." Jonathan stood to leave. "There is no reason this should be in the financial section. Isn't that right, Miss Price."

She grinned. "Yes, sir. The real story is not about the contracts but about the men working overseas. How will it affect their families? Also, the relationship between not only House Weldsmore and the king of Abyssinia but the relationship of all the Great Houses with the world." Miss Price thumped her pencil on her notepad. "This is a human-interest story with enough politics mixed in for the front page."

Mr. Gordon gaped at the two of them in bafflement. "I suppose we could take that approach."

"More people will read it, sir." Miss Price chimed in. "And the circulation will increase. People love a good human-interest story."

"Listen to the young lady, Mr. Gordon." Jonathan headed toward the door. "I expect it to be in the paper no later than the day after tomorrow."

Mr. Gordon leapt up from his chair. "It'll be in tomorrow's edition, sir. I promise."

"I'll hold you to that."

Jonathan exited the room knowing full well that Miss Price would receive a dressing down, then be ordered to write the best story of her life. Based on her enthusiasm, he surmised that she would not only dig into his story but do research on the other Great Houses and their economic dealings overseas. It might reveal information that House Tillenghast would rather not see in any paper, causing them a minor scandal or embarrassment. Or at least he hoped.

Back in the car, Jonathan recognized that this would only distract Tillenghast for a short time. He would come at Jonathan again. But where and how Jonathan would have to figure out soon.

15

Elizabeth had changed back into a casual dinner dress made of pink silk with embroidered rose brocade on her corset and accents of freshwater pearls. She had to admit that the Middle District dress and jacket she had been wearing the last few days was far more comfortable. It might be worth her while to talk to her seamstress about altering her day dresses, especially if she and Samuel were to be spending most of their time at the docks with the new business.

There was so much going on, and she was thrilled at what she had accomplished. She didn't find her visions to be exhausting at all, unlike what Rachel and Andrew told her would happen. In fact, they filled her with such excitement and energy she couldn't wait to dive into another one and discover where the missing children and the other South Siders were. She not only felt a sense of purpose, but wonder and awe. However, right now Elizabeth had to decide how much she should tell Samuel about what had happened today. 'Parse information out carefully,' her father used to say. 'But always hold something back so you have the advantage.'

There came a knock on the bedroom door.

"Come in."

Sampson entered carrying a tray with a teapot, one cup, and dried mint tea leaves tied in a bundle.

"Sally should have brought that. I'm sure you have much more important things to attend to."

He gave her a slight bow then walked over to a small inlaid wood table and set the tray down. "I wanted to speak to you, miss. I'm sorry . . . Mrs. Hunter."

"Don't be silly. Mrs. Hunter is too formal."

Sampson poured hot water into the porcelain cup. "With the challenges your family is facing right now, if you ever need me, all you have to do is ask."

Elizabeth walked over and patted his arm. "You are the best, Sampson. I don't know what Father would do without you. Or me, for that matter."

Sampson dunked the mint leaves in the water several times. "If you and Mr. Hunter are ever faced with the unhappy task of running House Weldsmore without your father, I will help in any way I can." The tea having reached its desired color of green, he handed her the cup.

"That's because you know where all the bodies are buried." Elizabeth teased him.

"Miss!" Sampson pretended to be shocked, then looked serious. "Well, yes. Your education has focused on the politics and society of the Great Houses, which is of vital importance. On day-to-day operations you may not be as knowledgeable. Such as which employees you can trust. For instance, Mr. Evans but not any of the undersecretaries."

"Duly noted, sir." She gave him a mock salute and smiled.

Samuel trudged in, taking off his jacket in the process. "Sampson! What do I have to do to get some of Jonathan's good whiskey?"

"Ask and you shall receive," Sampson replied with a subtle grin as he left the room.

"Did you learn anything about Thomas?" she asked.

"He definitely has money in one of the banks in Liberty Row. How much?" Samuel shrugged. "Your father should be able to find out." He sat on the bed and pulled off his boots and dropped them on the floor. "But why would he have money there and not where it's easily accessible in Chicago where he works? It's not like he doesn't have job security."

He got up and walked into the bathroom where Elizabeth heard him wash his face and finish getting dressed for dinner. She sat at her vanity and adjusted a few pins in her hair until satisfied with the result. Finding herself with a spare bobby pin, she placed it into an ovoid-shaped cobalt-blue glass bottle and put the stopper back on. She peered at it for a minute.

"What if he was saving for a rainy day?" She called out to her husband.

"What?" he yelled back over the water running.

"What if he were keeping the money for a special occasion?" she yelled back.

Samuel walked in wiping the water from his face with a fluffy white towel made of Egyptian cotton. "He's clearly saving it for a specific reason. But why hide it from Tillenghast? Wait." He stopped wiping his face. "You said rainy day."

Elizabeth stood up, took the towel from him, and dried off the spots he'd missed around his neck. "Yes, in case something happens and he can't access it from the banks in Chicago."

"Or he doesn't want anyone to know he's pulling money out. Or an unusually large amount." Samuel kissed her hard on the lips. "You're brilliant."

"But why?' Elizabeth tapped a finger against her cheek. "He has everything. And why ask Father for money?"

"He needs more than he expected. Like for a mistress. Someone Tillenghast wouldn't approve of."

"No. They wouldn't care." Elizabeth shook her head. "Not unless it was one of Tillenghast's daughters, and the only one who lives in Chicago is Charlotte, Hal's wife. So I don't think that's it."

"Wait. What if he's planning to leave the country?" Samuel paced. "What better place to keep it than at a major point of departure. Especially if he can convince my father to let him berth on one of our ships. And no one would ever question a guest of your father's."

"Exactly." Elizabeth batted her eyes at him for fun. "Didn't I tell you we'd make a good team?" She leaned over to kiss him.

"But the question is why?" Samuel put a shirt on. Elizabeth buttoned it up for him.

"With all that's going on, it could be a number of reasons," Elizabeth remarked. "Or something we've never considered." She frowned. "Do you think he knows anything about the missing South Siders?"

"That's a leap, don't you think? Which reminds me, how did it go today?"

"Good. I found Mary, Mr. Owen's sister. She's a medium, and I was sort of able to talk to her. But I still have no idea where they are being held."

Stunned, Samuel took a step back. "And you're just now telling me that? Have you told Mr. Owen?"

"No. Not yet. I didn't want to give him false hope. Plus, trying to explain how I knew this would have been awkward." Frustration seeped into her voice. "We were so close, but I also saw Abigail, the little girl from the candy store."

"I talked to the owner. He said she had a fit outside the store. That's about it. I tracked down some of her friends she went clamming with. One boy remembered a blond man in ill-fitting clothes loitering about." Samuel put on his dinner jacket. "I want to see if anyone else has seen him. Though he's probably just from the Middle District looking for a, ahem, lady of the night."

"Samuel, you can say the word *prostitute* in front of me. I won't melt." Elizabeth returned to the vanity and picked out a necklace with a small ruby at the center of a circle of diamonds on a gold chain. "This is worth at least two truckloads of food and clothing," she commented as she put it on.

"Probably more. You plan on selling it? It does look good on you."

"Maybe. What do you think about opening more schools on the South Side?"

Samuel shrugged. "You're asking me? That's Great House politics."

"Hummm . . ." Elizabeth frowned. "I'll need more than charm to have that approved."

"I'm afraid so." He headed toward the door. "Ready?"

"Go ahead. I'll be down in a minute."

Samuel nodded then walked out, closing the door behind him.

Elizabeth sat down at the vanity again and pretended to check her makeup. Part of her wanted to tell Samuel everything that had happened, but she couldn't bring herself to do it. This ability to enter visions on her own had taken a very personal tone, and she didn't want to share all of it. This was her achievement not Samuel's, nor her father's.

From the looks that Rachel and Andrew had given her today, they were surprised at her rapid progress. Shocked even. Was she as powerful as the older, more experienced, medium? Or was she more? And would Rachel try to hinder her to keep her in her place? The more

Elizabeth thought about it, the more absurd she realized it was and tried to shake off the idea, but it kept gnawing at her.

And what about the thing that had tried to communicate with her? Not the man who'd whispered in her ear, but whatever had left the handprint on her boot and pulled on her dress. If that wasn't a cry for help then what was? Perhaps it was even one of the missing people like Mary.

Elizabeth sat up straight and stared at her reflection. What she saw was a strong, attractive woman capable of doing anything she wanted as long as House Weldsmore permitted it. That's when she decided that she would no longer be dictated to by a Great House or anyone else. It was time to steer her own course no matter where it led her.

***

Sampson passed by the open door and noticed that Elizabeth had not gone down to dinner. He circled back and was about to announce himself when he saw her staring into her vanity mirror as if she were looking at a person other than herself. It was odd. He waited a moment or two before knocking in case she needed any assistance. From where he stood, he could see her reflection, but she was not able to see him. Sampson raised his hand to knock—and froze. Elizabeth's eyes had changed. One minute they were her normal hazel color, the next a swirling morass of amethyst. Alluring and repulsive at the same time, Sampson had the urge to reach out and stroke her hair and gaze deeper into those eyes, but he shook it off.

Frightened, he turned and fled down the staircase and didn't stop until he reached the bottom.

His first thought was to inform Mr. Weldsmore, but what *would he say? Your daughter's eyes changed color?* He'd think Sampson had lost his mind. Not to mention it could be construed as inappropriate to be staring unseen at a woman in her private rooms. Even telling Samuel might end in Sampson being dismissed. No, he wouldn't tell anyone. Not yet. He would watch over Elizabeth like he had done all her life. Whatever he'd seen, she was still acting fine as far as he knew, and as long as she remained that way, he would have nothing to tell anyone. However, if she was threatened in any way, he would act.

Elizabeth might be Jonathan Weldsmore's daughter in name, but she was Sampson's in spirit.

***

The look on Elizabeth and Samuel's faces at dinner when Jonathan told them he had gone to the newspapers to announce his business deal with the Abyssinians was worth the trouble it would cause. Or so Jonathan thought.

The next day he had Sampson remove the phone from his office after two hours of nonstop calls from other newspapers wanting interviews, the heads of several Great Houses, and the Senate chairman of the Foreign Defense Committee for the Great States of America. Edgar Monplasir of House Monplasir barged in with his usual pack of followers without so much as a courtesy call, ranting about how was he supposed to ship his crops overseas if Congress shut Jonathan down for treason? Jonathan assured him that nothing of the sort would happen. His contracts with His Majesty were legal and did not violate any preexisting trade agreements.

Monplasir finally left in a huff with his trail of sycophants behind him, but not before they had touched, manhandled, and commented on every piece of furniture and artwork in the foyer and Jonathan's office.

His contracts with the Abyssinians would have leaked in time, but he still believed getting out in front of it was the smartest thing. It would also throw House Tillenghast off guard. They wouldn't expect him to announce a deal that on the surface smacked of treason. The truth was Jonathan Weldsmore had beaten them to a market no one had ever considered or were too afraid to consider. Once he cleared the path, other Great Houses would follow in his footsteps to exploit foreign markets. Why colonize and conquer when it was easier to do business and make a profit?

The heads of House Du Pont and Bridgeworth and a few others either sent telegrams or called to praise his ingenuity and brashness, but most either expressed their outrage or stayed silent. Jonathan suspected those who were quiet were waiting to see how this all fell out before they acted.

He found it interesting that House Zhou from San Francisco sent a message written in Chinese that when translated said, "Strength and Good Fortune." Most of the West and East Coast Great Houses had little interaction unless it came to cross-country transportation. House Zhou built their own ships out of San Francisco but did not have as large of a shipping yard as House Weldsmore, nor the wealth—yet. House Espinosa in the northern part of California produced wine and had little interest in the political machinations of the East Coast as long as it did not interrupt production. This would all change as more of the population moved west.

Now, Jonathan waited for the other shoe to drop. And it did, but much more rapidly than he expected.

By the end of the day, he was served with a summons by an official congressional courier to appear in Washington, DC the day after tomorrow in front of the House Foreign Defense Commission. He would have to face questioning by the same men he'd helped to elect on whether his contracts with the Abyssinians were legal or not. He'd expected such a summons, but not for at least a week. That would have been plenty of time to prepare. It annoyed him that he would have to scramble to put his allies in place to fight to keep the contracts intact.

The entire proceeding had House Tillenghast written all over it. No one had known he would go public since he had only decided himself a day ago. The only way this summons could have arrived so fast was if it had already been approved, which meant House Tillenghast had played every angle and had come out ahead. Tillenghast had likely heard about the contracts before the paper even went to press.

Jonathan had thought he understood what Tillenghast's true end game was, but now he wasn't so sure. It didn't surprise him that someone had leaked information that the contracts existed, but not the true nature of the ship or the new weapons he was building. Then again, perhaps Tillenghast had had just enough information to make an educated guess and deduced the rest. It was more likely he was using the summons as a means to force Jonathan to reveal more about what he was working on. Jonathan needed to remain calm and not run out to where the new weapons were being built to check on their progress. Jonathan was sure he was being watched, and he had no intention of leading spies to his secret facility.

Sampson and Mrs. Owen ordered the staff to prepare his clothes and transportation to DC while he arranged for Mr. Evans to contact a few of the less influential Great Houses that had supported him in the past. Even with the flurry of activity around him, Jonathan phoned as many of his colleagues as he could to solidify his base among those who wielded more power, such as House Du Pont, House Carnegie, and House Griswold. He found it most advantageous that Samuel had saved the life of one of Carnegie's sons-in-law. Jonathan would have to remember to thank him later, but now he had to say goodbye to Elizabeth before she left to continue her lessons with the medium.

"Looks like someone lit a fire under your butt, little brother." Hal leaned against the doorway to Jonathan's study with a smug look on his face. "How does it feel to be humiliated?"

"Hal, I'm not humiliated. This is just business as usual." Jonathan put the initial ship diagrams into his briefcase and pulled the flap over to close it.

"Getting your name plastered on the front page of the *Boston Times* isn't humiliating?" Hal scoffed. "You've certainly changed your tune about publicity."

Jonathan stood up and looked at his brother with utter contempt. "I went to them. Did you even bother to read the story? It was a human-interest piece. Every Middle District shipworker up and down the coast has been submitting applications to work for House Weldsmore. Mr. Evans and the rest of the staff are swamped. I wouldn't be surprised if we get offers from other countries looking for help to build their navies. This whole enterprise is not only good for House Weldsmore, it's good for the country."

Hal chuckled. "You've fallen into his trap."

"Why are you still here?" Jonathan asked. "I thought you'd be off to sponge off of Tillenghast's distant relatives by now instead of gallivanting around every night club and brothel in town."

"You really think you're clever, don't you? With your spies and informants all over the country. Why do you bother to spy on me? Nothing I do is very interesting."

"You think I didn't know that Tillenghast wants to institutionalize your wife?" Jonathan shot back. "Was that the deal? You bring me into the fold and you get to keep your wife at home? Why didn't you ask for my help?"

Hal's face turned mottled shades of crimson. "Because I hate you."

"Selfish idiot. It would have been easy enough to get you and Charlotte out of the country. Go home, Hal. You don't belong here. You haven't in a long time."

As he walked away, Hal put a hand on his arm to stop him.

"Tillenghast wants to centralize all airship and sea vessel production here in the States. If you start setting up facilities in other countries, it makes it harder for him to control." Hal leaned in closer to whisper in Jonathan's ear, like a snake slithering in for the kill. "He will push you harder than ever to join him. Don't wait too long, little brother, before he decides to get really nasty."

"He's already tried to kill me once, and that didn't work."

Hal sneered. "Idiot. If he wanted you dead then you'd be dead. Otherwise, it was just a feint."

Jonathan sniffed as he shoved Hal away. "I've tried to be kind, considering your situation, but you make it too difficult. You still think if I die he'll let you run this House? Sampson can do a better job than you."

"I don't doubt it. His talents are wasted being your lap dog."

Fed up, Jonathan lashed out. "Pack your bags. Leave today on the first train or airship back to Chicago. Mr. Rochester may go at his convenience. He at least knows how to behave like a gentleman."

"He's just as arrogant as any Great House flunky."

"At least his arrogance didn't almost get his entire family killed," Jonathan snarled at him.

As Hal marched out, he yelled back, "Watch yourself, little brother. Tillenghast will always hit you where you least expect it."

16

Elizabeth did her best to stay out of her father's way as he prepared to leave for Washington. To an outsider, he looked serious yet calm and unconcerned, but she could tell he was worried by how his eyes crinkled. It was something no one else would notice but her.

When she overheard his fight with Hal, Elizabeth fled back up to her room until he left.

She had come down to discuss the Abyssinian contracts. It annoyed her that he hadn't informed her about them, but in all fairness, there had not been enough time. Between setting up a new business, learning how to control her visions, and taking care of her social duties as well as interviewing the families of the missing, life was spinning upside down and sideways. While she fiddled with the drapes, Elizabeth made a mental note to hire a personal secretary as soon as possible.

Movement caught her eye. Sampson hovered at her door with a distinctly guilty expression on his face.

"Sampson! What are you up to?" she asked, giving him a playful smile.

"Ah, I . . . Are you feeling well, miss?" he stammered.

"Never better," she replied. "But you look like a little boy who broke his mother's best china."

"I've done no such a thing." He stood up even straighter than usual. "I've come to tell you that Mr. Hunter is finished with his breakfast and the horse carriage is waiting."

"Did my father say when he was returning from Washington?"

"No, miss. But these proceedings rarely last more than one or two days. The committees usually have their minds made up before anyone arrives. The rest is just going through the motions. Though I'm positive your father has his people lined up to support him."

"I'd forgotten how well versed you were in Great House and congressional politics." Elizabeth raised an eyebrow. "How would you like to be my personal secretary?"

Taken aback, Sampson blinked a few times in surprise. "I'm not sure your father would approve."

"Let me take care of him. Are you interested or not?"

"No, miss. Not really. I enjoy running the house, and when your father needs a sounding board, I am happy to oblige. As I would with you. Is there perhaps something you'd like to discuss?"

Elizabeth shook her head. "No. And now that I think about it, you're overqualified for the position. I need someone to help with not only my personal scheduling but our new detective agency once it gets off the ground."

"There are several young ladies I can recommend when you are ready."

"Excellent. Thank you." Elizabeth pursed her lips. "Where is Samuel? Is he making Mrs. Owen cook another breakfast for him?"

"I heard that." Samuel poked his head into the room. "And no, I didn't eat all of her muffins, but lunch made it into the carriage. Mrs. Owen was nice enough to pack one for our driver and guards as well." He offered his arm to Elizabeth. "Shall we go?"

She strode over and took it, but as she walked out Elizabeth noticed that Sampson looked at her like he was seeing her for the first time and wasn't sure if he liked what he saw. It disturbed her that the family's most trusted servant would act that way, and she wondered what she had done to warrant his odd behavior. Had her offer of being her personal secretary offended him? If that was the case, she was determined to find out why. Sampson adored her, and she loved him as if he were her real uncle. It was settled. Tonight when she returned, she would set up a time to have tea with him. Then all would be made right again.

***

When Elizabeth and Samuel arrived at Rachel's, she noticed a hush had fallen over the tenement whereas before the sounds of life had rung through the doors and walls. It unnerved her.

The door to Rachel's apartment was open, and Andrew paced inside, stopping every once in a while to peer out the window. The front room had chairs tossed over, a table smashed, curtains torn, and the contents of the cupboard emptied onto the floor. Whatever had happened, it wasn't good.

Andrew turned when he saw them arrive.

"Someone took her," he announced.

"Who? Rachel?" Elizabeth asked.

"Aye." Andrew wrung his hands. "I came a bit early like I always do to talk about what she had planned for you today. But when I arrived, the door was open and she be gone."

Samuel studied the debris as he inched his way around the room. "Anything missing?"

"They took her jewelry. Wait . . ." Andrew hesitated, then rushed over to the small kitchen and searched through a sea of broken glass and canned food on the floor. When he didn't find what he was looking for, he reached up into the back of the cupboard. He pulled out a tin can that was still sealed. With a resounding pop, he opened it, and several hundred dollars in cash spilled out.

"Whoever it was, they wanted to make it appear like a robbery," Samuel commented. "Searching everywhere for valuables, but only taking the most obvious."

Andrew nodded. "That be true. She kept her jewelry box in the other room."

Elizabeth stepped forward, but Samuel held out his arm to stop her. "Wait."

He tiptoed around the broken furniture and pulled back the curtain to show that the table had been cleaved in two by what looked like an axe. There was a small amount of blood on the floor. Whoever was bleeding wasn't dead, but they were hurting.

"It's all right. You can both come in," he called out.

Elizabeth entered ahead of Andrew and surveyed the room. It gave her a chill knowing she was so close to violence, although . . . She was surprised to realize another side of her seemed to enjoy the thrill of it. She shoved those ugly thoughts out of her mind as she studied the scene. Something shined next to one of the broken table legs. She walked over and kicked it aside. Underneath laid Rachel's trinity knot necklace.

"Look!" She picked it up and placed it in the palm of her hand. "She must have lost this in the struggle. What if she was kidnapped by the same men who took the others?"

"It's possible," Samuel replied. "But we need more facts. Did she have any enemies? Unsatisfied clients?" He eyed Andrew.

"Aye, there always be one who don't like the future Rachel spelt out for them or those who she refused to work for. Usually that ended up in a shouting match, not kidnapping. Besides, she be responsible for bringing in food and clothing to the South Side. Most will overlook any grievances for that."

Elizabeth stepped in front of Samuel. "Rachel was special like the others. It makes sense they would take her. Especially, if they were able to control her in some way."

"Aye." Andrew agreed. "If it be those devils, then you two be gettin' too close to the truth."

"Which means Elizabeth is in danger." Samuel grabbed her hand. "We're leaving."

She yanked it back. "There is no reason to believe I'm in danger yet. No one knows about my abilities except you, Father, Andrew, and Rachel. As far as anyone else is concerned, I'm here to get my fortune read."

"Then I say let the police handle it," Samuel declared.

Both Andrew and Elizabeth looked at him as if he had lost his mind.

Elizabeth placed her hand on his arm with all the gentleness of a loving wife. "Samuel, they won't care. And if you're worried about me, may I remind you that we have two very large Irishmen outside who are highly motivated. And I have a very capable ex-Pinkerton husband. I think I will be fine for the time being."

"If your father . . ."

"I won't tell him if you don't," Elizabeth replied.

Samuel stared at her, his nostrils flared, then sighed. "Fine. But if there is a hint of danger, you're going home." He turned to continue examining every detail of their meeting area.

Andrew gestured for her to come back into the other room. Not wanting to cause any more of a fuss, Elizabeth followed.

One undamaged chair leaned against the wall. Andrew righted it and motioned for Elizabeth to sit. Grasping the trinity knot necklace to her chest, she sat down and watched Samuel as he took a small notepad out of his jacket and jotted down notes.

"I could help," she called out to him. "Isn't that part of my job as your partner?"

"Not this time." Samuel's face softened. "Think of it as training. Detectives do have to learn how to deal with boredom and frustration."

"Aye, lassie. You might be a wee bit of a distraction," Andrew added. "Seems like the lad knows what he's doing, and if he be needing our help, he'll ask."

Elizabeth squirmed on the uncomfortable wooden chair. While waiting for Samuel to discover more about Rachel's disappearance, she realized that she held a clue in her hand—the trinity knot. Rachel may not have lost it in a struggle but left it there for her to find.

With Andrew engrossed in Samuel's examination of the room, Elizabeth closed her eyes and caressed the trinity knot between her thumb and forefinger. She traced the edges of the charm, taking particular care to notice the ridges and any flaws in the workmanship. The metal grew warm as she rubbed it, while every inch of her mind tried to connect with this object and the woman who owned it in the here and now and not in some future vision.

At first, all she heard was Samuel puttering around in the other room searching for clues—the scratching of the pencil on his notepad and how the soles of his shoes scuffed across the floor. The sounds became louder and louder until they stopped. In the background she noted the faint sound of water dripping. She opened her eyes to discover she was back in the basement where all the missing people were kept.

This time it was different. Everyone milled around like windup dolls with no direction or purpose. They muttered words over and over again that she couldn't quite make out. Elizabeth tried to move the body she was in, but discovered that her hands and feet were bound to the bed. She jerked on them, but the ropes were too tight and wouldn't budge.

"Stop it. You be hurtin' me," a voice from the person she inhabited whispered. It was Rachel! "I know you're there. It feels like a bee buzzing around my brain. And I can smell your perfume." The medium chuckled "This be strange. I wonder if all those you visit feel this way."

Elizabeth thought the answer was no. So far, only Mary had sensed her presence to the point where she was able to communicate.

Rachel moved her head sideways so Elizabeth could get a better look at the room, but the crowd obscured her view.

"I didn't see the faces of the men who grabbed me," Rachel offered. "But they were Irish by the sound and the stench of them. They threw me in a cart with a potato bag tied over my head." she grumbled. "There be another. Sounded like one of yours."

Someone from a Great House was involved? Perhaps it was the man whose hand she'd seen helping Abigail up. Could it also be the same man who'd whispered, "Gotcha?" It didn't make any sense. Why would a Great House kidnap these people?

Her mind swirled with ideas of how to communicate with the medium to get more information, but they all came up short. There was no way to question Rachel in her current state.

The door opened and shut, then footsteps headed in their direction. Rachel closed her eyes and pretended to sleep.

"Wakey, love." It was the voice of the Irishman whom Elizabeth had seen before.

Cold water splashed Rachel in the face. She sputtered and opened her eyes to see him leering at her.

"You be a handsome woman. And I hear you not be mad like the rest." He gestured around him. "Too bad. You will be when he's done with the likes of you."

"You idiot! Get away from her!" the same clipped authoritative voice from before yelled at him from across the room. "Cover her eyes! Someone may recognize you."

There was something about the voice that seemed familiar. Elizabeth racked her brain for where she might have heard it before, but her thoughts were interrupted when a cold, damp cloth landed on top of Rachel's face, covering her eyes and nose. It reeked of mold and urine. Rachel gagged.

"That makes no sense," the old Irishman remarked. "Who's she going to tell if she does know who I am?"

A cuffing sound made her wince.

"Ow! No need to be hittin' me."

"Do not question what you don't understand. Make sure her eyes remain covered," the younger man ordered. He paused. "Oh, she's back." His voice took on a seductive tone.

The sound of footsteps came closer to the bed. Elizabeth recognized the sharp heels of custom-made shoes. A lone finger traced its way from the crook of Rachel's elbow to the palm of her hand. The restraints on her right arm were released. Smooth fingers lifted it up and caressed the palm before he brought it to his lips. His breath, warm and humid, sent shivers through Elizabeth's entire body. His tongue flicked across her—Rachel's—fingertips. Both she and Rachel yanked them away.

He laughed. "That wasn't for you, Irish whore, but the one who married far beneath her—Elizabeth Weldsmore Hunter."

If Elizabeth could have gasped, she would have. Whoever this man was, he not only realized she was there, but who she was. Terrified, she did her best to calm herself and focus on the image of the trinity knot in her mind. It calmed her, and she concentrated on returning to her own body. There was a moment of release then something yanked her back.

"No you don't, Elizabeth. You're staying right here with me and all these lovely people."

"Ah, sir. Who you be talking to?" the Irishman's asked with a worried tone.

"Go tend to the others," the younger man snarled. "Make sure they don't shit on themselves."

Elizabeth heard the other man shuffle off in a hurry, then felt the cot sag as this mysterious man sat down next to her. He held Rachel's hand in his again.

"Now, Rachel. I want you to let Elizabeth speak. It'll be hard at first. Maybe even a little painful, but I know you can do it. You are both extraordinary mediums."

"I don't know what you be talkin' about." Rachel tried to yank her hand back again, but the man held on tight. "Let me go, ye bastard. Or I'll have all the South Side lookin' to put your arse in a grave."

"Oh, Rachel. This is so perfect. Never in my wildest dreams did I think I'd be able to kill two birds with one stone." He gripped her hand harder; pain shot up Rachel's arm, echoing in Elizabeth's head. "Now . . . let . . . her . . . speak."

The mental image of walls torn down, brick by brick, floated through Elizabeth's mind. She had never noticed them before, but now she understood why Rachel taught her how to construct her own metal barriers. The medium was allowing her to access parts of her psyche she had never allowed anyone to see before. The loss of privacy and control had to be devastating. Elizabeth decided Rachel should not have to make such a sacrifice. She refocused her efforts on returning to her body, but the man's psychic hold was too strong. It was as if he had hooks in her mind, and every time she moved they tore a piece of her away.

Rachel cried out, her breathing rapid and shallow. "Please stop."

"It will once Elizabeth stops trying to escape." He sighed. "If you keep this up, you just may kill your Irish friend here. And who knows where you'll end up."

The thought of giving in to his demands sent Elizabeth into an unexpected rage. It filled her with such hate and violence that all she wanted to do was reach out and squeeze his heart until it burst. And then it occurred to her that if she could enter Rachel's mind, perhaps she could enter his.

As she refocused her efforts on reaching out to him, she felt one of the metaphorical hooks slip away. Someone or something else was with her. It was the same presence she had encountered before, the one who had burned her boot and grabbed on to her skirt. Whatever it was, it was trying to help her.

The young man gasped, dropping Rachel's hand as he jerked up.

"No, it's not possible. How are you doing that?" he screeched. "If you leave, I'll kill Rachel!"

A rumble came from deep within Rachel's chest that turned into harsh laughter. "You won't be killin' me else I'd be dead already. Go, lassie. I'll be all right."

Another hook slipped away, allowing her to free herself from the man's psychic hold. She soared into Rachel's psyche, sending a flood of warmth and strength to her, then fled.

Elizabeth expected to open her eyes and find herself back at the tenement apartment with Andrew and Samuel, but that didn't happen. Instead, she floated around in the spirit passageway surrounded by a churning purple-and-green mist. Elizabeth reached out to touch it, but it swirled away to form the outline of a man.

"If you're the one who saved me, thank you."

The form extended its hand, pointed in a direction beyond her then back to Elizabeth. Though time, space, and direction had no meaning here, she understood that it was pointing the way home. With a massive psychic push, he thrust her in the same direction he had pointed to. Ahead of her was the image of the trinity knot. Her mind flew toward it, picking up speed and energy. Light and noise flooded her vision.

Samuel was yelling at her. "Elizabeth! Come back! Come home!"

Andrew's hands gripped her shoulders; his fingers digging into her scapula.

She opened her eyes and took a deep breath. "I'm here."

Samuel knelt in front of her, his face awash in fear and worry. He collapsed onto the floor. "Where did you go? What did you do?" The words came out in gulps.

"I found Rachel. The same men captured her as the others. And I think a Great House is involved."

Andrew released his grasp on her and stumbled backward. "If that be true, we be in a whole lot of trouble, laddie."

Elizabeth filled them in on what she had learned. It was clear there was a larger plan for all the victims. It disturbed both of them that not only did this mysterious man know another medium inhabited Rachel, but he recognized it was Elizabeth. For some reason, she was a target, though none of them understood why.

"We need to up your security and inform your father. They may try to kidnap you."

"We still have to find out where they're keeping Rachel and the others. Whatever they're planning, I can't imagine any of those people will survive it. I need to contact Rachel again to learn more."

"Absolutely not!" Samuel stood up and straightened his jacket.

"Samuel!" Elizabeth could no longer keep her fury in check. "They need my help!"

"I don't care about them, Elizabeth. I only care about you. And what the hell do you think you were doing attempting a vision on your own like that?" Samuel seethed.

Andrew shuffled his feet, his face taking on a pained look.

"You knew about this, didn't you, Andrew? You knew she could do this on her own. Why didn't either of you tell me?" Samuel demanded.

"She told Rachel and me, so there's no cause for alarm," Andrew tried to calm him.

"Are you insane? You lied to me!"

"Samuel, I decided not to tell you until I understood more about it. And I didn't want to worry you." Elizabeth calmed down and took his hand. "You've had so many changes and upheavals in your life. There was no reason to burden you with more. Please don't blame Andrew or Rachel. They did what I asked."

Samuel let go of her hand and crossed his arms over his chest. "We're done with this case. I'm handing everything we have over to the police."

"No!" Elizabeth stood up, knocking over the chair. "They'll never find them in time!"

"In time for what?"

"I don't know," Elizabeth exclaimed. "It's just something I feel. Like time is running out. The way he talked. His arrogance. And now they have Rachel."

"She be one of the strongest mediums in the city, laddie. And if they be collecting the likes of us for some purpose . . ." Andrew shook his head. "We might be in a world of hurt that we don't rightly understand yet."

Samuel paced around, then whirled and pointed his finger at Elizabeth. "Promise me you won't enter a vision without Andrew present again."

Elizabeth hated to do it, but she did. "I promise."

"Fine. Now, is there anything else you need to tell me? I can't work a case properly without all the information that is available. No matter how small it might be important."

Elizabeth thought about the entity that saved her. Convinced they would think her mad, she decided not to tell Samuel or Andrew about it. No need to worry them even more. But it was more than that. Right before the entity had hurled her back into her own body, it had put a spectral finger over its ghostly lips. Whatever it was, it understood the power of secrets just like she did.

"If it's important, I will tell you," Elizabeth replied.

17

Jonathan arrived at the Capitol Building in Washington, DC, with two hours to spare before he was to be questioned by the Senate Committee on Foreign Defense. His allies on the committee had arranged for a steam-powered car to pick him up at the station then take him to his hotel. He could have taken an airship, but for such a short distance the train was faster. Besides, it would have given Tillenghast operatives a perfect opportunity to have him "accidentally" fall over the railing on one of the viewing decks if they were so inclined.

The Greek- and Roman-inspired federal buildings awed the tourists, but Jonathan's frequent visits only reinforced his belief they were mausoleums for those who didn't realize they were dead yet. Entrenched in the power and political structure of Washington, the other Great Houses were averse to change unless it involved making money or enhancing their status. Jonathan couldn't fault them, but business was not for the faint of heart, and he thought it might be time for some new ideas. He hoped that he could use his relationship with the Abyssinians as a way to implement that.

As he entered the rotunda with four Weldsmore guardsmen flanking him, he noticed that the statues of Grant and Lincoln had been removed, but Washington was still there. Statues were rotated in and out depending on the political climate, but General Washington always remained as well as the painting of the surrender of Lord Cornwallis at Yorktown. Everyone knew it irritated the British ambassador, so it was kept as a constant reminder of England's embarrassing loss. However, given the chance, every British envoy liked to point out that the Great States of America had lost the War of 1812 though they were reluctant to admit it.

The tapping of heels coming in his direction caught his attention. A young clerk in his early twenties dressed in the traditional bureaucratic black wool suit with two bands of copper wire sewn into the cuffs of

165

his pants walked toward him. Most of the clerks came from Middle Districts throughout the country, but on occasion the third or fourth son of a Great House was assigned to the Capitol since their chance at inheriting was slim and they needed an occupation. It was a good way to educate one of their own who might eventually be elected to the House or the Senate.

The man stopped short and gave Jonathan a quick bow. "Mr. Weldsmore." He ignored the guardsmen as he glanced around, looking for something or someone. "Will your secretary be accompanying you?"

"No." Jonathan had left Mr. Evans in Boston and out of the committee's reach. No sense volunteering a potential witness when he hadn't even been summoned. Besides, he hated dragging along a bunch of useless assistants

The clerk's eyes narrowed. Jonathan could almost hear the man thinking out loud. Jonathan knew the man was trying to figure out what kind of tactic he was using. The clerk quickly gave up.

"Your security must remain here. If you would please follow me."

Jonathan gestured for his men to stay in the rotunda. Carrying his briefcase, he walked a few feet behind his escort as he led the way to one of the committee rooms. The marble floors echoed their footsteps. Only one other clerk passed them, which he found odd. It was quiet for the middle of the week.

"Are you on recess?" Jonathan asked.

"Of a sort, sir," the clerk answered over his shoulder as he approached a large oak door. He reached for the knob, pulled it open, and held it for Jonathan to enter.

A long rectangular room with a matching table that could seat over twenty men sat in the middle. Two cascading crystal chandeliers hung from the vaulted ceiling, which set off the baroque murals of Constantine Brumidi in all their glory. Jonathan had been here before and found both the room and the murals to be ostentatious. Baroque artwork gave him a headache.

What surprised him was the lack of the usual flunkies who normally surrounded the seven men and one woman who sat on the committee. Each was a long-standing member of the Senate, and all held positions of influence within their own Houses. The two who held the most sway were Everett Du Pont of House Du Pont and Bai Zhou, the lone woman and chairman from House Zhou in California. Jonathan had a cordial relationship with Miss Zhou, but he did not consider her an ally. A ship-building family like his, the Zhous focused their energy on expanding the Asian market, and they had yet to come into conflict. He knew it was only a matter of time before they became a threat to one another, but he hoped they would be able to work out a mutually beneficial deal before then.

The oldest on the committee and an expert negotiator, Zhou was a stickler for protocol, which should work in his favor. Everett was smart but not as smart as her, and even though he was an ally of House Weldsmore, Jonathan had seen the Du Ponts make some serious mistakes, much like House Carnegie. He had no doubt it would come back to haunt them in the future.

The rest of the committee was comprised of George Eastman from New York, Hank Carroll from Texas, Ernesto Garza from Arizona, Edwin Stellmacher from Oregon, William Hibbard from Illinois, and Justin Butler from Georgia. Senator Butler was one of three half Negroes in the Senate. Jonathan had had business dealings with all of them or the Minor Houses that were allied with them from time to time. Hibbard was a lackey for Tillenghast even though they were technically a Great House. They had been taken over in everything but name by the Tillenghast family during the House Wars. Jonathan suspected that House Tillenghast continued to prop them up to use them in situations like these so their influence was not quite so obvious to the outside observer. The government had to at least give the appearance of being unbiased to its citizens. It helped prevent revolutions.

"Mr. Weldsmore." Hibbard smiled. "Thank you for coming on such short notice. We wouldn't have asked you here if it weren't important. Please sit. We had water, coffee, and tea brought in." He gestured to the silver coffee and tea set in the middle of the table as Jonathan sat down. "Let me know if you need anything else."

Zhou burst out laughing. "Important? Nothing about this is important. You're the one who dragged us here, Mr. Hibbard. Please inform the committee what is so critical that I had to miss my train and cancel my plans."

"I was wondering the same thing, William," Everett chimed in. "Please enlighten us."

"I'll 'enlighten' the damn lot of you. This bastard is doing business with the enemy," Hank Carroll leaned forward on his elbows as he glared across the table at Jonathan. "Just what the hell do you think you're doing, boy?"

The Texan was broad shouldered, heavy set, and had a bulbous nose. At seventy-two years of age, he called any man younger than sixty "boy."

"So we are all clear, I'm assuming you are referring to the contracts I have to build ships for His Majesty, the King of Abyssinia," Jonathan replied.

"His Majesty, my ass. He's just a jumped up n—"

"Senator Carroll! That will be enough," Zhou growled at him. "That language is unbecoming of a senator. And don't think I don't know what you call me behind my back. Besides, I have not brought this committee meeting to order."

The Texas senator sat back, folded his arms across his chest, and curled his upper lip. "Fine. Get on with it."

"I bring the Senate Committee on Foreign Defense to order," Zhou announced. "Our first and only order of business is the legality of the contracts of House Weldsmore and the Abyssinian government. Please open your folders."

The lone clerk who attended the meeting passed around leather-bound folders to each of the senators as well as Jonathan. He opened it to discover a detailed report on his meetings and the two contracts he had with the Abyssinians: one for the ship he was building and one for the workers to be sent to Abyssinia to build a small fleet. He scanned the information and realized most of it had been gleaned from the newspaper article. Jonathan flipped through to the back and didn't see anything damaging.

Zhou and Eastman thumbed through it. Garza didn't even bother to open his, though Butler took the time to get out a pen to mark his up while Stellmacher looked bored.

"There is nothing against the law that says a Great House, or any business in our country, cannot conduct trade with a foreign government. We all do it." Everett threw up his hands in exasperation. "Why are we even here?"

"Because he's a liar and a traitor!" Carroll shook his finger at Jonathan. "Just admit it, Weldsmore. You'd like to see this country run by European dandies and so-called African monarchies."

Jonathan did his best to keep a straight face throughout the Texan's tirade.

"I want to review these contracts in more detail," Senator Butler announced in his soothing southern accent. "I suggest we recess."

Senator Eastman scratched his balding head in frustration. "We don't have time for that. This whole thing is ridiculous."

"I'm inclined to agree," Zhou interjected.

"But he hid them from us!" Carroll yelled. "What else can he be hiding?"

Zhou frowned. "Mr. Weldsmore made these deals public at the appropriate time. Do you make your deals public before all parties have come to an agreement, Senator Carroll?"

"Senator Zhou is correct," Garza interjected, his Spanish accent cutting through the din. "House Weldsmore has done nothing that risks the security of this country. And that is the question at hand, is it not?"

Jonathan watched as Garza gave him a nod of understanding. He didn't know much about the youngest member of the committee, which was something he'd have to rectify. Garza had the demeanor of a man who wanted more for his House and was willing to show his allegiance when it counted. House Garza had become a Great House a mere twenty years ago, so it was still young in the hierarchy, and allying itself with an older and more prestigious House would benefit it.

"He's hiding something. I can smell it." Senator Carroll grumbled.

"We are all hiding something, Hank." Everett remarked. "Can we call this a wash and go home? I have a play to catch in New York tonight." The senator from New York slid his chair away from the table.

"Yes." Zhou nodded. "All who agr—"

"I abstain," Butler announced.

"Very well." Zhou sighed and made a note in her agenda book. "Once again, all who agree that House Weldsmore is in compliance with the Foreign Defense Act of 1868, please raise your right hand."

As the four hands of Zhou, Du Pont, Garza, and Eastman shot up, Edwin Stellmacher cleared his throat in such a manner as to make everyone groan.

"Senator Stellmacher? Do you have a point of order?" Zhou asked.

"Yes. You failed to move that we accept this report as part of the record. Is that because you know it is inaccurate?"

"What are you implying, senator?" Zhou narrowed her eyes at him, suspicious of where this was going.

He sat up straighter in the high-backed chair and folded his hands across his lap, his every movement contrived to give the appearance of benevolent condescension. "Only that I think you're being a little hasty, Senator Zhou. Which is very unlike you."

Zhou did not bother to hide her desire to eviscerate Stellmacher for questioning her authority and her integrity. Jonathan suspected that the senator from Oregon's lifespan had just been shortened.

"I move that the report on House Weldsmore's contracts with the Abyssinian government be entered into the committee records. Second?" she asked, her eyes never leaving Senator Stellmacher.

Everett's hand shot up. "I second."

"Wait." Senator Butler waved his pen in the air as he pushed his glasses back up his nose. "What are you suggesting, Edwin? Is there something you'd like to share?"

Jonathan closed his eyes, sighed, then opened them again. He was beginning to see the pattern now. Hibbard was staying out of the fight but using Stellmacher as his proxy. Jonathan wondered what they'd offered him in exchange for his assistance in killing his deal with the Abyssinians. Senator Butler did surprise him, though. The little man could crunch numbers until they squealed, but he was not one for intrigue. What Stellmacher had done was cast enough doubt to make honest men question those they trusted.

Stellmacher shrugged. "Is it true, Mr. Weldsmore, that you have a group of men working on a secret project in Virginia? Or is it Maryland?"

"Everyone has secret projects, Stellmacher! It's called research and development," Everett snarled at him. "What's your point?"

"Do we have to explain patent law to you, Edwin?" George added without bothering to hide his annoyance.

Jonathan knew he had to let his allies fight for him, but it was time to put a stop to this line of inquiry. He waved his hand in the air to get their attention.

"Madame Chairwoman, may I speak?" Jonathan asked Senator Zhou.

"Please do."

"To answer Senator Stellmacher's question, yes, I do have several projects in development. Maryland, Virginia, New York, and other regions. It's not a crime to want to test and refine new ideas before bringing them to market."

Senator Butler squinted at him. "That I understand. However, is there anything about these projects that could be considered harmful to our country?"

Jonathan shook his head. "Of course not."

"But what if they are designed to be sold to a specific buyer overseas and not to the Great States of America?" Stellmacher threw that question at him like a lightning bolt.

"So what if they are?" Jonathan shrugged. "Not all products will sell here. It's time we as the leaders of this nation spend more time expanding our markets overseas. That's where future profits lie." He glanced over at Stellmacher, who had a hint of a smile on his face. Jonathan knew he wasn't done testing him yet. Stellmacher had picked up a pencil and now pretended to make notes on the report. Senator Butler, who sat next to him, leaned over and tried to see what he was writing.

It was all a distraction.

"What if . . . ? And this is just a 'what if' since I'm not privy to House Weldsmore's research. But what if he were selling weapons to foreign countries without our consent? That would be illegal. Isn't that correct, Senator Butler?"

"What?" Senator Carroll bellowed. "Are you out of your mind, Weldsmore?"

"Senator!" Zhou yelled back at him. "That behavior is not acceptable in this room."

Butler bobbed his whole body up and down. "Yes, yes. That would be true. But why would any Great House want to do such a thing?"

"I have no idea. Why don't we ask Mr. Weldsmore?" Stellmacher feigned deference and respect.

All of them turned to Jonathan.

Both Everett and George gave him a look of "we can't help you now," while Zhou pleaded with her eyes that he'd better make the next moment count.

"Senators. I would never jeopardize the safety of our nation. I've designed and will continue to design and build military ships for this country for as long as House Weldsmore stands," Jonathan responded with complete sincerity.

The truth of his words resonated throughout the room. Even Senator Carroll gave him a grudging nod, but Stellmacher wasn't done.

"Very nice, Mr. Weldsmore, but that doesn't answer the question. Are you or are you not building new weapons?"

Before Jonathan could reply there was a rustle at the door and a clerk ran in and over to Senator Zhou. As he leaned over and whispered in her ear, another clerk entered behind him with a message in his hand. He walked over to Jonathan and tapped him on the shoulder.

"For you, sir."

Jonathan took it from the clerk and ripped the envelope open. It was from Mr. Evans, his executive assistant He blinked a few times as he read it and reread it. The Abyssinian envoy Mekonnen was dead. His airship had never arrived in Abyssinia. Pieces of it had been found floating by a passing fishing boat. All aboard were presumed lost.

He folded the message up and tucked it away in his pocket.

"Mr. Weldsmore?" Zhou addressed him. "I believe that we just received the same information. I'm sorry. We will send our condolences to the Abyssinian government, but in the meantime several hundred Americans are dead in an airship accident, and we need to find out why."

Everyone in the room gasped in shock except for Stellmacher. He'd known it was going to happen, and he didn't care.

Stunned that Tillenghast and his stooges would be willing to kill so many innocents just to kill one foreign envoy to get at him made

Jonathan realize how far his adversaries would go to destroy him. He knew he and his family would always be targets, but he'd never thought they would kill so many in an attempt to destroy his plans. Their actions were horrific, and they had to be stopped.

"I move that we adjourn for two weeks. During that time we trust that Mr. Weldsmore will not have any dealings with the Abyssinian government until we rule out that they are not responsible for the destruction of an American passenger airship. Second?" Zhou asked.

"Second." Butler piped up, then turned to Jonathan. "My condolences, Mr. Weldsmore. It is always difficult to find good business partners."

"All in favor, say aye," Zhou commanded.

A series of resolute ayes echoed in the room.

"Then we are adjourned." Zhou scooted her chair out and stood up.

George and Everett stopped on the way out to shake Jonathan's hand. Stellmacher and Hibbard left not even bothering to linger and gloat. The rest scurried out as fast as possible, leaving Jonathan to contemplate his next move.

The contracts weren't scuttled yet but would take more time to finalize. Jonathan considered sending Mr. Evans to Abyssinia on his behalf to finish negotiating the workers' contracts. However, that wasn't his concern right now. The next target might be him or Elizabeth.

"Get me on the first train back to Boston," he ordered the lone remaining clerk.

***

Sampson watched as Samuel trudged through the front door with an older Irishman trailing behind him while Elizabeth chatted with two of the Weldsmore guardsmen. They followed them in to keep an eye on the newcomer until Sampson waved them off. The man didn't appear young or muscular enough to be one of their escorts, so Sampson assumed he was one of the mediums he had overheard them talking about.

Both men carried themselves as if burdened with a preordained duty, while Elizabeth radiated an energy that surprised him. She held her head high and breezed in as if she'd had the best days of her life.

"I have no doubt that you'd both like to rest. I will have one of the maids bring tea and some food up to your room," Sampson said as he cut the trio off before they reached the staircase. "Would this gentleman like to go to the kitchen for some refreshments? I'm sure Mrs. Owen still has muffins left over from this morning. Or I can have a fresh sandwich made." He smiled graciously at the Irishman.

"Sampson, this is Andrew O'Sullivan. He's . . . helping us on our first case," Samuel volunteered.

The house manager gave Andrew a polite nod. "Mr. O'Sullivan."

"Some tea and a bit of food sounds good," the man replied. "Laddie, you'd best make sure the missus gets some rest. It be a hard day."

"Any word from my father, Sampson?" Elizabeth asked.

"He should be on his way back."

Elizabeth cocked her head to one side and studied him. "Something's wrong. What is it?"

Sampson kept a measured tone in his voice so as not to give away the fact he was the one who had sent the message that Mekonnen was dead. "Nothing that cannot wait until after your father has returned. However, he did request that you remain in the house until he does."

She scowled. "But we have work to do. We have to find—"

"We have to eat and rest. Where does he keep the good whiskey?" Samuel cut her off. "How about it, Andrew? Mind if I join you downstairs after I steal a bottle of House Weldsmore's finest?"

"I know where he hides it," Elizabeth chimed in. Instead of heading upstairs, she dashed off toward her father's study.

"Elizabeth!" Samuel called after her, but she had already disappeared.

Andrew frowned. "You need to be keeping a steady eye on the lassie."

Elizabeth ran back into the foyer holding a bottle of Jameson's. "I used to sneak a bit of this when I was a teenager." She giggled.

"I know." Sampson deadpanned.

"What? You weren't supposed to." Elizabeth scowled at him, then grinned. "Thank you for not telling my father."

Sampson gave her a smile and a brief nod of his head.

"Elizabeth, why don't you give me the bottle and go upstairs and change?" Samuel suggested. "I'll bring you up a glass."

Sampson watched as her back tensed up as if she was going to argue with him, then she relaxed.

"Good idea." She leaned in and gave her husband a kiss. "I am a little tired."

Samuel looked surprised at this public display of affection but didn't seem to mind.

As Elizabeth headed up the stairs, Sampson saw a slight change in her posture, as if she were pretending to walk like someone else. Andrew had noticed it as well and frowned as they watched her saunter up the stairs.

Samuel held the bottle up to Sampson. "Care to join us?"

"No, thank you, sir. Though it is appreciated, I have work that still needs to be done."

"Sampson, I'm going to the library to have a drink, then I'll head upstairs. Could you have dinner sent up to the rooms?" Samuel asked.

"Yes, sir."

The house manager led Andrew down to the kitchen where one of the kitchen girls was already preparing a light meal for him. Made up of several rooms, the men entered the central kitchen where the food was prepared. Boasting two gas stoves, four ovens, a sink big enough to handle two crates of vegetables, and a large oak preparation table with several stools around it, the room was designed to create meals for an army. The adjoining rooms were for storage and a dining area for the servants.

"Ah. What a place where everyone knows what's to be done before anyone else does," Andrew hooted.

"That, sir, is the very definition of a well-run House."

As Sampson seated Andrew at the servants table, one of the kitchen girls screamed and dropped a plate of cut lamb. Both men looked up to see Thomas Rochester limping in through the servants' entrance. His face bloodied and bruised, he hugged one arm to his chest as if it were broken.

"Where's Weldsmore?" he gasped right before he collapsed onto the floor.

18

Elizabeth sat in a robe on the edge of her bed and rocked back and forth, torn between doing what was reasonable and secure and what was needed to save people's lives. All the men in her life sought to protect her, and she appreciated it, but it was time to step out of what was safe into what was right.

She had secreted Rachel's trinity knot in a pocket in her dress when they left the South Side. She decided to use it again to find out where Rachel and the others were. Only this time, she'd have help. The entity, or whatever it was, that she'd met in her psychic limbo had come to her aid once, and she was certain he would do it again. Whether it was a "he" or not, she wasn't positive, but Elizabeth was sure she'd sensed a masculine presence.

Nevertheless, Elizabeth was convinced that whoever "he" was, he must be a medium who had either gotten lost in that psychic limbo or was searching for others like himself. Perhaps he didn't even live in the Great States, but in another country. She fantasized that he could be an emissary of sorts. And what if she was the first medium he connected to? The whole idea filled her with exhilaration and pride.

A knock on the door interrupted her thoughts. Sally, her maid, entered carrying dinner. She placed it on the table then arranged the plates, utensils, and food.

"Just leave it."

The young Irish girl bobbed a little curtsy. "Yes, Mrs. Hunter."

"Is my husband on the way up?"

The girl bit her lip. "He and Mr. Sampson are . . . are . . ."

"Ahh, I understand. It's time he and Sampson got to know each other better anyway."

"Do you want me to draw you a bath?" Sally asked.

Elizabeth shook her head. "No, thank you. I'll take one later. You go on. Get your supper."

"Yes, Mrs. Hunter." The girl left.

Elizabeth got up from the bed and walked over to the door. She cracked it open to see if anyone else was in the hallway, but all she saw was Sally heading down the stairs. As she closed it, Elizabeth considered locking it but did not want Samuel to get the wrong idea. She also might need help if she found herself lost in one of her visions. Elizabeth could tell by Samuel's and Andrew's glances that they were worried about her, and she respected that. It would be stupid of her not to allow them to save her if she needed it.

She hopped back onto the bed, propping up the pillows so she could sit comfortably. Resting her head, she contemplated going to sleep, but the idea of Rachel trapped with that man drove her to dig out the trinity knot from her pocket.

Warmed by her robe, the metal felt smooth and supple to the touch. She placed the piece in her palm and rubbed it with her thumb. The action calmed her, and any lingering exhaustion fled. Elizabeth closed her eyes and concentrated on Rachel. The Irishwoman's image floated around in her consciousness like a random spark, but it was as if Rachel had become the brass ring on a merry-go-round Elizabeth kept missing.

Elizabeth opened her eyes and frowned. She was certain Rachel was deliberately keeping her away, making sure they couldn't connect. But why would she do that? Didn't she want to be saved?

Elizabeth had an idea. Instead of searching for Rachel, she would search for the emissary, as she'd decided to name him. Perhaps he could help her find the medium.

Once again she closed her eyes, but this time she cleared her thoughts of everything but him. Her mind slipped from her body and entered that mysterious realm of darkness as the trinity knot blazed white hot and burned its image into her hand.

***

Samuel and Sampson helped Thomas off the floor and into a chair from the adjoining room.

"Claire, get Mrs. Owen's emergency kit," Sampson ordered the girl Thomas had frightened. She regained her composure and ran into the next room to return with a toolbox filled with iodine, bandages, needles, and thread.

Andrew grabbed it before Sampson had a chance. The house manager grumbled.

"Let him handle it, Sampson. He's more experienced than you," Samuel informed him. "Which is a good thing, by the way."

The Irishman pulled out a needle and thread. "Aye. Though Rachel be a mite better at this than I am. Lassie, hot water and towels. Let's get his jacket and shirt off."

Fading in and out of consciousness, Thomas resisted them as they tried to remove his jacket. "No, stop," he grunted. Blood oozed from his mouth, and his eyelids swelled from a terrible beating.

"Stop fighting us!" Samuel ordered. "We're trying to help you."

Thomas passed out again and fell off the chair and back onto the floor. An odd sound of metal hitting wood reverberated across the room.

The three men and the kitchen maid all look at each other, puzzled, but continued to help the injured man.

"Well, this makes it a wee bit easier to work with him on the floor," Andrew commented.

He reached into the emergency kit, pulled out a pair of scissors, and immediately started cutting away Thomas's jacket and shirt. As Andrew peeled the blood-soaked material off, he stopped suddenly and looked up at Sampson. "Send the lass away."

The house manager frowned then gestured toward the girl. "Claire, that will be all. Go to bed, and not a word of this to anyone. Do you understand?" His tone lingered on threatening.

"Aye, Mr. Sampson." Claire blanched, then bobbed her head and made a brief curtsy before she scurried off.

None of the men said a word until the girl was gone.

"Andrew?" Samuel's implied question hung in the air like a dense fog.

The medium pulled back the torn and bloody shirt to reveal several damaged interlocking metal plates where Thomas's left shoulder and part of his chest should be. Andrew continued cutting the shirt away. Finally getting it off, the men saw how Thomas's entire arm was made of cables of various thicknesses and a multitude of gears. The cables sparked and hissed where they had been ripped out. Old burn scars were seared into the fleshy part of Thomas's chest, while fresh blood poured from stab wounds—some deep, some shallow.

"Aww," Thomas groaned as he regained consciousness. He sat up and spit blood and mucus out onto the now slick floor. "I'm sorry, but you should never have seen this."

Sampson grabbed the whiskey bottle from the table and poured a glass. When he handed it to him, Thomas grabbed it with his normal arm, gulped it down, and thrust it back at Sampson.

"More, please," he gasped. "Where's Jonathan? I need to speak to him."

Samuel squatted down next to him. "He's in DC for the night. Now, don't you think you should tell us what the hell is going on?" he demanded.

Thomas shook his head. "No. It's safer that you don't know any more than you do."

The house manager poured another glass and handed it to the injured man. "I think we are past that, Mr. Rochester."

"Aye, laddie. Mr. Sampson has the right of it." Andrew worked to remove the blood, dirt, and swatches of fabric that were wedged into Thomas's flesh, picking debris out of the gears and the chest plates though he was careful not to touch the loose cables.

Thomas leaned against the chair and sighed. "Tillenghast must have found out I was planning to leave the country and hired thugs to bring me back. Fortunately, they were not well informed about my capabilities."

"Ah, that explains the money in the Liberty Row bank." Samuel stood up and loomed over the hurt man, frowning. "You could have told us and not made up a story about gambling debts."

Thomas arched an eyebrow at him, wincing at the effort. "There was no reason to have any of you involved."

"Well, it's too late for that." Samuel grabbed a nearby chair and sat down.

Thomas set the glass down on the floor. "There's no going back once you know."

Samuel clasped his hands together. "We can't protect ourselves if we don't know the truth."

Thomas nodded. The words came out haltingly at first, then sped up as if the desire to talk outweighed his fear. "I liked working for Tillenghast. He gave me everything he promised. My own department to design and create the new era of flight. I had total control and little interference from any of the family. Even Hal and I got along. As outliers, we were natural partners in crime, so to speak. We had a good time." Thomas sipped his whiskey again. "There were rumors about what House Tillenghast had done before and during the House Wars. Horrible, vile things, all in the name of their House and the Great States of America. I never believed any of them. Like most, I thought it was propaganda. Stories to terrorize their enemies. Until we demolished an old building to build a hanger." Thomas shuddered as if the memory were still fresh. "The men called me over when they found their first set of human remains. Then another and another. It had to be an old cemetery they'd forgotten to mark, but when I looked at the bones and decaying bodies, I saw they weren't quite right."

Samuel frowned. "What do you mean?"

Thomas flinched as if remembering a bad memory. "They were altered. Holes in their chests where their hearts should have been. Remnants of mechanical devices grafted into bones. Missing limbs. Mostly men, but maybe a few women as well."

Andrew took all of this in without comment while Sampson turned pale.

"Mr. Rochester, there must be a logical explanation for what you saw." Sampson scowled. "I have a hard time believing a Great House would use its employees in such a manner."

The memory of what the Great Houses were capable of drove the darkness Samuel tried to contain to the surface, squeezing his heart. He realized he was holding his breath and forced himself to relax. He shoved the hate and pain out of his mind until it felt like an echo of a memory. There were more important things to deal with right now than his own failings. "You are very fortunate to have worked for Jonathan all these years, Sampson. Most Houses are not as forgiving, old man."

Thomas nodded. "We boxed up what the men had found to show to the operations manager, assuming he'd give us a reasonable explanation. But when we arrived at the site the next day, the boxes were gone and where the men had dug, a new foundation had been poured. The manager who had approved of demolishing the building disappeared, and the men who worked on it changed from a normal crew to a bunch of nervous and paranoid workers. Everyone was looking over their shoulders, including myself. I thought it was my imagination." Thomas sighed. "Then there was the accident. I was told later that a spark ignited one of the hydrogen cells due to arcing and faulty insulation."

"Oh, hell," Samuel spat out. "They tried to kill you and failed."

Thomas grimaced as Andrew bandaged his wounds. "I woke up to the smiling face of a woman I'd never seen before nor was ever introduced to, but I believe . . ." He lifted the metal arm a few inches off the ground before letting it drop down with a loud thump. "That I have her to thank for this."

"That must have cost a pretty penny," Andrew remarked.

Samuel pursed his lips. "You're an investment now. And Tillenghast likes to keep tabs on his investments. So he made Hal your watchdog."

"Maybe yes, maybe no," Thomas replied. "I asked Tillenghast if I could accompany Hal on this trip. I told him I'd keep Hal out of trouble. But yes, Hal may have suspected I was going to run and betrayed me." Thomas used his metal arm to prop himself up as he struggled to stand. "I can't stay here."

"No, you can't. But I'm not sure there's any place you can hide from him forever." Samuel shifted on the chair. "You'd be running for the rest of your life."

"Why don't the lad do what most of the Irish and the Negroes do?" Andrew asked.

All three men stopped and stared at the Irishman.

"We be hiding in plain sight." Andrew chuckled. "No one takes notice of us unless we make it a point to be noticed. Or we be in a place we don't belong."

"So he should go to Liberty Row?"

Andrew shrugged. "Or somewhere like it. Change your name,

clothes, and start acting like everyone else. No one will care about you unless you get in their way. But I'm afraid your days of wearing fancy clothes are over, laddie."

"Have you done any other work?" Samuel asked. "What can that arm do?"

Thomas lifted his mechanical arm about a foot of the ground. The gears whined as the remaining cables jerked it up, then he slammed it into the floor, crumbling the wood beneath it.

Stunned, Andrew, Sampson, and Samuel stared at him and the floor.

Sampson recovered first. "May I suggest boxing, sir."

The remark got a chuckle from everyone.

Samuel smiled grimly. Laughter always drove his personal demons farther out of his mind. "Let's put you into one of the servant's quarters for the night. Sampson?"

Sampson took Thomas by his good arm, but Andrew stepped in. "Just point me in the right direction. And we'll get to work getting some clothes on you."

Thomas closed his eyes and sighed as they exited.

Samuel watched as the men hobbled out. He motioned for the house manager to follow him.

"Sir?"

"We need to contact Jonathan as soon as possible. Can you or his secretary find him?"

"I'll get a hold of Mr. Evans then telephone and send a courier."

"And please inform the staff that Thomas left when Hal did."

"Understood, Mr. Hunter. I will pack up his things."

"Be sure to burn his clothes and all his possessions. Thomas Rochester no longer exists. I'll take care of creating a new identity for him."

"Very good, sir."

"Damn it!" Samuel realized he had forgotten something very important. "I was supposed to join Elizabeth for dinner."

"I'm sure she's asleep, sir. There's no need to worry."

Samuel clapped him on the shoulder. "Of course. Thank you. Sampson. Now, let's get to work."

***

Elizabeth floated in the psychic abyss, unafraid and relaxed. The region's complete lack of light or substance no longer frightened her but gave her a sense of peace and freedom. She did not want to leave. Not long after she had those thoughts, she chided herself for wallowing in this safe place when she knew Rachel needed her help. She concentrated on the image of the trinity knot, and its reflection appeared far off in the distance. It faded in and out of view as if a fine mist passed over it. She willed herself forward, finding she had arrived in what one might consider a blink of an eye even in a place where time might not exist. She reached her hand out to touch the knot only to have a brick wall construct itself in front of her. Startled, she yanked her hand back.

This could only mean one thing: Rachel did not want to be contacted.

Her mentor was trying to protect her, but her life and all those who had been kidnapped depended on Elizabeth finding out where they were. It was time for everyone to stop shielding her and for her to embrace her abilities to their fullest.

Her body had no real form here yet Elizabeth could sense it. Rachel had taught her she should always imagine having a body in this limbo so her mind had something to center on. Elizabeth pulled back her arm and thrust it forward with the palm open, imagining she was pushing the wall down. It wavered, but otherwise the effort had no effect. She tried again using both arms. This time she blasted a few chinks out of the wall, but it remained standing. Frustrated, Elizabeth realized couldn't do this alone.

She needed the emissary.

There was a shift in the fluidity of the spirit passageway as though the air had been sucked out then shoved back in the space of an instant. She whirled around to see the image of a man outlined with stars, his body a miasma of emerald green and mauve. The sight made her head hurt, but she was so enthralled she didn't consider what it might mean.

"You came!"

The emissary pointed toward the wall.

"Yes. I'm trying to get to Rachel. She needs our help."

He stepped closer to her and offered his arm. The act sent a thrill through her she had never experienced before. Without hesitation she took it.

She couldn't feel it, but the miasma flowed like a snake over and around her forearm and hand. As they stood in front of the wall, the emissary raised his arm and pointed at the only thing between them and Rachel. A surge of power ran through her. Out of the palm of her hand, a blinding white light flowed, melting the wall as if it were thick, molten honey. The emissary withdrew his spectral form from hers and gestured for her to go forward to where the trinity knot glistened like it was brand new.

Elizabeth wavered, savoring the remnants of the power that still lingered in her psyche. If one could breathe in the abyss, it would have stopped her heart.

The emissary motioned again, but with greater urgency.

"Thank you."

Elizabeth faced the trinity knot. "Rachel! I'm coming!" In her mind's eye, she imagined herself merging with the image and pushing through it to reach the Irish woman's mind. As she exited the abyss into what she hoped was Rachel's psyche, Elizabeth felt a sharp pain and a tug in her neck, like she had been pinched by a brooch. She reached back to feel if something was there but was distracted by the force of her entry into Rachel's mind.

The medium and the other victims were screaming.

With her eyes still covered, Elizabeth could tell that Rachel had been forced to her feet and was being whipped by an unknown assailant.

"Shut the hell up! You're nothing but trouble. The whole lot of you!"

She recognized the voice of the man who had shrouded Rachel's eyes when she was last there. The medium dropped to her knees in anguish. For Elizabeth, it felt like every lash was on her own body.

"There be your proper place." The man put his foot on her back and shoved her to the ground.

"I won't cause any more trouble. I promise," Rachel pleaded.

He leaned forward, his onion breath wafting over her. "No, ye won't. Not after *he's* done with you." The man grabbed her arm, yanked her up, and threw her on the bed. He tied her up again, making sure the ropes dug into her flesh. "Now stop messing with their heads and quiet them down, or I'll start cutting off bits."

The other victims turned eerily silent. Elizabeth could hear them shuffle off. Their cots creaked as they lay down.

He kicked Rachel's cot then marched off in a huff. Elizabeth waited so long for Rachel to say something, she feared the medium did not know she was there. She was wrong.

"You stupid girl. You shouldn't have come back," Rachel whispered. "I still don't know where we be at, but I think it be on the South Side. Must be a warehouse on the wharf."

Elizabeth heard a door open then close.

"They be moving us soon. Don't know where, but the other one—the medium. He's powerful. Stay away from him. He controls the lot of us. Including me."

Rachel took deeps breaths through the rank cloth that covered her face, then froze. "Wait. There be someone with you." Elizabeth felt the medium twist at her bindings. "Oh, no. Get it away." Her voice rose in a panic. "Elizabeth! Get it away!" she yelled.

The door opened again. "Stop yer hollering or I'll beat you again."

"I'll take care of it," the voice of the younger, educated man echoed across the room.

Terrified that he might confront her again, Elizabeth fled Rachel's mind. As she did, an ethereal presence swept past her. It did not touch her, but skimmed through her mind and into Rachel's. Something about it was familiar and comforting, yet she could have sworn she heard Rachel cry out like a wounded animal.

Elizabeth opened her eyes to find herself back in her bedroom. The pain in her hand snapped her out of the trance. She held it up to see that the trinity knot she held had burned her palm and left an imprint. Elizabeth jumped out of bed, knowing she would have to bandage it before Samuel came up. Fearing that Rachel might have been seriously injured, she decided that this time she was going to tell him everything.

When she got to the landing, Elizabeth saw the lights had been turned down for the evening. There was no movement, so she assumed the servants had gone to bed. She hurried down the stairs to see if Samuel was still in the library. Not finding him there, she headed toward the kitchen. Three flights of stairs later, the only thing she found were a few wet kitchen towels.

Alone and exhausted, Elizabeth climbed up the stairs to her room. Samuel must have gotten a lead on the case or else her father needed him for something. There was no other reason he would leave without telling her.

By the time she got back to her room, Elizabeth staggered through the door and shut it behind her. As she walked past her vanity mirror on her way to bed, she thought she saw a pinpoint of emerald green-and-mauve miasma swirling deep within her eyes. Elizabeth stopped and stared at the mirror, but saw nothing unusual.

"My eyes are playing tricks on me now," she said out loud, as she lurched over to her bed and fell into it, falling asleep almost instantly.

19

Jonathan stood on the train platform with his four guardsmen the next morning. By the time the committee meeting had concluded last night, the last train with a Great House car attached had already left. Not willing to risk his safety or his guardsmen, he'd decided to stay the night at his DC apartment. He had informed Mr. Evans, who would call Sampson.

A wooden awning covered the entire platform, and benches were placed equidistance apart from each other flush against the station. Cast-iron hexagonal lampposts stood guard at the edges to light the area during the evening hours. Jonathan sat in a roped-off section set aside for Great House passengers. There was a separate class for Middle District and foreign tourists, but they never shared the same car with the families of the Great Houses. Associates were allowed to ride with family members if invited, but even they were relegated and often more comfortable riding with others of their class.

All the Great House train cars were equipped with reinforced iron walls and had guns mounted on the top and were checked at odd intervals for explosives and any tampering with the brakes or other vital mechanical parts. Jonathan liked the separate cars because they were quiet and allowed him to get work done. They also made him wary as they were a big fat target even though they were armed and guarded by his own House and the federal government. It was the latter that worried him.

As he watched the crowd milling about, Jonathan thought about Mekonnen and the other passengers on the airship that had gone down. It occurred to him that whoever had done that would not lose any sleep over destroying an entire train to kill him. But was Tillenghast behind this or was there a new player?

The blast of a steam engine approaching distracted him from his thoughts long enough to check his watch. The train was right on time.

The engine pulled past him and stopped at the platform. Several federal agents inspected it alongside his own security team. They were all very thorough and professional, but it felt wrong. Maybe he was getting paranoid, but perhaps not.

He heard yelling in the distance. A telegraph agent ran at him full tilt.

"Mr. Weldsmore! Mr. Weldsmore!" he yelled.

Jonathan panicked for a moment, thinking something had happened to Elizabeth.

The agent handed the telegram to him. He ripped it open to find a message from Mr. Evans. It read, "Mrs. Owen burnt your breakfast and is unable to cook more. You'll have to eat elsewhere."

Working to maintain a nonchalance he didn't feel, Jonathan folded the paper up and placed it in his pocket. "Sawyer," he spoke to the nearest guardsmen.

"Sir."

"Get a car. We're heading over to the Du Pont's residence."

The man jogged off to do as ordered without question.

His nerves and muscles tightened to a fever pitch, Jonathan nodded at a few passersby as he exited the holding area and headed toward where the better taxis were lined up. He would have had one of his own cars here, but hadn't bothered since it was supposed to be such a short trip. Now he regretted that decision. Indeed, *regret* might be an understatement. His life might depend on it.

In Mr. Evans's coded message, Jonathan had learned that His Majesty, the king of Abyssinia, was dead and that his shipyards had been destroyed. Jonathan and Evans had developed this manner of correspondence years ago for whenever Jonathan was traveling and phones were not available. They updated the messages for every trip, including this one. But as clear as the note had been in one regard, there was an underlying meaning. There was a chance Jonathan would be the next target and that the attempt might occur on the train. Whether they would try to blow it up, he did not know, but he would not risk the lives of the other passengers for his own convenience.

His guardsmen swarmed two unsuspecting taxi drivers, commandeering their cars. They searched the men and gave the vehicles a thorough inspection. Once they were satisfied, they escorted Jonathan to the first taxi, where one guardsman sat with Jonathan while the other rode shotgun. The other two guardsmen seized another taxi, promising the driver it would be returned with appropriate compensation. Together the cars sped off toward Du Pont's Eleutherian Mills residence at Hagley in Delaware.

It took over two hours to get there, but it gave Jonathan time to plan his next move. As soon as he arrived at the Georgian style estate of his longtime friend, he would phone Elizabeth and order her to stay at the house. Next he would talk to Sampson or Samuel, whoever answered first, and find out anything else that might have happened. Then he would contact Mr. Evans to instruct the men working on his ships to go home and to lock down the shipping yards. Spies were in the work crew, but all of Jonathan's informants had said they were there to glean information, not blow things up. However, their orders could change, and he needed to protect the workers and his assets.

The Du Ponts were far more powerful than House Weldsmore and wielded an immense amount of influence both here and abroad. Their nearest competitors for the top spot were House Carnegie, House Kennedy, and House Tillenghast. Each House had their strengths and weaknesses that balanced the power and provided each with an incentive to work together. However, Jonathan suspected in the future they would be challenged by the Great Houses in the West.

After being inspected by Du Pont security at the main gate, Jonathan and his guardsmen drove up the long paved driveway to the front entrance. They were met by several men wearing Du Pont livery and guardsmen dressed in their traditional uniforms of long maroon wool jackets with matching pants accented with black piping. Each had the Du Pont crest of a clock face sewn on their lapel. Unlike other Great Houses, the crest had nothing to do with their main business, which was manufacturing gunpowder. It was an homage to Pierre du Pont, a watchmaker and the man who had immigrated from France to the Great States of America to establish what became one of the most powerful families in the nation.

Everett's house manager, Dawson, met him as the footmen opened the car door.

"Mr. Weldsmore." The house manager's sea-green eyes assessed the situation and the look on Jonathan's face. "Mr. Du Pont is in his study. If you will follow me . . ."

Dawson always reminded Jonathan of a human praying mantis with his razor-thin build and elongated arms that swung like they could latch on to anything. He had been with Everett for as long as Sampson had been with Jonathan and he suspected bore many of the same responsibilities and access to critical information. House manager was often a position of tremendous power, though in some Great Houses their only duty was to safeguard the efficient running of the household.

The interior of Eleutherian Mills was not as impressive as most would expect. With wooden floors and Persian carpets, it was not as ostentatious as most Great Houses, including his own. Dawson led him to Everett's study, which had antique French tables and chairs arranged to highlight the walnut desk that sat in front of two recessed windows. Jonathan found it to be refreshing and one of the things he liked about Everett. However, he had heard his wife had decided that the house was not grand enough and was interviewing architects to build a palatial estate in Pennsylvania.

"Sir." Dawson gave a curt nod to both Jonathan and Everett before he marched out of the room, closing the door behind him.

Everett took off his glasses as he stood up and shook Jonathan's hand. "Jonathan, I thought you were on your way home. What's happened?"

They both sat as Jonathan filled him in. Everett ran his hands through his short, spiky gray hair before he reached for the telephone and called his son, William, who was a senator and a member on the Foreign Security Committee. The conversation was brief, but confirmed what Jonathan already knew—His Majesty, King of Abyssinia was dead and his shipyards destroyed. Hundreds of people had perished, and the port city of Massawa was still in flames.

"I'm so sorry, Jonathan." Everett offered his condolences. "I can't imagine how much money you've lost. I'm only glad your men weren't there."

"Yes. A lot of talent would have been lost as well. Any idea yet how it was done?" he asked.

"Some sort of accident, but the consulate said they've never seen a fire burn so hot or so fast. They barely got out in time." Everett scratched his temple. "He did say something odd though."

"What?"

"He was running toward the car, and he turned to make sure his assistant was behind him. The fire was two blocks away, so they thought they had enough time if they didn't dawdle. Out of nowhere, a tunnel of flames surged right down the middle of the street, setting fire to everything in its path. His assistant swore he saw a man inside it."

Jonathan tensed up, gripping the arm of his chair. He willed himself to relax before Everett noticed, but it was too late.

"What is it?" Everett asked while peering over the tops of his glasses. The Du Pont heir might not be as brilliant as his predecessors, but he was very observant.

"You don't want to know," Jonathan replied. The last thing he would tell him was that demons might be involved. That would only result in Everett calling Jonathan's doctor and having him committed, and he had no time for that.

"Which really means either you think I won't understand or you're too embarrassed to tell me."

"Everett, you're my friend and my ally. You need to steer clear of this. At least for now."

"Don't you think I'm aware that Tillenghast has been pressuring you to ally with him?" Everett sat back in his chair and tapped his fingers his nose. It was a gesture that meant he was going to say something that would sound like a suggestion when it was in fact an order. "You should do it. The two of you would control all the shipping on the eastern seaboard."

"Why would you want that? It would put you at a disadvantage."

"Not at all. I'd save money by paying for combined air and sea trade shipments." Everett winked at him. "Think about it. But if you do decide to do it, keep Hal out of it. Your brother is a nightmare when it comes to business."

Jonathan frowned. "Tillenghast doesn't ally, he absorbs Houses."

"Then don't let him do to you what he did to Hibbard. They were weak. You're not."

"Everett, what if I told you I believe Tillenghast is responsible for assassinating the king and setting fire to the shipyards."

"Do you have proof?" Everett's face hardened.

"No."

"Tillenghast thinks far too much of himself, but even that's a reach for him," Everett remarked. "Besides, he couldn't get his men or their lackeys over there without someone noticing."

"He may have had a different kind of help."

Everett pursed his lips, waiting for him to say more, but Jonathan stayed silent.

"Fine. Don't tell me, but you're worried about what he'll do next. I'll have my men drive you up to Philadelphia to pick up one of my train cars to Boston." He touched a button under his desk, and Dawson reappeared again.

"Dawson. Mr. Weldsmore and his men will be taking our train to Boston. Have the taxis returned to their owners in DC." Everett turned to Jonathan. "You want to eat lunch here or in the car?"

"Car."

"Dawson? You heard him. Go!"

The house manager left again at a fast clip.

"Thank you, Everett. May I use your phone? I need to call home."

"Of course." Everett stood up and gestured for Jonathan to use his desk. His tone turned serious. "I think you're wrong about Tillenghast, but I'll look into it. I'd hate to think the House Wars were simply a precursor to a world war."

"So do I."

Everett left the study to give him privacy. Jonathan called the house only to discover that both Samuel and Sampson were out on a mysterious errand and Elizabeth was still in bed. The footman who answered said she had not been feeling well but was eating soup and crackers, according to Mrs. Owen. He also confirmed that his brother was gone as well as Thomas Rochester. Puzzled at Thomas's sudden decision to depart, he was nevertheless satisfied that Elizabeth was safe. Jonathan hung up and called Mr. Evans.

One of the undersecretaries answered and promptly put him through to his executive assistant. He had locked down the facilities and sent the men home on a brief vacation. They feared they were losing their jobs, but Mr. Evans took it upon himself to tell them it was a belated celebratory present on the occasion of Mr. Weldsmore's daughter being married. He said he hinted that it was her idea. Before he hung up Jonathan approved of his initiative and promised a bonus at the end of the year.

Dawson knocked on the door and poked his head in. "Mr. Weldsmore, the cars are ready. Mr. Du Pont is sending along additional security for both the trip from Philadelphia and to Boston. Our cook prepared enough food to feed your men as well."

Jonathan stood. "It's much appreciated. Is Everett still available?"

"I'm sorry, Mr. Du Pont had to attend to other business and regrets not being able to see you out." The house manager bowed stiffly as Jonathan brushed past him.

As he exited, Jonathan glanced back to see Everett watching him from one of the windows on the third floor. He raised his hand to wave goodbye, but Everett turned away. That was all the proof he needed.

Somehow Tillenghast had gotten to his friend. Jonathan's alliance with House Du Pont was severed.

***

Samuel spent the morning with a forger having new identity documents created for Thomas. He had arranged for Andrew to return that morning to help Sampson check Thomas's wounds and then buy clothes and a small trunk for him. Elizabeth had been sound asleep when he got up, so he'd left her a note telling her he was following up on a lead for her father. He and Sampson had decided not to tell her the truth about Thomas. It might upset her, and she had enough to deal with right now.

He hated to admit it, but Elizabeth's visions were the only thing giving them leads on locating the missing South Siders. They did not have enough manpower to search an area as large as the South Side, and even if they did, it would tip off the kidnappers. That might cause them to release their victims or kill them. Samuel didn't like having his wife so deeply involved in all this, but they might not have any choice.

The forger took longer than expected, and Samuel did not leave his apartment until noon. He was on the far side of the Middle District and had to hire several carriages to get there and back. Samuel hoped

Jonathan had returned so he could talk to Thomas himself before he left. If he wasn't, Samuel would send Thomas on his way so as not to increase the risk to the family.

By the time he arrived back at House Weldsmore, it was almost two o'clock. Sampson had ordered most of the servants to take the afternoon off, leaving himself, Claire, and a footman inside. He'd used the excuse that in the upcoming weeks the House would be especially busy, so he wanted to make sure they took care of any personal business they needed to attend to so as not to inconvenience the family. Outside, he had doubled the guardsmen as per Jonathan's orders.

As they entered the servant's section, Sampson informed Samuel that Jonathan was taking the Du Pont train from Philadelphia and would be back later. Samuel asked the house manager why Jonathan wasn't leaving from DC, but Sampson didn't know as an underbutler had taken the call. Mr. Weldsmore had not deemed it necessary to give the young man any details.

When Samuel entered the servant's room, Thomas sat on a bed eating a light meal of stew and bread while Andrew packed up the small trunk with the used clothing he had purchased.

"How are you?" Samuel asked as he handed Thomas a leather pouch with his new work history, letters of recommendation, and proof of his parentage and their freedom documents.

"I'll live." Thomas put the stew down on the bed and rifled through the paperwork. "You are a thorough man, Mr. Hunter." He squinted at one paper. "Interesting, the freedom documents are accurate, just with different names."

Samuel nodded. "It's best to stay as close to the truth as possible when you are lying."

"It also be easier to remember." Andrew snapped the trunk shut.

Samuel pulled a third-class train ticket out of his jacket and handed it to Thomas. "Sorry for the cheap accommodations, but it's something you'd better get used to. And don't tell anyone where you're going."

"Aye. That be true. Will you be needin' me for anything else, laddie? I need to go see about a job," Andrew remarked, looking at Samuel.

"Yes, I do, and I'll pay you for your time. If you wait in the kitchen, I'll talk to you in there. Sampson, please have Claire check on my wife."

With both men gone, Samuel sat on the lone chair across from Thomas, who held the train ticket like it would light on fire any second.

"Montreal? You're sending me to the Queen's Canada? Are you out of your mind?"

"Thomas, no one will recognize you there, and you can get a job in a factory that builds parts for airships. Or work as a rigger at a regional airship company. There is a large Negro population there of American ex-patriots. You'll blend in."

"Samuel, I have never 'blended' in. Even Philadelphia was too small for me. And now you want me to go north?"

"You don't have any choice. The two Irish carriage drivers that have been working for me will take you. The locals are used to seeing them, so it won't draw any undue attention. Can you walk?"

Thomas grimaced. "After a fashion. I'm sorry to be ungrateful, it's just that I hadn't expected my life to change so drastically. Any chance I'll be able to withdraw my money from the bank in Liberty Row? Or if I can't get it, perhaps leave permission for Jonathan to withdraw it for me."

"I'm sure Tillenghast will have figured out where you've been hiding your money and have people watching the bank. I would. And as for Jonathan, you mention his name, and he'll have even a bigger target on his chest."

Thomas winced again. Samuel wasn't sure if it was from physical pain or the knowledge that he'd probably never see his money again.

"One more thing. Do you know if anyone with your abilities is working for Tillenghast?" Samuel asked. "I'd like advance notice in case I run into one in a dark alley."

Thomas shrugged. "I have no idea. But God, I hope not."

Samuel stood up as he gestured to the leather pouch. "I put enough money inside to pay rent on a small apartment for a few months and feed yourself until you find a job." He offered his hand. "Goodbye, Thomas, and good luck. I hope you'll be able to use your talents again someday."

They shook hands then Thomas went back to eating. Samuel thought it best to leave him to come to grips with his new situation.

He understood a little of what it meant to have your life turned upside down, but in his case he'd had the privilege of marrying up while Thomas had been taken down a peg or two.

Exhausted, all Samuel wanted to do was to go to sleep, but he had to talk to Elizabeth and make sure she was all right. He trudged down the back stairs that led to the kitchen to find Andrew sitting next to the staff's dining table waiting for him.

"Where's Sampson?"

"He be manning the phone in case Mr. Weldsmore calls again."

Andrew handed him a glass filled with an amber liquid. Samuel leaned in and smelled the heady aroma of whiskey. He downed it in one gulp.

"That's no way to treat a fine whiskey," the Irishman grumbled.

"It is when you're tired." Samuel put the glass down on the table with a loud *whoomp.* "I know neither one us likes the idea, but I need you to anchor Elizabeth again. She needs to make contact with Rachel, Mary, or any one of the kidnap victims. They may be running out of time."

Andrew shook his head. "Laddie, you don't know what you be askin'. I fear the lass might be in over her head."

"Then what do you suggest?" In frustration, Samuel paced. "We've run out of options. Would Elizabeth really be in any danger?"

The medium rubbed his hand over his face, thinking. "Rachel and I never be faced with something like this before. It's hard to say. But the lass is strong."

"If she gets into trouble, can you pull her back?" Samuel asked.

"I have before." Andrew bobbed his head. "Aye. I can."

"Let me go upstairs to see if she's ready to do that. I'll send for you."

Andrew's eyes crinkled up in amusement. "I hope you don't think I be coming up to her bedroom for this?"

Samuel gaped in bafflement for a second until he understood what Andrew was getting at. "Ah, yes. The bedroom of the female heir to a Great House would not be the appropriate place for a male South Sider. I'll let Sampson know we'll need the library. Will that do?"

"A little fancy for my taste, but I won't be gettin' killed over it."

"Before I forget." Samuel reached into his trouser pocket, pulled out a hundred dollars in twenty-dollar bills and handed them to the Irishman. "Here. I put aside some money to pay you for your time."

Andrew stared at it, unmoving.

"Please, take it. You've more than earned it. Besides, didn't I hear you say something about a wife and daughter?" Samuel placed it on the table.

"Aye. Erin and Caitlin."

"Good. Go buy them something nice."

Samuel left the room, sparing Andrew the embarrassment of knowing he saw the older man wipe tears from his eyes.

***

As Samuel walked down the hallway to their bedroom, a sense of foreboding swept over him. He had kept his worries at bay by working nonstop, but now it forced him to slow down and take deep breaths. Each step he took felt like he trudged through molasses. He had to shake it off. There was too much to do, too much at stake.

But it nagged at him. The mental anguish bore down on him, yet he refused to be overwhelmed by it and forced himself to the door. It stood ajar, and Samuel pushed it open to see Elizabeth sitting on her vanity stool in her robe, staring into the mirror. In the reflection, he saw green and purple undulating through her eyes.

He stopped breathing. If he could describe a color that reflected the malaise that fell upon him, this would be it.

Elizabeth whirled around, jumped up, and ran over to him. "Samuel! Are you ill? You look terrible!" She hugged him.

Samuel held on to her as if she was the last person on earth.

"What's wrong?" she asked.

"Nothing." He inhaled a few times, calming himself. The malaise lifted as quickly as it had descended. He looked into her eyes. They were clear and bright. "I'm fine. I think I'm just exhausted."

"From what Sampson said, you've been running around all day on an errand for Father. What was it?" Her face radiated love and concern.

Samuel swallowed. "I'll tell you all about it later. But right now I need you to meet with Andrew in the library. The trail's run cold. It's time to find Rachel and the others."

"I'm not sure I can, but maybe one of the children."

"Why not?"

"Please don't be angry. I tried before by myself, and I found Rachel, but she forced me out. She's not letting me in anymore. I was going to tell you this morning, but you had already left."

Too tired to reprimand her, Samuel kissed her forehead. "You were right to try. But you've got help now."

"Let me get dressed and I'll be down." Elizabeth dashed over to her closet. "Will Father and Thomas be here for dinner?"

"Probably, though Thomas has gone." Samuel tried to make his tone as neutral as possible so as not to give her any clues that something else might be wrong.

"What? When?" She grabbed a day dress.

"He left with Hal earlier today. Business back in Chicago." Samuel headed for the door. "Do you need help dressing? I can send Claire up since Sampson sent most of the staff out on an afternoon holiday."

"No. I mean, yes. It will make this easier."

He fled the room before she asked any more questions he didn't want to answer.

20

Elizabeth breezed into the library as if she were holding court. Other than her mother's little garden, it was her favorite place in the whole house. Two stories tall with floor-to-ceiling mahogany bookshelves, Persian carpets, two loveseats, four French Renaissance desks with matching chairs, and a globe so large she could not reach her arms around it. The room brought back memories of both her mother and father reading stories to her and playing games on the floor. Now her husband and the Irishman sat on two chairs they had pulled out from the desks, waiting for her to appear. Andrew sat as stiff as a board with his knees together and his hands clasped in his lap. Elizabeth thought if he breathed too hard, something would break. Samuel had his legs spread apart with one toe tapping in nervousness. Her husband had a long way to go before he was comfortable here. Andrew never would be.

"Gentlemen." Elizabeth waltzed over to the loveseat, smoothed down the back of her dress. and sat down with her ankles crossed underneath her skirt. "I may have found the assistance we need to find the missing people."

Both Andrew and Samuel frowned, but the Irishman spoke first. "What kinda help would that be, lassie?"

"When I was in the spirit passageway, I met someone else. Someone who helped me get to Rachel last time."

Samuel looked over at Andrew. "Is that normal?"

The Irishman shook his head. "Not to my way of thinkin'. What did he look like? Did he have a name?"

"I didn't see his body. Just a manlike form. I call him 'the emissary' since we couldn't speak to each other, only gesture. I assumed that's how he saw me as well." Elizabeth's excitement grew even though she felt a little guilty about not telling them earlier. "He must be another medium. Why else would he be there?"

"I don't like it," Samuel groused. "I may not be a medium, but why does this feel odd?"

"It be the first time I be hearing anything like this, but you be a lot stronger than I am. Rachel knew we had just touched on your gifts, lassie." Andrew shrugged. "Maybe it be another medium. Can't think of what else it could be."

"We don't have a choice. We have to find the missing before they are moved, even if I have to enter the mind of someone else." Elizabeth insisted. "Unless one of you has discovered another way to solve this mystery."

Both men shook their heads.

Andrew squinted at her hand, then motioned for her to show it to him.

"It's nothing." She hid the burned hand in the folds of her skirt. "I burned it on a hair iron."

"You don't use a hair iron. Sally does." Samuel scowled. "What did you do?"

"Nothing."

"Elizabeth?"

Resigned to having to show it to them, Elizabeth pulled her hand out to reveal the imprint of the trinity knot on her palm. "It doesn't hurt much, but it'll probably leave a scar."

"That be Rachel's charm." Andrew pointed at it. "What happened?"

"I don't know. I think it may have had to do with the emissary helping me reach Rachel."

"This is way beyond anything we've discussed." Samuel stood up, shaking his head. "We need to find another way."

"Stop it, Samuel. I'm fine. If the emissary had meant to do me harm, he would have already done it by now." Elizabeth's eyes narrowed in frustration.

"That does not make me feel better."

"And you need to trust in me. This is who I am." She insisted. "Don't box me in like my father has all these years. I'm more than just Jonathan Weldsmore's daughter. And I can save those people."

Samuel knelt down in front of her and took her hands. "I know that.

And I believe in you. I also love you, which is why I worry." He sighed and kissed her hand. "So what do we do?"

"First, we need to do this before Father gets home and sees Mr. O'Sullivan here," Elizabeth urged them. "He's not as broad minded as you think he is."

"I don't think he's broad minded at all," Samuel retorted. "But you're right. Let's get this done."

Andrew stood up and walked behind Elizabeth, placing his hands on her shoulders. His touch was so light, yet a warmth emanated from his fingertips that spread down her back and arms. It made her feel safe and secure.

"I understand why Rachel uses you as an anchor. Your presence is very calming. Like a nice cup of hot tea," she remarked to him.

Andrew chuckled. "Now if only me wife thought the same, life would be perfect."

"What do I need to do?" Samuel asked.

"Make sure we're not disturbed. And let Sampson know we're in here and that if my father arrives, he's not to come in until we are done."

"He knows, but I'll lock the door anyway."

"I'll try to reach Rachel again, but if I can't, I'll search for Abigail or the boy," Elizabeth added.

"As you can tell, the lass has it all well in hand," Andrew reassured Samuel. The Irishman took a deep breath and exhaled. "Let me know when you be ready," he told Elizabeth.

While Elizabeth closed her eyes to concentrate, she heard her husband get up, lock the door, then sit back down again. He began to fidget.

"Samuel, you need to be still," she told him with her eyes closed.

"Sorry."

Confident in her ability to reach at least one of the missing people, Elizabeth relaxed her mind and allowed it to flow into the spirit passageway. She imagined tendrils of light searching for kidnap victims and was surprised at how easy it was to find and recognize them. They appeared as scarlet beacons of light writhing in the distance. She wondered if she were getting stronger or if something else had agitated them, thus making them easier to find.

Elizabeth cast her thoughts out for the emissary, but she got no response. She hoped if she needed him, he'd appear like before.

The beacons sparked then settled down. Something was happening. She had to get to Rachel. With a force that startled her, Elizabeth thrust her psyche toward the beacon. Her hope was that Rachel had left it as a signal in the passageway, but when she arrived there was only a cascade of scarlet stars, so she chose one and poured her mind into it.

When she opened her eyes, Elizabeth found herself once again in the room that held the missing people. This time they were on the move. They shuffled and stumbled forward in uneven lines between the cots toward the door. Elizabeth looked down and recognized the hands of the girl called Abigail. She tried to take control of the girl's body, but it was impossible. Somehow, the girl's mind had been blocked off by someone who knew how to do such things. It was as if Abigail and the others were sleepwalking. Elizabeth suspected the well-bred man she had encountered before had something to do with it. She would have to avoid him if at all possible.

Abigail kept her head down as the door opened. One by one they filed out. When Abigail got near the door, the stench of fish and rotting trash assaulted Elizabeth's senses. It was then she realized where they probably were. There was an old refuse site by the bay that had been used to deposit waste and other unmentionables from the city. She had thought they had closed it down after the sewage system was built, but she'd obviously been wrong.

About ready to return to her own body with this information, Elizabeth stopped when she heard two men talking. One was the older Irishman who had beaten Rachel; the other was the educated one. She had to learn what they were planning without being detected.

"Where be my money?"

"Here."

The jangle of coins in a leather pouch distracted her as Abigail stepped forward in the line. There was a snort, then a grumble as the sound of small metal pieces hitting the wooden floor then rolling away.

"Is this be a joke? What you playing at?"

"I play at nothing."

Out of the corner of her eye, Elizabeth saw a short-lived scuffle. The older Irishman screeched in agony and fell to the floor, spittle drooling from his mouth. She assumed he was dead.

"Stop!" The young man's voice rang out. "Look here!"

Abigail's head involuntarily cranked up, but the man in front of her blocked Elizabeth from seeing who was speaking. However, she recognized the woman standing next to him—it was Rachel.

"This is your leader. She will guide you. No one is to stop you. If they do, what will you do?"

"Kill!" The group said in unison.

"You will march through the Middle District and to Beacon Hill. What will you do there?" His voice rose with a little more passion.

"Kill! Destroy!"

"What?" he yelled.

"Kill! Destroy!"

"Very good. Rachel . . ." Elizabeth saw the man squeeze her mentor's hand. "Lead these people out of here. And be a dear and try to kill Jonathan Weldsmore for me. That should please my uncle." Rachel's nose twitched as if she was trying to encourage a fly off her face. "Don't be that way and fight me. You're not strong enough. Now go!" he ordered.

Rachel marched like a wooden nutcracker as she turned and led the group out of the building.

Torn between wanting to stay and help Rachel or fleeing back to her body to warn the others, Elizabeth made the safe decision to return. As she prepared her mind to leave Abigail, she felt a hand on the girl's shoulder. For a second she thought it was Andrew, but when it passed across her face, grabbed her by the chin, and yanked it up, it shook Elizabeth to her very core.

"Oh, you're not going anywhere, Mrs. Hunter."

Elizabeth stared up into the eyes of Leland Tillenghast, the young dandy who had bumped into her at the Gardner party. The image of him kissing her hand and then feeling nauseous afterward made sense now. He was medium. House Tillenghast must have known about her ability and sent him to trigger it. She was mortified that a Great House would threaten and terrorize not only herself, but Rachel as well. But why? The only answer she could come up with was that they were trying to take over House Weldsmore.

"What perfect timing," Leland said with glee as he scooped Abigail up in his arms. "I can't believe my luck. Just like at the Gardner party when I sensed what you really were."

Elizabeth tried to push out of Abigail's body, but it was as if he had put a massive wall around her psyche. She was trapped.

"Now, now. We can't have you wandering off again. This is glorious. It's like killing two birds with one stone. Or a hundred birds." With a chuckle, he carried her to the door. Elizabeth watched as his army of sleepwalkers lurched out of the warehouse and into the twilight. Men, women, children—they all did his bidding, with Rachel leading them into certain death. Once the violence began, the police would crack down hard and not think twice about killing a band of marauding South Siders.

"You, there!" Leland called out to a young man in his early twenties who shuffled over. "Take her," Leland ordered. "I want you to keep her safe until you reach Beacon Hill, then let her go. The police will do the rest." He dumped Abigail into the man's arms. "It'll be interesting to see what happens to the real Elizabeth Hunter when this girl's body dies. Will you die? Become a vegetable or just go mad? I guess we'll find out, won't we? Goodbye, my dear."

A horse whinnied. Then came the sound of hooves galloping off. Leland must have left to watch what chaos this plan of his would bring. *What was he going to do with all these people?* Elizabeth thought to herself. *And why?*

Elizabeth poked round in Abigail's head searching for a way out. Her mind generated the image of a brick wall to represent her prison. Using the techniques Rachel taught her, she focused her psychic energy through imaginary hands and blasted the wall. It wavered, so she hit it again. A piece of brick blew off. Emboldened by even a bit of success, she blasted it again. By the time she had bored a small hole through it, she noticed that Leland's army had entered the lower part of the Middle District. Most people stared at them but did not interfere. She knew that would end soon.

A flash through the hole she had made caught her attention. She peeked through it and saw the swirl of amethyst and emerald green stars. The emissary had returned.

***

Sampson paced outside the library door as instructed by Mr. Hunter. Additional guardsmen had been stationed outside and throughout the house, but none of that would be useful if something went wrong with these visions Elizabeth had. He knew they had saved people, but since seeing her eyes change, he wondered if these visions had affected her. What if the little girl he had loved and watched grow up was becoming a threat to House Weldsmore, and specifically her father? What would he do? Whom would he chose to protect? The very idea of making such a decision horrified him.

He had decided to inform Mr. Weldsmore about what he had seen as soon as he returned home. Attempting to explain something like this would be impossible over the phone. So he paced. And he waited.

***

Jonathan watched the steam from the engine blow past his window as the train rumbled down the track. He had a difficult time enjoying the well-appointed Du Pont train car knowing those alliances he had depended upon for support might no longer exist. As he jotted down a diagram of the relationship between the Great Houses and the minor ones who had changed their allegiances over the last few decades, a pattern emerged. While he had been looking outward to other countries for new business and other ways to expand, the most powerful Great Houses in America had been methodically consolidating power since the House Wars. Even seeing it on paper, the changes were almost imperceptible.

But why target House Weldsmore now? What was different?

Jonathan sighed. His mind shuffled through the various pieces of information he'd discovered over the past few days and paused over something possibly significant. Demons. Did they really exist? And if so, had Tillenghast discovered a way to control them? And what the hell could Jonathan do against an enemy like that?

As for why, perhaps Tillenghast had decided the new ships or weapons Jonathan was working on could thwart his plans. That had to be it. If Alfred Tillenghast believed this were true, then House Weldsmore would of course be in in his crosshairs.

Jonathan jotted down a few notes on whom he could approach for support. Perhaps it was time to solidify his relationship with the western Houses. Most were subservient to larger Houses in the Midwest and the east, but they would not stay that way forever. So why not reach out to Zhou, Garza, and even Stellmacher? The idea of a federation of Houses with broad base support from their constituents who no longer had to kowtow to the Great Houses had a certain appeal to him. He chuckled to himself. Perhaps he was a Republican after all.

All of these political machinations were well and good but did not solve the immediate problem of House Tillenghast working against him. They might take the easy way out and try to assassinate him, but tearing him down and letting him suffer was more Tillenghast's style.

"Sir?" One of his guardsmen approached. "We'll be in Boston in twenty minutes. Do you want me to telegraph the house to send a car to meet us?"

Jonathan shook his head. "No. I don't want anyone who is watching the house to know we are arriving. We'll pick up taxis at the station."

"Yes, sir."

He finished making notes about how to handle the financial loss of the Abyssinian contract then glanced out the window and saw several airships docking on their mooring masts. Different colored Clegg lights signaled their distance and direction to usher them into the airship port. A bright white light swept across the bow of one to reveal the numbers HT-147A. It was a House Tillenghast passenger liner.

No matter where Jonathan looked, that man infected every part of his life.

Jonathan closed his notebook and placed it back in his leather briefcase as the train pulled into the station. Both Du Pont and Weldsmore guardsmen scurried off to inspect the platform and the surrounding area before he exited. Even if House Du Pont were now working with Tillenghast, he doubted that Everett would do anything so crass as kill him on his own personal train. It would make the Du Ponts appear weak and vulnerable if they were not able to protect a valued guest.

"Mr. Weldsmore?" Sawyer, his lead guardsmen, approached him. "We're ready."

Jonathan followed him through the station platform set aside for Great House use and into the Boston and Providence Depot. Not as dynamic as the one in New York, nevertheless it was a handsome building with vaulted ceilings braced by cherrywood support beams, an interior that was three stories tall, and an entire lobby lit by gas lampposts on the second floor. A massive mechanical timepiece hung above the entrance, its gears whirring and clanking every time the minute hand moved.

There was some commotion as they walked through the station, as Jonathan rarely took public transportation. He preferred to use his own vehicles even when traveling out of state. A few people smiled, but most gawked at him and his entourage. He tipped his hat at a few and got curtsies and slight bows of the head in return. Jonathan reminded himself that he was the largest employer in the state and that perhaps he should spend more time with the people who worked for him. It would be a good place to build popular support for the days to come.

They exited the depot and headed straight for the taxi his men surrounded. As Jonathan ducked his head down to enter the car, a group of people rushed inside the depot, gesturing behind them and shouting, but he couldn't quite make out what they were saying. Scooting into the back seat, he leaned forward toward his driver.

"Did you hear what they were talking about?"

"No, sir. Would you like me to find out?" the guardsmen replied.

"No, that won't be necessary. Take me to the shipping yards," Jonathan ordered.

"Not the house, sir?" The guardsman voice shifted, like he was disappointed.

Rather than reply, Jonathan immediately slipped out of the car. "Sawyer!"

His guardsman, who had been ready to ride shotgun, ran around the car to Jonathan. "Mr. Weldsmore?"

"Find me another car. Let the taxi driver do the driving. And fire him." He pointed to the guardsman inside seat. "He's a spy."

Sawyer motioned to the other guards to huddle around Jonathan.

After a brief and quiet discussion, two of the guards opened the driver's side door and dragged the unsuspecting guardsman out of the car and across the street. They stripped him of his jacket, any weapons, and identification. With only the shirt on his back, they shoved him down the street until he took off running.

It didn't take long for Jonathan and Sawyer to settle into a taxi with a driver who looked stunned at having the head of a Great House in his car. He recovered enough to drive them through traffic safely.

"Sir, how did you know?" Sawyer asked.

"One, he questioned me. Two, he sounded displeased that we were not returning to the house. And he pretty much confirmed it when he failed to protest after he was pulled out of the car and stripped of his belongings."

"Yes, sir."

They bounced along, but the driver avoided the worst of the potholes, for which Jonathan was grateful. That is until the man slammed on the brakes, throwing both Jonathan and Sawyer up against the back of the front seat.

"Have you lost your mind!" Sawyer yelled at him.

The driver, a wispy man with gray eyes and mottled brown hair, apologized like his life depended on it. "I'm so sorry, Mr. Weldsmore, but the carriage in front of me stopped short. Are you all right, sir?"

Jonathan peered through the front window and saw a woman running between the cars toward them. Behind her, several men did the same thing. More came after that. All of them panicked.

"Sawyer?"

The guardsman got out of the car, shutting the door behind him. He climbed on top of the roof to get a good look at what was happening. The driver started to complain, but thought better of it and hunkered down next to the steering wheel. After a minute, Sawyer slid off the roof and opened the passenger door.

"Mr. Weldsmore, it's time to leave."

Jonathan reached into his jacket and pulled out a couple of hundred dollars and handed it to the driver. "For your trouble."

He took the money and mumbled a thank you as Jonathan got out of the car.

"Sir, it looks like some sort of protest. We need to get you over to the shipping yards for your own protection."

"Are they heading toward Beacon Hill?"

"I can't say, sir."

All thoughts of protecting himself went out of his head. He knew Elizabeth was at the house with Samuel and his security staff, but he had to see for himself. Or at least get to a phone. "No, we're going home. Even if we have to walk there."

Sawyer gave him a look, then nodded and rounded up the other guardsmen. They formed a phalanx around Jonathan to get him through the ever-growing crowd running at them. His men shoved and pushed their way through, only stopping when they got to a cross street. Jonathan was bumped a few times, which horrified his guards, but he assured them he was fine. The depot was three miles from Beacon Hill and they needed to walk through one of the nicer sections of the Middle District to get there, so Jonathan wasn't worried, just frustrated.

They rounded a corner only to have a mass of people shift directions and rush up behind them. Whatever was coming, it had started in the South Side. Jonathan and the other Great Houses in Boston had discussed the possibility of protests, but none of their informants had warned of any. There were always the disgruntled and disaffected, but protests were often preceded by a slow build of righteous anger. In this case, there had been none. It puzzled him how he could have been so misinformed.

As they worked their way through another intersection, a truck honked numerous times to nudge the throng along. Jonathan peered over Sawyer's shoulder to see the emblem of House Gardner on the side of the truck. His guardsmen flagged it down and identified themselves as House Weldsmore. The driver and his partner were more than happy to let him climb into the cab, but Jonathan insisted on riding in the back. He then complimented them on their timing and said he would inform Gordon Gardner of their good deed.

They inched along for ten minutes before the enclosed truck was forced to stop. Jonathan peered out through a small window in the back to see over a hundred silent people all dressed in the same type of old woolen clothing march lockstep down the street. They did not chant, carry placards, or otherwise behave in a way normal for a protest. It was unnerving, and the multitude of people around the truck sensed that as much as he did.

A woman at the head of the mob cocked her head up and stared straight at them. She stopped marching. The rest followed. Jonathan hoped that she'd decided to turn back, but that wish was short lived. The woman let out a scream, piercing his brain like a hot knife.

"Get us out of here!" Jonathan's chest constricted; he gasped for air.

With no further encouragement the driver of the truck shifted gears, mowing down any hapless bystander who got in the way. There were shrieks of pain and outrage, but the driver kept going. He soon found enough space to turn around, but he ground the gears and the steam-powered truck stalled. While trying to get the vehicle started again, he glanced up into his rearview mirror and blanched.

"They're coming."

21

Samuel must have stood up and sat down a dozen times as he watched Elizabeth in the loveseat. She twitched every once in a while but otherwise appeared serene. Andrew's eyes were also closed to help him concentrate in case Elizabeth needed him in this so-called spirit passageway she was traversing. Samuel's frustration at being useless gnawed at him.

He poured himself a glass of water and stared out the window at nothing in particular. He wanted a shot of whiskey, but he decided to stay clear headed.

A soft knock broke his self-pity. He walked over to the door and cracked it open. It was Sampson. The house manager motioned for him to come out. Curious, he did as Sampson asked and closed the door behind him without making a sound.

"Sampson? What's going on?"

The house manager frowned. "Mr. Weldsmore was forced to take the Du Pont train from Philadelphia instead of his usual route."

"So?" Samuel was unsure how this was a problem.

"He was due to arrive an hour ago, but I had word that a protest of some sort was marching near the train station. And it concerns me." An air of apprehension surrounded the older man.

"What are you not telling me?"

"It might be used as a pretext for an assassination attempt. Then again, it might just be the Great Houses flexing their political muscle to force him to join with House Tillenghast."

"Oh, hell," Samuel muttered under his breath as he ran toward the stairs. "I need two trucks without the House emblem filled with guardsmen and two more guarding that door." He pointed to the library. "Now."

"Yes, Mr. Hunter."

Samuel dashed up the stairs to their bedroom and threw open the bottom drawer of his dresser. Inside was a pair of pistols. They had intricate yet sturdy gears supported by a barrel that held a small bandolier of bullets. There was no hammer to cock back, but a switch Samuel pulled to load it automatically. Next to the pistols sat a shoulder harness.

Samuel took off his jacket, put on the shoulder harness, then grabbed the pistols along with some ammunition. He holstered the guns and put his jacket on again as he walked out the door. By the time he got to the bottom of the stairs, he heard trucks rumbling up to the front of the house. He had no idea how Sampson had gotten them there so quickly but would thank him later.

Sampson opened the door for him as he dashed toward the first truck. "Keep watch over Elizabeth while I'm gone. And give Andrew whatever he needs."

Samuel slid into the passenger seat as an older guardsman hunkered down over the wheel with the engine on. When he was inside, the driver shifted gears and took off.

"The train station, sir?"

"Yes. Follow any of Mr. Weldsmore's usual routes. If he's not there, take his alternate ones."

The driver grunted in acknowledgment as he sped down the street barely safe enough to avoid hitting carriages and other steam-powered cars.

"Where are you usually posted?" Samuel asked after they had driven a half mile.

"The shipyards. But Mr. Weldsmore always has a few of us on standby."

"He is prepared, isn't he?" Samuel mused.

"That he is, Mr. Hunter. That's why he's still alive." The man gave him a half grin, then glanced back at the road. He slammed on the brakes. "Whoa!"

A stream of panicked civilians ran for their lives past the truck. The guardsmen swerved to avoid them. "Damn!"

Samuel hung on as they careened around a corner, narrowly missing two cars coming straight at them. By the time they arrived at the train station, the whole place was in chaos. Both Samuel and the guardsmen scanned the area for any sign of Jonathan and his men but found nothing.

"Since he didn't use the House cars to pick him up, then he most likely commandeered taxis for him and his men," the guardsmen offered. "There are a couple of ways he could have gone at that point."

"Prioritize them," Samuel ordered. "Then go."

The man's foot hit the pedal, and they shot forward. As they passed two abandoned taxis, the men gave each other a knowing look.

Soon they drove headlong into another mob, but this one was different. Their rage had a single-minded ferocity that Samuel had seen only once before: at the Homestead Steel Mill. His hands trembled, and he gasped for breath. He didn't have time to fall apart; lives were at stake. Samuel concentrated on forcing the encroaching despair out of his mind.

"There!" The guardsman at the wheel pointed at a House Gardner truck being attacked. Sawyer and several other Weldsmore guards fought to keep the mob at bay.

"He must be in there. And even if he isn't, we need to help those men." Samuel pulled out one of his pistols and loaded it.

"Hang on!" The driver yelled.

They drove through the mob not caring who they ran over and skidded to a stop behind the House Gardner truck. Samuel and the rest of the guardsmen jumped out, beating back attackers to get to the truck's back door. When they had cleared a path and met up with the men guarding the vehicle, Samuel pounded on the door.

"It's Samuel Hunter with House Weldsmore!" he shouted. "Let us get you out of here!"

He heard a creak then a clank as the door opened to reveal a workman with a wrench in his hand. When he saw Samuel, he sighed in unmitigated relief. "You be a sight for sore eyes." The worker opened the door a little wider. Jonathan stood crouched behind him ready to pounce, but relaxed when he saw Samuel.

Samuel motioned for two of his guardsmen to help Jonathan while the others helped Jonathan's guardsmen fended off the mob. Those who were able to walk jumped into the Weldsmore trucks and helped those who were injured. As Jonathan stumbled past him, he grabbed him by the shirt.

"Is Elizabeth . . . ?"

"We have to find her." Samuel shoved Jonathan inside the truck.

"What do you mean?" A panicked look crossed the older man's face.

"It's complicated. Now get in!"

As Samuel slammed the doors, a sense of dread fell over him. The mob of eerie attackers were dressed exactly like the people Elizabeth had described in her vision, which meant Rachel—and Elizabeth—were out there somewhere.

"Go!" he yelled, as he climbed into the cab.

***

Elizabeth's confidence surged when a stream of amethyst and emerald green stars poured through the small hole she had created out of Abigail's mind and back into the spirit passageway. Tendrils slithered through and to her side, attaching themselves to the psychic wall like an octopus. They gripped it, pulling it backward in an effort to demolish it. Not wanting to be the damsel in distress, Elizabeth once again imagined her arms thrusting a blast of energy.

In her mind, the wall melted layer by layer until it was weakened so much by their dual attack that it blew apart. In front of her stood the spectral entity she called the emissary. He was more defined this time. She could see the outline of a man, but his body was composed of an ever-shifting pattern of stars.

"Thank you," she said. "I need to find Rachel or something terrible is going to happen."

He gestured for her to leave Abigail's mind; the brick wall was rebuilding itself. She stepped through and stood next to him.

"A man is using Rachel, and he's blocked me from getting to her. Can you help?" Elizabeth thought she sensed him smile as he wagged an incorporeal finger at her. "Now, you're making fun of me."

The emissary made a gesture for her to go ahead and he would follow.

Elizabeth focused on the trinity knot, trying to detect where it was. If she found it, she could find Rachel. The problem of entering the medium's consciousness would come next. The emissary's body undulated around her like he was impatient. It was time to stop thinking and start doing.

To help herself, she drew the trinity knot in the air and put her palm in the middle. The psychic energy Rachel had taught her how to use flowed down her arm, out through her palm, lighting up the knot. A flare shot out of the top of it then burst out into sparkles, which descended like falling stars. As they fell, a light pulsated in the distance as if to acknowledge the call.

It was Rachel.

Elizabeth sped toward the beacon without hesitation, assuming the emissary followed close behind. It wasn't until she got closer to the true image of the trinity knot that it became apparent she had a new obstacle to face. Between her and Rachel's psyche lay a swirling mass of psychic debris. In it were images—the haunting memories of what must have been every person Rachel had connected with as a medium. When Elizabeth tried to touch the dark morass of broken dreams and hearts, it tore at her emotions. Had Leland stripped Rachel of all her memories and set them adrift in order to control her? Was that even possible? Or had Rachel thrown up one more barrier to stop Elizabeth from helping her?

The emissary was there. Once again, he offered her his arm.

Elizabeth placed her hand on top of it only to have it sink into the miasma of stars that filled the space where an arm should be. At first she felt nothing, and then a tingling moved through her hand and up her arm. Frightened, Elizabeth tried to remove it, but couldn't. The sensation crawled up her shoulder and onto her back. It whirled inside her neck, paused, then exploded into her brain. Terrified, Elizabeth used all her strength to pull herself away from it, but failed. Her consciousness flailed in confusion as the entity she had named the emissary cascaded into her thoughts and memories. Familiar images of her mother, Sampson, her father, and finally Samuel whipped around her as if she were viewing them through a kaleidoscope. She latched on to the image of Samuel, but it was subsumed by the miasma of stars she recognized as the emissary. They were becoming one.

As both their consciousnesses intertwined, raw power surged through her. It spun her around with such force Elizabeth thought the emissary was stripping her memories from her. Panicking, she tried to flee what she could only describe as a torrent of stars fused with emotion. She focused on sweeping the stars away to find a way home—until a wave of calm swept over her. It was the emissary. He was trying, she realized, to show her how to use their power together. With that understanding, her fear abated and she let herself float among the stars. Now she understood. Together they could destroy this barrier that kept her from Rachel.

Elizabeth composed herself then thrust both of her hands forward. A stream of light with flecks of the emissary's energy and hers collided with the psychic debris around Rachel's mind. It disintegrated bit by bit until it dissipated into the passageway as if it had never existed. With the trinity knot exposed, Elizabeth reached out her hand and placed it in the center again.

She assumed the emissary would leave her at this point, but when he didn't, she thought little of it. Their bonding brought her a sense of completeness she had never felt with Samuel.

She focused on the trinity knot and Rachel as her mind slipped from the passageway and into the medium's psyche. It was quick and painless . . . but what Elizabeth saw through Rachel's eyes horrified her. Slaughter, vandalism, and anarchy raged through the streets. The kidnap victims had become a mob and laid waste to whatever and whoever they came across. Even Rachel, who led them, took turns kicking and beating a man who curled up on the street with his hands protecting his head.

Elizabeth called out to the medium to try and make her stop, but Rachel wouldn't listen. It was if the part of her psyche that controlled empathy and compassion had been locked away and all that was left was the rage born of decades of mistreatment toward the Irish and those beneath the boot of the Great Houses. Shame overwhelmed Elizabeth as she searched for a way to stop Rachel and the mob.

"Elizabeth." A voice echoed through her as though she was a hollowed-out shell.

"Is that you? The one I call the emissary?" she asked.

"I see you, Elizabeth."

It wasn't the emissary; it was Leland Tillenghast intruding into her mind.

To stop Rachel might mean killing her, and Elizabeth didn't want to do that. Instead, using the combined power of the emissary and her own, she carefully but firmly imposed her will on Rachel and took over her body. Subconsciously, she apologized for the harsh intrusion, but she had to find Leland.

She craned her neck around, but there was nothing to see but increasing chaos. The mob surged forward, taking her with them as they split apart into smaller groups, now directionless and meandering. It occurred to Elizabeth that Rachel had been their focal point, and without her they were leaderless. Though she had disrupted Leland's hold on Rachel, the medium still functioned as a beacon to these poor souls. Leland must have planned it this way so the mob wouldn't follow him but a South Sider, one who was a powerful medium in her own right.

"Let's play hide and seek, Elizabeth," Leland taunted her.

Elizabeth kept Rachel's head down as she walked forward searching for Leland. To her surprise, the thought of killing Rachel to stop this madman now simmered in her like water about to boil over. Gentle nudges from the emissary urged her toward that violence. But she had a better idea.

She wasn't going to kill Rachel; she was going to kill Leland Tillenghast.

The emissary flooded her mind with confidence. He agreed with her plan.

The mob reformed and ran in the direction of a steam-powered police carriage Terrified that they might kill the unfortunate men inside, Elizabeth forced Rachel's body to move though a rib was cracked and there were bruises up and down her sides where Leland's flunky had beaten her. She pushed and shoved her way through the crowd that pressed against her, fleeing in the other direction. By the time she caught up with the mob, they had taken hold of both sides of the carriage and were rocking it back and forth like a teeter-totter.

Two police officers were dragged out of the front seat. They pulled out their billy clubs to fend off their attackers, but they were quickly overwhelmed. The mob descended upon them like piranhas and there was nothing she could do to stop them.

Elizabeth scoured the crowd looking for Leland, knowing he couldn't be far. His ego wouldn't allow it. He'd want to be there to watch this disaster he'd created unfold. Elizabeth knew those like him. She'd dined and danced with them and understood the mindset of one born to a Great House—one of her own.

Laughter echoed nearby. Real laughter. Not in her mind or coming from the spirit passageway. Leland was behind her.

"There you are, little bird," Leland jeered. "I was hoping to meet you again. Though, I must say the body of the real Elizabeth Hunter is much more attractive than this old Irish hag."

"Let these people go." The words Elizabeth spoke came out as a croak in Rachel's voice.

He smirked as he leaned forward with his hand to his ear. "What's that, little bird? I can't hear you."

Elizabeth took complete control of the medium's body and hoped the woman would forgive her. She shook out her arms and stood tall and confident.

"I said—" Her voice carried authority. "—release these people."

"Oh, look at you. Pretending to be like a man. It's so cute," he mocked her, feigning a serious tone. "Release these people. Blah, blah, blah."

"This makes no sense. All this just to destroy House Weldsmore?"

He put his hands on his hips. "Yes. This will prove to my uncle that I belong in his inner circle and not left to be treated like a poor relation begging for scraps at his door. When he sees what I can do . . . what I've accomplished . . ." Leland rubbed his hands in glee. "I almost did it earlier by manipulating some poor drunken sop to throw the bomb at your father's car. But this is much better, and I'll finally have what I deserve. A seat at the table."

"All this death and destruction just to impress your uncle, Alfred Tillenghast? Are you mad?"

"I'm quite sane, little bird. The bonus is that with you dead or a vegetable, your father will pine away into nothing. Or die. Unless I kill him first," he crooned. "Uncle Alfred will be more than happy to hand over control of House Weldsmore to me."

"You fool! Tillenghast would never hand over House Weldsmore to you," she snarled at him. "And you'll never be able to kill my father!"

"Really? How long do you think it will take this mob to make it to Beacon Hill?" he asked as he loomed over her. "I will make sure they burn your house to the ground and everyone in it."

A fiery rage consumed her. She would not allow this Tillenghast minion to kill her father, Samuel, and everyone she loved, even if it was by proxy. He was not worthy of being in the same room as her father or Samuel, let alone the same city. Elizabeth reached her mind out to the emissary and found he was still there, watching and waiting.

"I would kill this man, emissary," she declared.

Elizabeth sensed his intense joy at her request. At first that bothered her, but a surge of power filled her entire being, thrusting away any concern. She felt invincible as every part of her body tingled as though an electrical current ran through it.

"What's happened to your eyes?" Leland asked, his confidence wavering.

Elizabeth grinned, though she wasn't sure if it was her or the emissary. "You're pathetic. Did you really think you could kill a Weldsmore?" Without thought, she reached out with her mind and forced it into Leland's without ever entering the passageway. Some small portion of her mind was astounded that the combined psychic power of her and the emissary allowed her to do this. But it was quickly forgotten in the task at hand. What she found in Leland's mind was what she expected: a bully masquerading as a charming man.

Leland grabbed his head, writhing in agony as he lurched back. "No! How can you do this?"

The mob had gone quiet and now staggered about unsure of what to do as Leland's power over them faded. He attempted to wrest his mind away from hers, but Elizabeth matched his brutality. With a snarl, she imagined her fingers were red-hot pokers as they skewered his brain. But it wasn't enough.

"Fire," her voice croaked. Her psychic fingertips flared and burned away his eyesight, then his hearing, and then his ability to speak.

Leland opened his mouth to scream, but nothing came out. He fell to the ground, writhing like a worm. Elizabeth sauntered around him, enjoying his agony. She could feel the emissary relishing every moment as their bond deepened.

Finally, Elizabeth decided to end it. With no more than a flicker of thought she reached into the center of Leland's brain and squeezed it until his consciousness was nothing but mush.

Drool dribbling out of the corner of his mouth, Leland gaped like a fish gasping for air. His eyes remained open, but he saw nothing. He breathed, but only a shell of the man remained.

Elizabeth heard a child wail. She turned to watch as each of the people Leland had held in thrall regained control of their minds and bodies. Realizing it was over, the survivors assisted the injured. Several of the bystanders saw a chance for revenge on the poor souls who had been controlled by Leland and attacked them. Being that she was dressed like the mob and was their leader, they came for Rachel first.

Her first instinct was to lash out at the attackers, and it took all of her strength to stop herself. The joy it gave her destroying Leland's mind was heady, and she wanted more. But it was the thought of what Samuel and her father would think of her that brought her to her senses. She was better than this, and her work here was done. Leland could not harm anyone ever again. Her bloodlust abated just as three men carrying makeshift weapons approached her.

Elizabeth did what any intelligent person would do; she ran.

Bottles, bricks, and cobblestones were thrown at her as she darted through debris and fallen bodies. She heard yelling as a new mob formed. She hadn't gotten far when she saw Abigail, the girl from her visions, standing in the middle of the street crying for her mother. Elizabeth swept her up in her arms and ran behind a trash barrel as a gang of angry citizens sprinted past looking for their assailants.

"Shh! Abigail. You must be quiet," she begged the girl.

She heard sirens in the distance. Hoping they were safe, Elizabeth darted out of their hiding place grasping Abigail's hand.

"There she is," a rough male voice yelled. "She's the one who led them."

Five men, each holding a makeshift weapon, bore down on them.

"Please, we mean you no harm," she pleaded with them.

"That's rich," said a stout man wearing the clothes of a longshoreman. He headed an unusual mix of lower-class and Middle District workers, all of whom were bloodied and angry.

"None of these people meant to hurt you. They were forced."

"Forced! I don't see anyone holding a gun to their heads."

The men grumbled and moved in on her and Abigail.

Two trucks swerved in behind Elizabeth, blocking any escape. Her heart sank as she realized they had nowhere to run. She had a choice: return to her own body and let Rachel deal with these men or stay and fight. Elizabeth crouched down and crushed Abigail to her chest.

"Close your eyes, sweetheart."

The bloodlust she had contained bubbled to the surface of her consciousness. Elizabeth could hear the emissary's voice like the faint echo of a faraway stream. It was time to release that power once again.

Footsteps drew closer. A shot fired.

"Back away and leave the woman and girl alone!" Samuel's voice bellowed from behind her.

Samuel's voice shot through her like a jolt of electricity. Her desire to kill these men diminished with the memory of his unconditional love for her. The emissary and all her emotions connected to him seemed to vanish. Elizabeth's eyes snapped open to see her husband pointing his pistols at the men who threatened them. Two nondescript trucks sat behind him with Weldsmore guardsmen piling out.

"How can you protect them?" The longshoreman demanded.

"I have no problem shooting you where you stand. Now back away!" Samuel ordered again.

The men hesitated then backed up a few steps.

"And drop your weapons!" Samuel glared at them.

One by one they dropped them. The clatter made Elizabeth wince.

Several House Weldsmore guardsmen ran forward and helped Elizabeth and Abigail to their feet. They escorted them to the back of one of the trucks while Samuel continued to hold off the men, who looked like they might grab their makeshift weapons again if given a chance.

Once Elizabeth and Abigail were safe, Samuel handed Sawyer one of his guns as he hurried over. One of the other guardsmen lifted Abigail into the back of the truck.

"Elizabeth?" Samuel asked, peering into what she knew he saw as Rachel's eyes. "Are you in there?"

She nodded. "Yes. Did Father send you to help?"

He put his hands on her shoulders. "Elizabeth, your father's with us. His transport was attacked and we rescued him."

"What? No!" She tried to shove him away, but he wouldn't let her go.

"He's fine. It's time for you to return to your own body. I can't imagine this has been good for you or Rachel. You need to go back. Now."

Elizabeth craned her neck around him, trying to see her father, but Samuel refused to budge.

"Please come home." He brushed her cheek with his hand and smiled. "I miss you."

Although she desperately wished to see her father, Elizabeth realized doing so in Rachel's body could cause complications. Frustrated, she gave in. "You'll take care of Abigail and Rachel?"

"Of course."

She stepped back. "See you soon."

***

Rachel collapsed into Samuel's arms, trembling and twitching.

"Rachel, is that you? You're safe now." Samuel lowered her to the ground, keeping her head up. "We'll get you to the hospital."

She gasped and grabbed on to his jacket. "Elizabeth . . ."

"She's back with Andrew. He'll take good care of her."

"No . . . danger," Rachel whispered right before she passed out.

22

Samuel picked up Rachel in his arms. Two of the guardsmen helped carry her inside the truck and set her down next to Jonathan. The look of apoplexy on his face would have amused Samuel if the circumstances hadn't been so dire.

"Get everyone in this truck to the nearest hospital. I need the other one," Samuel ordered.

"Samuel, what's going on? What are these people doing in here?" Jonathan demanded as he winced from some unseen injury.

"I'll explain later." Before Jonathan could ask any more questions, Samuel slammed the door shut. "Go!" he yelled.

The truck sped off, and Samuel jumped into the driver's side of the other one.

A young guardsman hopped in beside him. "Sir, do you need me to—"

"Hang on." Samuel shifted the car into gear and accelerated.

The guardsman gripped the roof through the open passenger's side window as they rushed through the city as fast as they could and not injure anyone else.

***

Elizabeth closed her eyes and imagined seeing the spirit passageway in her mind's eye. She'd left Rachel's mind hoping the medium was not too badly damaged after her ordeal with Leland. The darkness of the passageway surrounded her, but ahead lay a warm beacon of light. Elizabeth had no doubt it was Andrew.

As she approached it, the emissary detached from her and coalesced once again into an outline of a man filled with the amethyst-and-emerald green miasma. His presence now gone from her psyche, Elizabeth felt a wave of horror pass over her. She did not regret killing Leland, but the way she had done it mortified her on one hand, and on the other—she didn't want to admit to herself how it really made her feel.

The emissary pointed to the beacon then to himself. He wanted to come with her! The idea sent a shiver of excitement through her mind. She was giddy at the thought. Think of what they could do together.

Then she thought of Samuel.

"No. You can't. Not yet, anyway. But thank you for all your help. Perhaps you can give me an image of where you live. Then we can finally meet in person. I have so many questions for you."

He reached over and touched her forehead. Images of fire, chaos, and beings without form overwhelmed her mind. She backed away, terrified.

"I don't understand. Where is that? Who are you?" Elizabeth chastised herself for her naiveté. Could she have been mistaken about his intent?

The emissary held his hand up. Inside the swirling miasma of his palm, an image formed. It showed Elizabeth and Samuel walking together in her mother's garden. Then their bodies merged into a shapeless blob of the same miasma that his body consisted of.

"I don't understand."

He placed the same palm on her chest. It sent such a rush of power through her it made her psyche writhe in pleasure. The experience was so potent it brought her to the edge of ecstasy. She didn't want to leave, but something pinged in her mind. Andrew's beacon called to her.

She pushed away from him. "No, this isn't right. I don't know what you are, but I must go home." Elizabeth turned and dove into the warm light of the beacon.

When she opened her eyes, she was back in her body and sitting in the loveseat. Andrew was kneeling before her clutching her hands.

"Ah, lassie, you were gone quite a long time. You be all right?" Andrew asked. His eyes were sunken from exhaustion.

"I think so. It was all . . . rather very frightening. My father? Is he all right? And Samuel? Is he back yet? Have you heard anything?" Elizabeth stood then sat down again from dizziness.

"Not a thing, but I'm sure your man Sampson will stay on top of it. And you should sit in case you fall over, lassie." He put his hand on her shoulder to steady her.

Elizabeth opened her mouth to tell him about the emissary then stopped herself. Embarrassment and shame overwhelmed her. This was too intimate, too humiliating to share with the Irishman. Or anyone else.

There was a soft knock as the door slid open. Sampson leaned in.

"I heard voices, so I assumed I could enter." The house manager looked to have aged ten years in the past twenty-four hours. "Can I get you anything?"

"The lassie be needing some fruit juice if you have it."

"I'll have a footman bring some for both of you. And a light snack." Sampson tugged on a rope that signaled to the staff downstairs.

"Could you order a carriage for Mr. O'Sullivan? I'm sure he'd like to go home."

"Of course." Sampson left.

"Andrew . . ." Elizabeth bit her lip and touched his shoulder lightly. "I'm not sure how Rachel faired in all this. I had to be . . . how should I put it . . . not very delicate with her. I needed to use her to stop the man who kidnapped all those people."

Andrew squinted. "You mind telling me who caused all this trouble?"

She studied him before answering. "I can't. It's too dangerous for you. It's something I'll need to discuss with my father."

"What about Mr. Hunter?"

"It might even be too dangerous for him."

Andrew bowed. "Spoken like a true lady of a Great House. There be anything else?"

She gave him a tired smile. "Yes, but not tonight. We're all exhausted. Thank you, Andrew. We'll call on Rachel soon. Please let me know if you or she needs anything. And reassure her that the shipments of food and clothing will continue."

He gave her a short bow then shuffled out.

Elizabeth waited a few minutes for the juice to arrive, but when it didn't, she made her way up to her room to take a bath. Her battle with Leland made her feel cold and dirty, but the encounter with the emissary was something else entirely. He had touched a part of her that gave her such pleasure. Yet . . . there was a cruelty behind it. She had no doubt now that he had been manipulating her. Elizabeth decided she would not enter the spirit passageway again until she had found a way to protect herself from him. When she was ready, she would discuss it with Rachel and Andrew. Perhaps the time for secrets was over.

Elizabeth walked into her bedroom and sat down at the vanity to remove her jewelry. As she went through the routine motions, however, a strange sensation came upon her. Her chest heaved as the air seemed to thin and her ears plugged up. It was as if the barometric pressure had suddenly dropped—something she knew was impossible. Confused, she shook her head and yawned, trying to pop her ears and relieve the pressure. When she glanced up into the mirror again—a miasma of stars had consumed her irises.

Her first thought was that she was going mad. She closed her eyes, trying not to let fear overwhelm her. *It must be a hallucination*, she thought to herself. She was exhausted and distraught over what harm she might have done to Rachel. That had to be it.

She opened her eyes and faced the mirror again. Emerald and amethyst lines swirled.

"No!" she screamed, jumping up and knocking over the vanity stool. Dizzy, she gasped for breath. It was if she had suddenly been tossed up onto a mountain top. Nauseous, she careened around the room as panic overtook her. "No, no, no. This can't be real." Stumbling back to the vanity, she picked up Rachel's necklace and clutched it to her chest as if it could protect her. "Get out!" she cried out.

Above her a huge gash appeared in the air as if the giant talon of a predatory bird had ripped the fabric of her world attempting to escape another. A blast of wind from the opening pushed her back, and she held up her hand to protect her eyes. As she peered through her fingers, she saw the empty blackness of the spirit passageway. A figure of stars took shape inside the rift.

It was the emissary.

How can you do this? Elizabeth thought as she trembled with fear. *What are you?*

"I am what you wish to be." For the first time his voice echoed in her mind. "Deep in your heart you know this."

The emissary possessed more power than Elizabeth had understood, she now realized. Immense power. He had given her a taste of it to defeat Leland and was now using it to seduce her, to make her want more.

To make her want to do his will.

And she knew: a being such as him running rampant in Boston or anywhere else would be catastrophic. This new understanding horrified her. She had to stop him.

The emissary's hands reached out toward the edges of the rift. As he did, his thoughts melded into hers as he reinstated their psychic connection. It was tenuous since she was not in the spirit passageway, but she heard him calling to her like the sirens of myth and legends. He wanted her to return. She created an imaginary brick wall in her mind to stop him, but a pulse of energy swept over her and she faltered.

"No!" she yelled at him, building the psychic wall higher and thicker. She imagined metal poles reinforcing it, but his mental assault was too great.

He blasted through it like it was tissue paper.

The emissary tormented her with images of Samuel being ripped apart by an angry mob. Blood vomited out of her husband's mouth, and his eyes were burned out of his skull. She saw her father decapitated by a ghostly sword, yet his body lurched around as if to find his head. Fires erupted through Boston. Driven by rage and hatred, city dwellers from every walk of life killed and maimed each other—

And the emissary fed on it. His power grew by consuming the life force of the city and its inhabitants. This was how the emissary survived. The terror and horror of it all twisted her soul and squeezed.

Although she feared it wasn't enough, Elizabeth reached down for every inch of strength she had. Piece by piece she rebuilt her brick wall, this time layering it with cement. The being's assault slowed. Elizabeth lurched back to the vanity, hoping the miasma had gone from her eyes, but it was still there.

Elizabeth could sense the emissary's frustration and his determination to break her. He would not stop—ever. But why? What was so special about her? In a corner of her mind, she ran through the times she had interacted with the emissary, seeing the way he had followed her—no, stalked her, then urged her to kill. She now understood that the burnt handprint on her boot had been him trying to follow her into to her world. But that attempt had failed. So he wasn't invincible, just very powerful. He needed Elizabeth to succumb to his offer of power in order to pass through to this world and use it to feed on.

But why her and not Rachel? Or any other medium? What was special about her? Elizabeth realized that didn't matter. The emissary needed her. That was his weakness.

Another blow to her psyche shoved her to the floor. She gasped in pain, curling up into a fetal position. Every nerve felt raw, searing as if on fire. She clawed at the floor in desperation. She tried to call for help, but no sound escaped her lips.

"You cannot defeat me, woman. You are a lesser being. Only worthy of being my vessel until I merge with the one who truly deserves that honor." His voice echoed in her mind.

At that moment, a brief glimpse of who that person was flashed by. Now everything made sense to her. It also made her angry, and that anger gave her strength. Ideas of how to defeat the being tumbled through her mind until she latched onto one. Elizabeth knew her will would fail at some point and she would no longer be able to hold him off. She wasn't strong enough. But if he needed her, she'd give herself to him—just not in the way he expected.

"Stop! I beg you. I'll come. But please, give me a minute," she said in her most plaintive voice, hoping that he would not see through her ruse.

The psychic assault abated but did not disappear. His presence hovered over her psyche like a swarm of mosquitos ready to extract every bit of what made her human. Elizabeth took those few moments to walk around the room and touch Samuel's clothing, smell the fabric, clutch it to her breast. She wanted to remember everything about the man she loved even if it was just for an instant.

"I'm ready."

Elizabeth closed her eyes and willed her mind into the passageway. Unlike before, the miasma overwhelmed the darkness. It swirled and twisted into so many shapes and patterns that in the real world it would have made her dizzy. The emissary's manlike form emerged from the haze and offered him his arm. Her hesitation was real and not part of her plan, but it made her acquiesce believable. Once again she took his arm and merged with him.

The same rush of power returned; if one could breathe in this place, it would have taken her breath away. The being released all of his primordial strength into her. Piece by piece the woman known as Elizabeth Weldsmore Hunter fell away as the emissary took over. Still, she fought to retain some vestige of control over her own psyche, otherwise her plan would not work. In one corner of her mind, she tucked away all that she was and the people she loved. She encased it with the strength borne of her father and her husband. She embraced the emissary, distracting him from her true purpose.

Protecting Samuel.

She knew now: the darkness that had haunted her husband all these years had been this creature attempting to claw his way into his soul, turning his thoughts troubled and violent. Something Samuel had done or been exposed to in the past had made him the perfect vessel for this creature. She was merely the conduit to achieve the emissary's goal of transforming the man she loved into an unstoppable destructive force.

Elizabeth refused to allow this. It was time.

With an urgency grounded in desperation, she formed the image of the first bricks under their feet. But these were not just any bricks. She used her anger to reinforce them with the image of the steel that built her father's ships. From there she built upward. In her mind, she constructed a cocoon of interlocking metal bricks in the shape of an egg all around them—trapping them both. Too late emissary flailed against it, trying to use his power to destroy it. When that didn't work, he tried to extricate himself. He lashed out, pummeling her psyche to force her to release him, but Elizabeth held onto him and stood fast.

She knew it had taken both of them to destroy Rachel's psychic wall, and without her to help they were both trapped.

The emissary screeched and writhed in her mind, but she didn't let go until the last brick was locked in place. When she finally released him, he wreaked vengeance upon every part of her psyche, torturing her with images of Samuel's death unless she helped him break out. But Elizabeth knew in her heart it was all a lie. She had saved, at least for a time, Samuel, her father, and the city she loved—Boston. Elizabeth had no doubt that someday the emissary would escape, but by that time she prayed there would be someone stronger than her who could stop him.

The violence of the being's attacks grew more savage. She knew the death of her mind was near. How long it would take for her body to die, she had no idea. Elizabeth could only hope that Samuel and her father would work together to protect House Weldsmore.

Now it was time to let go to make sure her trap was complete. So she did.

***

Samuel leapt out of the truck as it screeched to a halt in front of the Weldsmore mansion. Another truck pulled in behind them, and he saw Jonathan being helped out of the back. Obviously his father-in-law had countermanded his order and had raced home. So be it. Samuel had no time to confront him.

Instead Samuel sprinted over to the entrance doors without waiting for the footman to open them.

"Elizabeth!" he cried out as he stumbled into the foyer and ran as fast as he could up the stairs. "Elizabeth!" Every step was agony as the darkness he had bottled up emerged to drag him down, but he kept going. He raced down the hall, paused at the bedroom door, looking for any sign of her.

And there she was. She had collapsed on the floor, but what hovered over her could only be described as a rift in the universe. The sight shocked him. What had she done? What was it?

He staggered toward his wife, knelt down next to her, and gathered her up in his arms. Her breathing was rapid and shallow.

"Elizabeth? Can you hear me?" His voice broke with emotion. "Someone!" he screamed toward the doorway. "Get a doctor. Now!"

He brushed the hair away from Elizabeth's face then looked up at the rift. Inside lay darkness and a miasma of stars. He turned back to his wife. "Elizabeth, come back. Please come back."

The rift began to shrink.

Jonathan lurched in. He saw the rift and gasped. "What the hell?"

It closed, leaving the room as if nothing had ever occurred there.

Samuel felt Elizabeth's last breath leave her body. "No. It can't . . .

No." His body heaved in despair as tears ran down his face. "We're too late."

"Elizabeth?" Jonathan stared at Samuel holding his daughter in his arms.

Samuel looked toward him. "She's gone."

23

Samuel sat across from Rachel at the same table where his wife had once sat during her lessons with the medium. It had been repaired since the last time he was there and the rest of the apartment cleaned up. Andrew leaned against the wall next to Rachel, his hands clasped in front of him. All were in mourning as Elizabeth's funeral had been two days ago.

It had been a somber yet grand affair, suitable for a head of state or royalty. The heads of all the Great Houses from Boston had attended as well as a few others from New York and Pennsylvania. Others sent condolences and enough flowers to overflow the foyer and parlor at the Weldsmore mansion. Most of Boston came to mourn. It surprised even Jonathan to see how much she was loved.

A small contingent of South Siders had arrived to pay their respects, but was kept out of the church and the cemetery. When Jonathan saw the Irish, he'd ordered his men to clear them out. Samuel tried to stop him, but the look the older man gave him chilled him to the bone and he let it go.

At the reception, Samuel had overheard that someone from House Tillenghast had been caught up in the riots and had been injured so gravely he was carted off to an asylum. Samuel thought it odd but was too distracted to give it any consideration.

The one happy note to the whole incident was that Mary, Mr. Owen's sister, and the girl, Abigail, had survived the riot and returned home. Many others did not.

Rachel was still weak from her ordeal and looked frail sitting across from him.

"Can you remember anything?" he asked.

She shook her head and glanced down at her hands, which kept twitching. Obviously embarrassed, she hid them under the table. "I be terribly sorry, Mr. Hunter, but I don't remember much. There be a man controlling us, but who he was and what he looked like . . . I just don't remember." She closed her eyes. "There be so much pain in that room. It was hard to keep it out."

"You must remember something," Samuel begged, desperate for any information to help him track down who or what had killed his wife. "Who did you warn me about? How did you know she was in danger?"

Rachel opened her eyes and turned to Andrew.

"Tell him, lass. He'll believe you."

She gulped. "When Elizabeth entered my mind, there be another with her. Riding along like a leech. I'd never felt its like before, and I hope to God I never do again."

"Another medium like yourself?" Samuel asked, his interest piqued.

"That's what Mrs. Hunter believed, but she be wrong. It was . . . It was . . . as close to the devil as I've ever come." Sweat broke out on her brow.

Andrew got her a glass of water. "Rachel, be calm, lass."

Rachel sipped like she was trying to avoid speaking. When she composed herself, she put the glass down. "Mr. Hunter, whatever that thing was, it not be a man or beast."

"Do you think you could enter this spirt passageway again? Find out more about this thing?"

Rachel's face took on a profound sadness. "I lost it all, Mr. Hunter. My gift, my reason for being . . . It be gone. Ripped from me. I . . . I . . ."

Andrew stepped forward and touched her shoulder as if he could ease her pain.

Samuel considered telling them what he'd witnessed in his bedroom, but thought better of it for now. The woman had been through enough. There would be time to discuss it later.

"I'm so sorry, Mrs. Callahan. Please let me know if you need anything." Samuel stood up to leave.

"You'll still make sure the bairns get the food and clothing your wife promised?" Her eyes pleaded.

He nodded. "Of course. I'll take care of it myself."

Samuel left the building and got into the carriage to go back home. *Home.* He scoffed at that idea. House Weldsmore was no longer his home with Elizabeth gone, but he still had business with Jonathan and a killer to find.

***

Jonathan sat in his office chair, turned toward the window with an empty whiskey glass in his hand. The other arm hung in a sling. On his desk lay an empty bottle of Ireland's finest. He stared out the amber-colored window at nothing in particular.

He'd gotten word from Mr. Evans that his secret workshops had been discovered and destroyed. Most likely it was Tillenghast and his minions, but he'd never be able to prove it. The money he had sunk into those projects was lost. The Abyssinians were in disarray and had cancelled their contracts until further notice. Other Great Houses were keeping at arm's length until the political fallout had settled. House Weldsmore wasn't bankrupt but was in financial trouble. If he didn't act soon, his legacy—or what remained of it—would disappear. Not that it mattered.

Tillenghast, Du Pont, and whoever else they were working with had gotten exactly what they wanted. His only heir was dead, and the future of House Weldsmore lay in jeopardy.

He heard Sampson clear his throat.

"What do you want?" The words came out more like a grunt.

"Sir, Mrs. Owen would like to know when to open the house to visitors again. So that she might plan appropriately."

"Tell Mrs. Owen to fire half her staff, and you need to fire half of our footmen as well. We will no longer be receiving guests."

"Sir? I don't understand."

Jonathan glanced back over his shoulder at the house manager. The older man's unshaven face looked haggard. "I thought I was perfectly clear. You can leave now."

"Yes, sir." Sampson turned, but stopped. "Mr. Weldsmore, please accept my sincere condolences on the loss of Miss Elizabeth. She was very dear to me and the rest of the staff. I loved her like she was my own."

"I know, Sampson."

The house manager hesitated before a slew of words poured out of him. "Sir, did this have anything to do with her being a medium?"

Jonathan stopped breathing for a moment then inhaled sharply. Hatred and fear radiated from him like an over stoked furnace. "You have no right to interfere in family affairs."

"There is little that happens in this house that I don't know about, sir."

"How dare you! You have no right!"

"I loved her." Sampson held on to whatever control he had left. "I saw something strange a few days ago. Miss Elizabeth's eyes changed. They seemed almost otherworldly. My eyes must have been playing tricks on me," Sampson said as doubt creeped into his voice. "They were, weren't they?"

A fury rose through Jonathan that he could not stop. "How could you say nothing and claim to love her? What kind of man are you?"

Sampson stepped back, grief and horror running across his face. "It . . . I . . . was ashamed."

"What are you talking about?"

"She was . . . It was uncomfortable," Sampson stammered.

Jonathan stood up as if a giant hand pressed down on his back. "My daughter is dead because you felt uncomfortable. Get out!" he screamed. "Get out! You're done. Pack your bags and go!"

Sampson's face went ashen. "Mr. Weldsmore . . . Jonathan, please. This is my home."

"Not anymore." Jonathan's voice edged toward a violence he'd never felt before.

Sampson fled.

Jonathan picked up the whiskey bottle and threw it against the wall so hard it shattered. "Damn you to hell!"

He collapsed into his chair and wept.

**

An obsidian banner hung down the roof of the Weldsmore house. Samuel watched it wave and twist in the wind as undulating clouds moved in over the city.

A storm was coming.

He entered the house with little fanfare. No one greeted him, and the lone footman made an excuse to scurry off. The joy Elizabeth had brought had vanished as if it had never existed.

Samuel trudged up the staircase and down the hall toward the bedroom he and Elizabeth had shared. There were only a few things he wanted to pick up, and then he would leave. He couldn't live here without his wife, and he was sure Jonathan didn't want him around. Samuel would leave Elizabeth's jewelry behind in case Jonathan ever remarried. The man was still young enough, but Samuel doubted he would do it.

As he walked into the bedroom, Samuel saw Sampson standing motionless in front of Elizabeth's vanity mirror. If that wasn't odd enough, he was not wearing the livery of House Weldsmore.

"Sampson? Is something wrong?"

"What happened here, Mr. Hunter? What really happened?" Sampson's melancholy tone almost convinced Samuel to tell him what he'd seen.

"None of it was your fault."

Sampson turned, tears running down his face. "I saw something, but I didn't say anything."

"Even if you did, the outcome wouldn't have been any different," Samuel tried to explain. "None of us really understand what happened."

"But you'll find whoever killed her, won't you, Mr. Hunter?"

Samuel gripped the house manager's arm. "I will not rest until I do." He released it and backed away. "Why are you out of uniform?"

Sampson wiped the tears from his face. "I am no longer in the employ of House Weldsmore."

"What? But Jonathan needs you."

"Not anymore. He made that abundantly clear." Sampson walked toward the door.

"Let me talk to him?"

Sampson shook his head. "No. It's done."

"Where will you go?"

"I have a niece in Philadelphia, and with the money I've saved over the years we can open a boarding house. She's been at me to retire and go in with her."

Samuel extended his hand. "Best of luck to you."

They shook and without another word, Sampson left.

A silence fell over the room after he was gone. The whole house was stone quiet, no movement or the soft laughter of the maids going about their choirs or footmen obeying the kind yet firm orders of Mrs. Owen. The qualities that had made House Weldsmore a home had disappeared without a trace.

Samuel spent a half hour picking out a few things to take with him: photographs of him and Elizabeth on their honeymoon in Europe, a scarf he had given her, and some of his clothes. He left the better clothing here as he would not need it where he was going. At the last minute, however, he packed one good suit. Elizabeth would have chided him for not having at least a spare. The memory made him smile.

As he stepped into the foyer with his suitcase, Samuel noticed that the door to Jonathan's study was open. He put his bag down and walked in. Jonathan sat with his back toward him in his chair with his feet up on the windowsill. The remains of a whiskey bottle glistened against the wall and floorboards.

"You didn't have to fire Sampson," he called out. "None of us would have understood if he'd tried to tell us. At least not until after what we saw in her bedroom."

"I saw my daughter die." Jonathan spat the words out of his mouth like a bitter aftertaste.

"Jonathan, he's been a loyal servant to you for how many years? Why would you do this?"

"It doesn't matter. He failed me. Now, what did the medium say?" Jonathan demanded.

Samuel shook his head. "Not much. The incident caused her to lose her psychic ability, but she thinks whatever attacked Elizabeth may have been from a place other than the spirit realm."

"So you've failed me *and* Elizabeth. None of this would have happened if you hadn't taken her to that medium."

"Jonathan, the visions returned and were even stronger than before. She had to learn how to deal with them. You agreed."

The head of House Weldsmore stood up and put his hand on the window, inspecting it like a bug. "As per Elizabeth's request, you will receive a small stipend from her estate. Now, I want you gone."

Samuel glared at Jonathan, debating whether or not to let his own grief make him lash out at this man who had lost everything he had ever loved. "I will find out what killed her, Jonathan. And you can keep the money."

He marched out of the room without looking back.

***

Samuel watched as the last of the furniture Elizabeth had selected for their new office was carted away. He'd use the money from their sale to purchase the food and clothing she had promised Rachel. Jonathan's animosity toward mediums and Rachel had made him cancel the orders of foodstuffs that Elizabeth had made prior to her death. It angered Samuel that the man could be so petty, but he'd also heard House Weldsmore had taken a financial beating over some secret projects and the Abyssinian contracts. Perhaps Jonathan just needed the cash.

What was left in Samuel's office was a desk, two plain wooden chairs, a table, stove, a cot, and a fancy newfangled ice box Elizabeth had insisted he have to keep foodstuffs cold. She knew they might be spending long nights on a case and had wanted to make sure they both had enough to eat. The fact that she was no longer here to share in these small things infuriated him. He would find out what killed his wife no matter what it took, but in the meantime he had to earn a living.

Samuel wandered through the rest of the warehouse and considered renting it out to one of the local fisherman. It still stank a bit of mildew and dust, so it would have to be someone who wasn't too picky. However, it was large and had plenty of storage space. He would ask around.

"Laddie! You be here?" A familiar Irishman's voice bellowed from the front of the warehouse.

Samuel walked back to his makeshift office to be greeted by a much healthier looking Andrew.

"I see you be making yourself right at home." Andrew remarked. "It suits you."

"I could never imagine living in that house without Elizabeth." Samuel heard the grief echoing in his own voice.

"Laddie, not all of us are made to live like that, though you and the missus were happy there." He assessed the room with a practiced eye. "I hear you still be opening up shop. That be true?"

Samuel nodded. "Besides needing to make a living, I thought being closer to people like you and Rachel could help me find out what killed Elizabeth. And why."

"Aye. That we could. Remember me telling you about how I used to work for a detective right here in Boston. We managed to solve a fair amount of cases together."

"Andrew, are you asking for a job?"

"Aye, laddie. I think I am."

Samuel's face etched out a half smile. "When can you start?"

24

Epilogue

Alexander Graham Bell hunkered over his new barometric pressure device. Smaller than most barometric devices, he hoped to sell this to the average family and not only scientists like himself. It was designed using two copper aneroid cells to act through a gear or lever train, which drove a recording arm with a pen attached at the end. The recording material was mounted on a cylindrical drum that rotated by clockwork. It was a side project that he liked to tinker with on occasion.

He heard a door slam and the sharp click of expensive men's shoes walking across the hardwood floor. Since his staff was gone for the night, it could be only one person: Thomas Edison.

"Alex! Why couldn't you come to my office to sign the contracts? You know how busy I am." Edison did not bother to hide his annoyance.

"I'm as busy as you are, Thomas. Now come over here and look at this."

Bell heard a sigh then felt the man leaning over his shoulder.

"It's a barometer. Why do I care?" he asked.

"See how small it is. Don't you think every family in the Great States of America would want to be able to know the day's weather before they head out to work?"

Thomas opened his mouth to say something obnoxious, but stopped. "Does it work? I'm sure I can market it. Have you thought of a price yet?"

"Slow down, Thomas, and let's turn it on."

Bell connected the final wire. It took a few minutes, but the cells began to rotate and the current pressure was recorded on the drum.

"Well done, Alex."

As the men studied it, the lever train spiked up off the drum, held for a minute, then plummeted downward. The sudden pressure change was so great that both men yawned to pop their ears. Even the air thinned, causing both to gasp for oxygen for a moment before the pressure normalized again.

They frowned, concerned that something occurred that they did not understand and could not explain.

"What the hell just happened?"

"I don't know Thomas, but I think we may have to find out."

ABOUT THE AUTHOR

Madeleine Holly-Rosing is a graduate of the UCLA MFA Program in Screenwriting where she won the Sloan Fellowship for screenwriting as well as other awards. She has also won the Gold Aurora and Bronze Telly for a PSA she wrote and which was produced by Women In Film.

Her comic Boston Metaphysical Society was nominated for Best Comic/Graphic Novel at the 2014 Geekie Awards and was nominated for a 2012 Airship Award as well as a 2013 and a 2014 Steampunk Chronicle Reader's Choice Award. Her novella, Steampunk Rat, was also nominated for a 2013 Steampunk Chronicle Reader's Choice Award.

Formerly a nationally ranked epeé fencer, she has competed nationally and internationally. She is an avid reader of steampunk, science fiction, fantasy, and historical military fiction. Madeleine lives with her rocket scientist husband, David and two rescue dogs: Ripley and Bishop.

Please follow her on:
www.bostonmetaphysicalsociety.com
Facebook.com/BostonMetaphysicalSocietyComic
Twitter.com/mhollyrosing
Instagram.com/mcholly1

ALSO BY MADELEINE HOLLY-ROSING

<u>Graphic Novels</u>

Boston Metaphysical Society: The Complete Original Series

Boston Metaphysical Society: The Scourge of the Mechanical Men
(*A Granville Woods and Nikola Tesla Story*)

Boston Metaphysical Society: The Spirit of Rebellion
(*A Caitlin O'Sullivan Story*) Coming 2019

<u>Prose</u>

Kickstarter for the Independent Creator
http://a.co/d2VYiKQ

Here Abide Monsters – A Boston Metaphysical Society Story
(Part of the *Some Time Later* Anthology from Thinking Ink Press)
http://a.co/9xSA2F9

The Underground – A Boston Metaphysical Society Story
(Coming 2019)

Boston Metaphysical Society: Spies and Airships
(Short Story – Coming 2019)